THEIR FROZEN BONES

BOOKS BY D.K. HOOD

Detectives Kane and Alton prequels

Lose Your Breath

Don't Look Back

Detectives Kane and Alton series

Don't Tell a Soul

Bring Me Flowers

Follow Me Home

The Crying Season

Where Angels Fear

Whisper in the Night

Break the Silence

Her Broken Wings

Her Shallow Grave

Promises in the Dark

Be Mine Forever

Cross My Heart

Fallen Angel

Pray for Mercy

Kiss Her Goodnight

Her Bleeding Heart

Chase Her Shadow

Now You See Me

Their Wicked Games

Where Hidden Souls Lie

A Song for the Dead

Eyes Tight Shut

DETECTIVE BETH KATZ SERIES

Wildflower Girls

Shadow Angels

Dark Hearts

Forgotten Girls

D.K. HOOD

THEIR FROZEN BONES

bookouture

Published by Bookouture in 2024

An imprint of Storyfire Ltd.
Carmelite House
50 Victoria Embankment
London EC4Y 0DZ

www.bookouture.com

Storyfire Ltd's authorised representative in the EEA is Hachette Ireland
8 Castlecourt Centre
Castleknock Road
Castleknock
Dublin 15 D15 YF6A
Ireland

ISBN: 978-1-83525-367-0
eBook ISBN: 978-1-83525-366-3

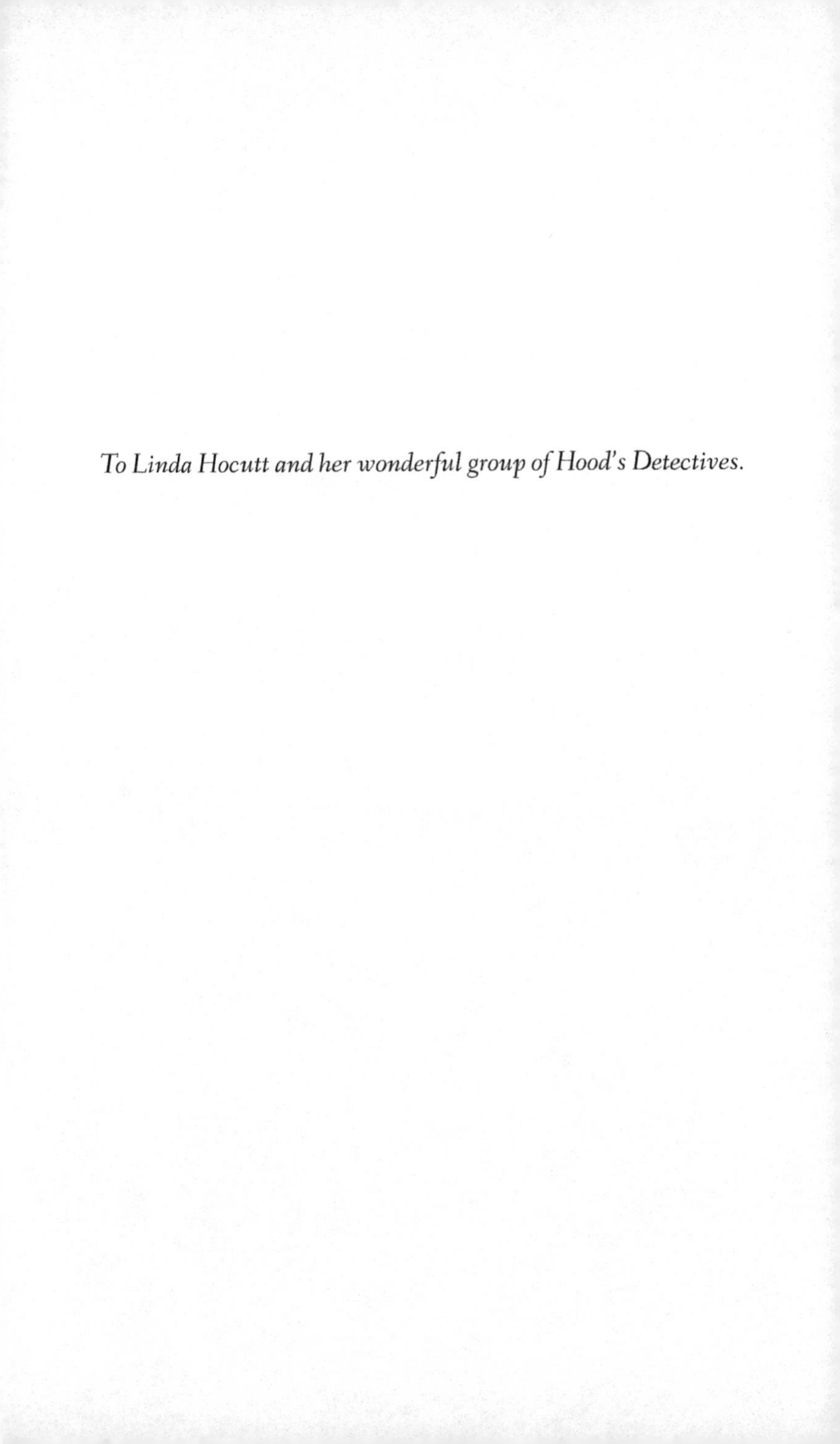

To Linda Hocutt and her wonderful group of Hood's Detectives.

PROLOGUE

SATURDAY

I'm going to die. Realization shuddered through Flora Hadley as she stared into the face of the man she'd trusted. Her lungs ached with each breath, but she forced words between cold trembling lips. "Why are you doing this?" Her teeth chattered as snowflakes melted on her cheeks and spilled down her face and into her collar.

He was everything she wanted in a man: tall, handsome, and attentive. She'd become so close to him and jumped at the chance of a romantic weekend at the Glacial Heights Ski Resort. It had only been three weeks but she'd trusted him. They hadn't arrived at the resort, but he'd acted mysterious and funny on the ride to a secluded cabin for lunch. The place had been beautiful, with outstanding scenery. Pines heavy with snow and views of valleys and frozen waterfalls went on forever. She'd wanted to take pictures, but he'd asked her to wait and promised to show her a view to die for. Now, she understood his meaning and it chilled her to the bone. She looked around, searching for a way to escape, but his pistol pressed into her stomach. He appeared to be enjoying dominating her, and acting scared would only encourage him. She had one small chance to outwit him by acting nonchalant. Hair blew across her face and she tossed it aside, pushing it behind her ears and then curling the ends in her fingers. Most men she'd dated took that gesture as a come-on. Could it work for him? Would he change his mind?

"Stop touching your hair." His mouth turned down as he ripped off her woolen cap and tossed it into a snowdrift. "Take off your clothes."

It was below freezing. She couldn't feel her feet. Uncomprehending, she gaped at him. "Have you lost your mind? I'm not undressing here."

"Shut your mouth." He slapped her hard across the face. "You'll do as I say or I'll hurt you."

Terror gripped her by the throat when he holstered his gun and pulled a long hunting knife from a sheath on his belt. Trembling, she stared at his grim expression. She had to try and sort out his problem with her. Had she said something, done something to upset him? "Talk to me. What are we doing here? What have I done to upset you?"

"If you're trying to analyze me, all you're doing is making me angry." He pushed her hard against a tall pine, making the snow on the branches plop down on her head, soaking her hair. "Don't move or I'll cut you." He stepped behind her.

Crying out as pain shot through her shoulders, Flora gasped as he dragged her arms around the tree and secured her with zip ties pulled so tight they cut deep into her flesh. "You're hurting me."

Instinct told her to fight but her training as an anger management counselor convinced her to try and talk her way out of the situation. Maybe this was some type of sex game. Apart from roughing her up a little, he hadn't actually hurt her too badly. His demeanor had changed again as he came round to face her. He unzipped her puffy jacket and then took his knife and slit her layers of thick clothes from top to bottom.

Shivering and too afraid to move in case he cut her, she watched in horror as he methodically removed every inch of clothing, peeling her like a banana. The frigid wind circled around her warm flesh, cooling her in seconds. Snowflakes drifted softly over her. The icy miracles of nature were something she'd loved to play with as a child. She'd lift her head and stick out her tongue to catch the frozen delights, but now they were frozen daggers cutting into her flesh.

As calm as if he had all the time in the world, the cruel unfeeling monster went to his backpack, took out a roll of gaffer tape. A scream hovered in her throat as he wrapped it around her chest and the tree. She couldn't move and the tape was so tight she couldn't breathe. When he did the same to her legs, she just stood there unable to move. It was as if one part of her brain was telling her to fight and the other part was in shock and too scared to move in case he cut her with a knife. Shivering, her teeth chattered as cold seeped into her, burning right through to her bones. Stiffness crept into her face. Breathing in the frigid air hurt so bad. Why was he doing this to her? The man she'd trusted was part of a nightmare that she couldn't wake up from.

Waves of terror surged through her when he finally straightened and stood in front of her staring at her face. Lip quivering, she met his cold hard gaze. "Please stop. Why are you doing this?"

He didn't respond but took the knife and hacked away at her hair. Fear made her dizzy as the knife nicked her scalp. Warm blood trickled down her cheek and she shook with uncontrollable sobs. All around her the snow was covered in long blonde strands. When he finally finished, he opened her backpack and took out her makeup bag. He extracted one of her lipsticks and walked toward her. He drew something on her forehead and then stood back and admired his work. He returned the lipstick to her makeup bag and retrieved a small mirror. He held it up in front of her. Trying hard to focus, Flora gasped in horror at her reflection. The long glossy blonde hair that had taken so long to grow was just spikes on a bald head. On her forehead he'd drawn a smiley face in lipstick. Tears fell hot on her freezing cheeks and breathing was becoming difficult. "Why are you doing this to me?"

"Because I can." Smiling and without a care in the world, he gathered dead branches from close by and used them to sweep away the footprints around where she stood as he backed away to the snowmobile they'd used to get to this secluded part of the forest.

Her mind refused to comprehend what was happening, but as shivers wracked her body, Flora stared at him. This must be a mistake. He loved her—didn't he? "You can't just leave me here. I'll die in this weather."

"That's the idea." He turned away and gave her a wave. "Enjoy the view while you can."

Desperate, Flora tried to scream through frozen lips, and she struggled as the sound of the snowmobile disappeared into the distance, but as the cold steeped into her body, movement was almost impossible. She couldn't escape and no one was coming to save her. A blizzard surrounded her, its icy grip claiming her last warm breath. She stared into a snowscape as beautiful as it was deadly, and as a single tear froze on her cheek, she surrendered to the inevitable.

ONE

The day Deputy Dave Kane, an off-the-grid special forces operative, arrived in Black Rock Falls, his life had changed dramatically. He'd encountered Sheriff Jenna Alton, an ex-DEA special agent in witness protection, spinning upside-down in her cruiser in the snow after an attempt on her life. Six years had passed since his reassignment to hide in plain sight as a deputy sheriff, and what an action-packed six years it had been. He'd found himself living in Serial Killer Central with a sheriff he'd been sent to protect and who was the last person who needed or wanted his protection. It was just as well his handler, Dr. Shane Wolfe, currently the medical examiner, was sent along to keep the peace. Not in his wildest dreams would he have believed six years later he'd be holding Jenna's hair from her face as she hugged the toilet.

After losing his wife in a car bombing during his time as a secret service agent, he'd never believed he'd love again, but the moment he'd set eyes on Jenna, something magical had happened. The opposite to him, Jenna was petite against his six-five, two-hundred-fifty-pound frame but they both had the same black hair and blue eyes. She just happened to be the most beautiful woman he'd ever seen. It had taken him four or more years to propose, but now they had an adopted son, Tauri, and Jenna was pregnant with their child. Hence the need to hold up her hair as she spewed. It had become a morning ritual. Watching her and not being able to stop her misery tore at his heart. He passed her a damp washcloth as she lifted her head. "Sit still for a while." He flushed the toilet and crouched before her. "Wolfe said it wouldn't last much longer."

"It wasn't supposed to start at three weeks but it did." Jenna pressed the washcloth to her face and leaned back against the tile. "Sandy's lasted for three months." She pulled down a small section of the washcloth and peered at him. "But she was having twins. What if I'm having twins?"

Jenna was referring to Deputy Jake Rowley's wife, whom he'd rather not use an example of pregnant bliss as she'd ended up delivering her twins in the morgue as the roads to the hospital were blocked during a blizzard. Kane shook his head. "There's no twins in our families, so I doubt it, but whatever sex or how many babies we have, they'll be a blessing."

"Easy for you to say, you're not hugging the porcelain every morning." Jenna covered her face again. "Two would be great. Three is a great number of kids to have and we'd get it all done and dusted in one go."

Grinning, Kane sat down beside her. "This is the easy part. Once the morning sickness has passed, you'll be back to normal for a few months before you start waddling like a duck." He chuckled. "Then you get to squeeze all the life out of my hands during labor. Rowley told me that it took him six weeks before he could move his hands again after being with Sandy during the birth of the twins." He took her hand and kissed her knuckles. "Don't worry, they say that as soon as the baby is put in your arms, you'll forget the morning sickness and the delivery."

"That's what women tell their husbands as an excuse for the verbal abuse they dished out during the labor." Jenna snorted.

"Now I know why in the olden times, the midwives refused to allow husbands to be present at the birth. The modern way must have been suggested by a woman just to let a man know exactly what we go through." She dropped the washcloth. "Why don't you want to know the sex of our baby?"

A tightness closed around his heart. His first wife had been pregnant with their son when she was killed. The loss of both of them was like a dagger to his heart for so long he didn't know how he'd survived. He tipped back his head and stared at the ceiling. "I already know." He touched his head. "In here, I can see you holding our baby. I know the name and that you'll want another the moment you lay eyes on our child." He touched her face. "I know you, Jenna. You're strong and capable. You're a wonderful mother to Tauri and you'll continue to be a great sheriff. Children, as we've discovered, only enhance our lives. We've been very fortunate to be parents don't you think?"

"Yeah, I want this baby so much, but I hate spewing, is all." She smiled at him. "I'm not worried about the labor, but it will take all my willpower not to discover the sex. When I have the scans, I'll be looking. I just won't tell you."

Kane pushed to his feet and held out his hands. "Have a few crackers and sit awhile in bed before you take a shower. I'll go and tend the horses." He glanced at his watch. "Tauri will be awake soon and I promised him he could watch while I fixed the Harley." He pulled her to her feet and handed her the mouthwash. "Will you be okay now?"

"Yeah." She squeezed his arm. "Same time tomorrow?"

Kane chuckled. "I wouldn't miss it." He headed for the door.

TWO

The last couple of weeks had been a stressful time for Wolfe. The workload as medical examiner had taken him all over Montana and had excluded him from a visit to Stockholm with his fiancée, forensic anthropologist Norrell Larson, to meet her family. Norrell's fifteen-hour-plus trip with the stopovers along the way would have been exhausting. It would be the same for his daughter, Julie. Her flight from Dallas had arrived in Helena late last evening and she'd stayed in town for the night before catching a turboprop aircraft from Helena to Black Rock Falls earlier this morning. It was a short flight, and she should be landing soon. The weather had been closing in for the last few hours, and flights canceled every few minutes. According to the local weather reports, a blizzard was hitting the mountain range, putting visibility down to zero. Had the small turboprop made it through? Anxiously waiting for both women to land was wearing at his nerves. He stared across the snow-covered tarmac as the jet aircrafts landed. When the board lit up that Norrell's flight from Salt Lake City had landed, he headed for the arrivals gate.

Checking his watch again, and staring at the arrivals board, a knot formed in his stomach. Julie's flight was late. He'd flown his chopper in bad weather and understood the problems. With a small aircraft a pilot would rather set the plane down in a field than risk flying over a mountain range in a blizzard. He'd call air traffic control the moment Norrell arrived for more information. Moments later, Norrell arrived pushing a cart loaded with baggage. His heart missed a beat at the sight of her angelic face. How a young woman like her wanted a forty-two-year-old man like him he'd never understand, but he thanked God every time he laid eyes on her. He held out his arms and she left her baggage cart and ran to him. He swung her around and kissed her. "I've missed you."

"I've missed you too." Norrell held up her gloved hand. "Pinky-finger swear we'll never go on vacations alone again."

Filled with emotion, Wolfe lifted his hand and linked her finger. "I swear." He hugged her close. "I'm waiting for Julie's plane to land. It's overdue. Her arrival time was before yours and she's only coming from Helena."

"We were getting updates on the blizzard all the way here." Norrell frowned. "It's bad and it's going to swamp Black Rock Falls within the next hour or so. She might have got through before it hit the mountains. What time did she leave?"

Wolfe checked his watch. "A little over two hours ago. The flight usually takes about forty minutes, add on a little more for takeoff. She should have landed by now. We'll go and stow your bags in the back of my truck. Maybe she will have landed by then."

As they walked out to the parking lot, snow chilled his face. He glanced toward the mountains, but before him was a sheet of white. Visibility was so bad he wouldn't even think of flying a chopper in these conditions. He pushed the bags into the back of his truck and then took Norrell's hand and ran back across the slippery blacktop to the airport waiting room. He checked the arrivals board again and then pulled out his phone. Being a chopper pilot had its advantages as he had plenty of contacts at the airport. He made a call to the air traffic control office. "Hey, it's Shane Wolfe. What can you tell me about a flight from Helena this morning? Can you get me an estimated time of arrival from the pilot? It's very late and my daughter is on board." He gave the flight number and waited. He could hear voices in the background.

"Yeah, we've been trying to reach that flight for ten minutes. The last call we had was for a weather report. The pilot could see the storm coming. Since then, no communication. No Mayday call. He could have ditched the plane in a field and the antenna is frozen. There could be a valid reason why he's lost communication. Right now, we have no contact. The blizzard is scattering the signal, but we'll be able to pinpoint the aircraft using other techniques. We'll be notifying the local sheriff's departments all through the mountain ranges to be on the lookout for the aircraft." The man sighed. *"Right now, all we can do is wait for the storm to pass."*

Dread dropped over Wolfe in an icy shroud. "Don't sugarcoat it for me. The plane is down, isn't it? If you've lost contact and can't reach it, it's down. The pilot would have followed protocol if he'd ditched it. He'd have sent out a Mayday and given his last coordinates. Stop wasting time and get people out looking for it. Give me its last position and I'll coordinate something from here." He pulled a notebook from his pocket and jotted down the numbers. "Call me if you have any news." He turned to Norrell. "They're not admitting it yet, but I believe Julie's plane went down over the Black Rock mountain range." He dragged in a shuddering breath and rubbed both hands down his face. "My baby girl is out there all alone."

THREE

The Black Rock Falls Sheriff's Department was on a skeleton crew this weekend. Maggie the receptionist insisted on coming into the office whenever it was open, but either one of Jenna's deputies would be on duty over the weekend. Both had decided to do half-day shifts on Saturday, and on Sunday the office would be closed and anyone who needed assistance would call 911. Deputy Zac Rio, a gold shield detective out of LA, was in the office this morning. He'd moved to Black Rock Falls with his two siblings to give them a better life and to keep them out of trouble. In the three years he'd been working for Jenna, he'd turned their lives around. Rio had a retentive memory, which made him super useful at crime scenes as his mind documented every aspect of the scene.

Nothing was better than Kane's pancakes, crispy bacon, and maple syrup for breakfast. Once her stomach had settled, Jenna had a ferocious appetite. She poured syrup over her pancakes and was nibbling at the bacon when Kane's phone chimed. She raised an eyebrow at him as he lifted it and mouthed the word *Wolfe*. It was unusual for him to call them this early in the morning, especially on one of their days off.

"Hey, morning, Shane. What's up?"

"Julie's plane has gone down over the Black Rock mountain range." Wolfe sounded frantic. *"In case you haven't heard the weather report this morning, we have a blizzard heading our way. We need to be organizing search parties ASAP."*

Horrified by the news, Jenna stared at Kane. Her heart twisted at the thought of Julie dying in a plane crash somewhere in the mountains. She pressed a hand to her mouth to hide her anxiety from her son. Julie was like her little sister. The thought of her out there alone cut deep. It couldn't be true, could it?

"Oh, sweet Jesus. Leave it to me, Shane. I'll get everyone organized. Give me the last coordinates and I'll contact search and rescue." Kane frowned. "Not that they'll be able to do anything until the blizzard blows through. The moment we get visibility, we'll get the choppers up. I'll contact Carter and Styles, but their coming here to assist will be contingent on the weather, as you well know."

"I know how bad it is, Dave, I feel useless not getting out there right now to search but it would be certain death by air." Wolfe moaned like an injured animal. *"There is one hope. If they ditched in the lowlands, the wireless could be blocked. You'll need to get out a media release so we have people on the ground looking out for the aircraft. Someone might have seen it crash or heard something in their area. Make sure they ask anyone with a snowmobile to assist in the search. I'll contact the snowmobiles enthusiast group in town and ask them for their assistance as well."*

"All those planes carry satellite navigation. The control tower at the airport should be able to coordinate the signals and give us a better idea of the location." Kane rubbed the back of his neck and stared at Jenna, his face holding an expression of deep concern. "I'll have everyone on standby once they give us the coordinates."

"You know any survivors won't last long out there in this

weather." The pain in Wolfe's voice was palpable. *"Help me find her, Dave. I can't do it alone."*

"You have my word." Kane stared at Jenna, who went straight for her phone to call Rio. "Jenna is arranging the media report now. Hang in there, Shane. We've got this." He sat down hard in the chair.

"Okay. We need to work out a strategy. Bring Tauri here. He'll keep Anna company, and if he needs to sleep over, he'll be safe here with my housekeeper."

"Okay. We'll see you soon." Kane disconnected.

"What's wrong, Daddy?" Tauri licked sticky fingers.

"Auntie Julie is lost in the mountains. We'll need to go and look for her." Kane ruffled his son's hair. "We could take you to Nanny Raya's or would you prefer to play with Anna today?"

Anna Wolfe was the youngest in the Wolfe family of three girls, the eldest being Emily, a medical examiner in training. Jenna waited for Rio to pick up and explained what she needed before turning to Tauri. In situations like this, they preferred to keep details away from their son. She smiled at him. "What's it to be? If we're held up, it might be a sleepover. Would you like that?"

"Yes, I like Anna and she'll be sad her sister is missing but you should call Uncle Atohi. If Julie is missing in the mountains, he'll find her." Tauri nibbled on a strip of bacon.

"I need to make a few calls." Kane stood and left the room, his thumb moving over his phone.

Atohi Blackhawk, a Native American tracker and now very much part of their family, had been the guardian of Tauri and, as a close friend, had been the one who'd brought her and Kane together with him. Their connection had been instant, and they'd made a long and arduous application for adoption. Tauri had officially become Tauri Kane over six months ago, and everyone had told her the moment she'd stopped worrying about becoming pregnant it would happen. Nothing had surprised and delighted them more than to discover Jenna had at last conceived. She loved Tauri with all her heart and welcomed another addition to their family with open arms. Since becoming a mother, her emotions had changed. Now she understood how losing a child would break a person's heart. Now she appreciated just how much Kane had suffered losing his wife and child. During a recent case, she had come too close to losing her husband and son, and her heart ached for the pain Wolfe must be suffering. Nothing could be worse than being helpless to do anything. Unless the blizzard broke, there wasn't a hope anyone could reach the aircraft before the survivors froze to death. She understood the seriousness of the situation and so did Wolfe.

Jenna looked up as Kane's phone chimed again when he walked back into the kitchen. She raised one eyebrow. Since she'd announced her pregnancy, her deputies avoided calling her with bad news. It was as if they figured the shock would harm her. Heavens above, she'd been pregnant when she believed Kane and Tauri had been killed. If she could cope with that shock, she could cope with anything. She looked at Tauri. "Could you do something for Mommy?"

"Yes, I'm big now." Tauri slipped from the chair and looked up at her.

Jenna smiled at him. "I know you are, sweetheart. Go and wash your face and hands and get dressed. I'll be along to pack a bag for you just in case we get held up."

She looked at Kane as Tauri scampered along the passageway to his room. "Why is everyone avoiding me?"

"It's Blackhawk." Kane shrugged. "I'll put him on speaker. Hey, Atohi, how's the blizzard where you are?"

"White and cold, but that's not why I called. I was out tending my traps when I saw an aircraft in trouble over the mountains. It disappeared out of sight and I heard tree branches breaking." Blackhawk took a deep breath. *"I figure it crashed*

some ways between Bear Peak and Bison Hump Bridge on your side of the mountain. I can see no way that you are going to be able to get to the crash site by chopper in this weather. I know people who live out of Bison Hump Bridge. They may be your only hope in this instance."

Trying to keep busy as chaos reigned around her, Jenna cleared the table. "We know about the missing aircraft. Julie is on board. Dave has called in all the emergency services available, but I'll see if I can contact anyone still living there. It's unusual for people to remain in the forest in winter, unless it's their only place of residence. We have issued a media report, so with luck if anyone else saw the plane come down, they'll call it in."

"The moment, I can head in that direction, I will." Blackhawk sighed. *"I hope we find everyone alive. I'll call the moment I have eyes on the aircraft."* He disconnected.

Saddened, Jenna stood and leaned into Kane. "This is going to be the worst Christmas ever."

FOUR

At an almighty crash and the gunshot splintering of trees, Johnny Raven ducked for cover and peered out between the branches of the pines heavily bent with snow. The ground shook under his feet and a ball of smoke rose into the air. Moments later charred fragments of flaming debris rained down onto the pristine snow-covered slopes. He ground his teeth and fought the flashbacks of war. It had been a time but loud noise and the smell of acrid smoke awakened memories he'd rather forget. His dog, Ben, an Alaskan Malamute, was never far from his side and whined, pushing against his leg. "That can't be good."

He picked up the frozen critters he'd collected in his traps and hurried back to his cabin. He didn't have much time if he planned on saving any survivors. The blizzard was setting in and visibility would soon be down to less than a foot in front of him. He had a good idea where the aircraft had hit the mountainside. He had often seen small aircraft coming through the pass on the way to Black Rock Falls Airport. Most flights would take the scenic route but in winter a blizzard could render the visibility to zero in a matter of minutes. He'd listened to the weather report before he'd set out to check his traps and there had been no mention of a blizzard heading their way. Such was the crazy weather fluctuations of late. He'd never seen storms of such magnitude or variations of temperature to such a degree as he had seen in the last three years. Winter had come late this year, with snowfalls barely reaching the towns until after Thanksgiving, but they had sure made up for it now. He had woken a week ago to drifts of six and eight feet blocking his front door. He'd needed to dig his way out and was glad that he'd made sure his dogs had suitable accommodation for the winter.

Without delay he packed his dogsled with medical supplies and blankets and drained the coffee pot into two Thermoses. He'd filled his pockets with energy bars and then headed out to the kennels. Housed inside a barn, the dogs had access to a large yard. These dogs he'd rescued and trained. Most of them were mixed breeds, strong and resilient with thick winter coats. He'd trained them to pull his sled in winter and to hunt with him, but he chose others to become personal protection dogs. It had become a lucrative business since Black Rock Falls had become Serial Killer Central. Not that he ventured into town often. He had a friend at the animal shelter who contacted him when a suitable stray was available and acted as a go-between if he needed to sell a dog. He preferred the solitary life and enjoying his own thoughts. His life in the military, and the discharge clutching his Purple Heart, seemed a lifetime ago. He'd retreated as far away from people as possible for three years before venturing into town and discovering his pension had been accruing in the bank. He'd purchased tools and other things he needed to extend his cabin and build the accommodation for his dogs.

The dogs were eager to be up and away. They enjoyed a run after being cooped up for a couple of days. He attached the harnesses, and with Ben bounding along beside him, they headed toward the downed aircraft. The trails on this side of the mountain were more familiar to him than the lines in the palm of his hand, although traveling through the forest in a blizzard was like living inside a snow globe. The dogs bounded over the snow, barking and creating a cloud of steam. Raven ducked the low branches weighed down by the snow and icicles. It was as beautiful as it was deadly. He needed to be on his game or he'd be knocked from the sled and out in the forest he'd die a fast and miserable death. Although he doubted Ben would leave his side. He'd trained him as K-9 from a pup during his rehabilitation and he'd become his constant companion.

Out with Ben one day, the dog had led him to a deserted cabin with a large mixed-breed dog chained outside. The dog was thin but had survived due to a drip-feed water supply from the adjacent river. Inside the house Raven discovered the body of a very elderly man and searched the place for any signs of friends or family. Finding nothing, not even one scrap of paper giving the man's name, he'd taken the dog and headed back to his cabin. The next time he'd ventured into town, he'd told his friend about finding the old man and ask her to notify the authorities, but no one had come by to claim the body. Months later, he'd returned, gathered the dried corpse, and given it a decent burial. Maybe someone would return the favor for him one day.

The dog had been the first personal protection canine he'd trained in Black Rock Falls and had started his lucrative business. He'd signposted the cabin and filed for possession. The cabin, a very old forest warden's dwelling, wasn't owned by the old man, and forestry had sold it to him for the filing fees of the paperwork. The old place had a good solid barn and a garage stocked with tools. He used the garage to store his truck over winter and to repair his snowmobile when necessary.

The smell of fuel and burning flesh seared his nostrils as he rounded a bend in the trail. The forest floor was littered with debris and he left the dogs to venture closer to the wreck on foot. The aircraft had hit the mountain and broken in half. The front section had burst into flames and the back section had slid down the side of the mountain in the thick snowdrift and was buried, the broken section opened to the elements. Bodies, some burned beyond recognition, lay half buried in the snow. One man had been thrown out of the back section, and although he appeared to be unconscious when Raven checked his vital signs, he'd died. Baggage was strewn all over. A set of pink suitcases caught his attention because all the people he'd examined so far resembled males.

Somewhere in this horror was a woman. He went to the back section and, glad of his thick leather gloves, grabbed the ragged edge and pulled himself up to peer inside. His gaze fell on a young woman with long blonde hair still strapped to her seat. He dropped back to the ground. She looked so still and waxlike but he needed to check life signs. Getting inside would be a problem. After gathering up the luggage, he piled it up alongside the aircraft and used it to climb over the edge. Once inside he kicked open the door. Immediately snow drove into the small area making the floor slippery. He slid down to the woman, removed his glove and pressed his fingers against her throat. He heaved a sigh of relief when a flutter pressed against his fingers. He removed his other glove and checked her for injuries. She seemed okay until he moved a large piece of the wing section that had cut through the side of the plane and covered her. The piece of metal had held her in place, but he suspected her leg had a clean break. As a medical doctor, the scene brought back memories of his time in the medical corps and flying into a battle zone. He'd need to splint the leg before he attempted to move her. He went back outside, hunting the wreckage, and found a piece of hard plastic, likely from a suitcase. He dragged the medical kit from the wall of the aircraft and used the bandages and plastic to splint her leg.

Before he moved her, he checked her again, lifting her eyelids and running both hands over her neck. She was bundled up in layers and wore a long sheepskin coat and a white knit cap. With care, he lifted the hood of her coat over her head. Her skin was so pale and her lips had turned blue. She resembled an ice queen. Like someone straight out of a fairy tale. A Nordic princess maybe. He guessed her age at maybe eighteen or twenty. Frightened he might break her, he lifted her with care and headed for the door, slipping and sliding on the snow-covered floor. He trudged through the snow and, reaching his sled, bundled her up in the blankets and then covered her with a foil blanket he'd retrieved from the first aid box. He ordered Ben to stay with her and went back to the aircraft, making many trips back and forth. He gathered the pink luggage and the first aid box and took the boxes of supplies the plane was carrying. No one would get to the plane before the melt, and the wildlife would devour everything edible by then. He could make use of everything, especially with another mouth to feed. With his sleigh packed, he made his way slowly back to his cabin. Tremors shook the ground and he stared at the mountain as snow shifted and slid down toward him in a wave of white dust. An avalanche would isolate him from the outside world. It had happened before, and of late, the seismic tremors had increased to frighteningly dangerous levels.

The intense blizzard was pelting the crash site with snow so thick and hard the charred bodies would be covered within the hour, maybe less. He shook his head, as emotion for the lost lives engulfed him. Tears stung the backs of his eyes. Families would be waiting for their loved ones to return home for the holidays. This young woman would be missed. He wiped a hand over his face. He had no form of communication at his cabin. He wanted to be incommunicado and deal with people under his own terms and when able to do so. When he wanted to speak to Breda Arnold, the woman at the dog rescue center, he walked to the dead man's cabin and fired up his CB radio. He'd purchased a battery and solar panel. There was no way he could risk the trail down the mountain to the old man's cabin. If he didn't make it, the young woman would die along with his dogs. He had no choice. Taking her home and nursing her back to health was his only option. The wind increased and snow fell so hard he couldn't see Ben running alongside him. He called to the dogs, encouraging them to keep going. They knew their way home. He looked at the blonde hair flowing from under the blankets. He'd find out her name and get a message to her family as soon as possible, but first he'd try and save her life.

FIVE

Smothering gut-wrenching grief, Jenna kept the conversation general as they traveled to Wolfe's house. She needed to chat about anything but what lay ahead. She glanced at Kane and raised both eyebrows. "Is it true that you will be replacing the Beast in the new year?"

Kane's tricked-out black truck had been supplied to him by POTUS and was literally bombproof. It had so many gadgets and other paraphernalia she couldn't imagine it being replaced by anything else. It had saved their lives so many times.

"I didn't plan on replacing the Beast. The decision was out of my hands and it's being replaced by something far superior. It wasn't my choice, it was an order." Kane turned slowly onto the highway. The Beast had a snowplow attachment on the front and towed a snowmobile trailer, hitched carrying their two vehicles and supplies. "It will still be my Beast and this one we've come to love will be returned to whence it came."

Frowning, Jenna appreciated just how much Kane loved his vehicle. "You've worked on this truck for years, making it better each time. Why would they want to replace it now?"

"It's over five years old." Kane flicked her a glance and

shrugged. "There have been many improvements in motor vehicles in the last five years, Jenna. If we're going to constantly put ourselves in danger, we need an upgrade. The new one will have everything we have now but with more technology. I was asked for what certain specifications I require and everything will be included. I'm looking forward to it."

Trying to keep her mind on anything but the plane crash, Jenna nodded. "When I lived in DC, I had a hankering for a Mustang." She sighed. "I'm not too sure it would go very well out here."

"In summertime it would be great to be tearing along the great stretches of highway we have in this state." Kane suddenly gave her a smile. "I figure you should have one. After all, I do have my motorcycles. You should have something for yourself that you will enjoy too. Everyone needs something nice in their lives. What is the point of working all our lives and not enjoying the fruits of our labor? We have more money than we need. Maybe it's about time we spent some of it on ourselves rather than constantly giving it away to charity. Surely one indulgence won't hurt?"

"I'm getting a mustang after Christmas." Tauri scratched Duke's ears. "Uncle Atohi told me it would be very gentle and we could all go riding together. We gave her the name Firebird. She is a mustang, and she's going to be mine."

Jenna bit back a grin. "The Mustang I was speaking about is a vehicle. A fast car."

"What would it look like, Mommy?" Tauri rubbed the end of his nose.

Jenna thought for a beat. "Oh, shiny black with silver stripes, tinted windows, maybe."

"That sounds like a plan." Kane nodded slowly. "Maybe a spoiler as well?"

Looking ahead at the recently cleared highway and the gray snow piled up along each side, her stomach dropped and grief filled her again. She nodded, trying to keep it together. "Yeah, that sounds wonderful."

"We'll find her." Kane took her hand and squeezed. "I'm sure as heck not giving up on her until I see her body. I know Julie and she is tough and resourceful. Wolfe, I, and Blackhawk have all trained the girls on how to protect themselves in the forest in all weathers. She knows we'll be searching for her." He scanned the landscape. "It's bad, I know that, but we have crews here that deal with rescues in this weather all the time. We need to trust in the system. Someone will find the aircraft and call it in."

Jenna pulled a tissue from her pocket and blew her nose. As sheriff, she had to act as an example to everyone on her team. She understood that her hormones were raging at the moment, but that was no excuse for falling to pieces on the job or upsetting her son. She nodded to him and sucked in deep breaths. Wolfe would be shattered and she needed to be strong. "I'm glad I have you, Dave. You put everything into perspective."

They blew through town with comparative ease. Not many people had ventured out into the blizzard and the snowplows had been working since sunup clearing the snow and keeping the roads open for emergency vehicles. As they turned into Wolfe's driveway, she spotted Rio's and Rowley's trucks parked outside. They headed for the door and at once Wolfe's housekeeper appeared and ushered Anna and Tauri into the kitchen to make cookies. Jenna watched him scamper away, glad he had someone to play with after being cooped up in the house with Nanny Raya for the past week. He loved being with his nanny, but he missed kindergarten and it had closed for the duration of the holidays. She headed into the family room and pulled off her coat. A log fire heated the room and everyone was in deep conversation. She went to Wolfe and hugged him and Emily. Norrell gave her arm a squeeze and the conversation stopped as all eyes went to her. "Okay, bring me up to date."

"We have a general idea of where the aircraft went down." Rio had taken charge. "Going on Blackhawk's sighting and a man driving into town from Bison Hump Bridge, we have triangulated a possible crash site. This being the case, search and rescue are on standby. Carter and Styles will be here the moment they have visibility. The snowmobile enthusiasts club is already heading in that direction. They are all carrying satellite phones. We have five snowmobiles and Blackhawk will be heading toward the coordinates from his side of the mountain. He'll meet with us at the area north of Bison Hump Bridge. The snowplows have cleared the way from town to Bison Hump Bridge and will continue to keep the road open for us."

"So what's the catch?" Kane tossed his coat over the back of a chair and removed his gloves. "If the roads are clear, why aren't we heading that way now?"

"The coordinates suggest the aircraft went down in a remote area. There are no fire roads or any way we can find to make it easier to get there." Rio's expression was like stone. "We're the most experienced team, so we're taking the most dangerous route." He looked at Jenna. "It might be better if you man the control center."

"Oh, for goodness sake." Norrell glared at him. "She'll be fine. I'm sure Jenna would appreciate it if you all stopped treating her as if she'll break. Being pregnant when a woman is strong and healthy isn't a problem at this stage. I might be concerned if she was in her last trimester, but right now this overprotectiveness is getting me down, so heaven knows how you're making her feel right now."

Looking at her team, Jenna smiled. "I know you care about me but I'm fine. I do appreciate your concern but right now we have Julie and the other people on that aircraft to consider. They are our priority, so let's move out."

"Does anyone need any supplies?" Wolfe looked around the

room. "Are your winter survival packs complete? It's darn cold out there. Is everyone bundled up?"

"Yeah, we make sure we have the backpacks fully stocked and the snowmobiles maintained well before the first snow." Kane picked up his coat. "The visibility isn't too bad right now. We should move out."

Jenna nodded. "Okay. Let's go."

SIX

In a world of pain, Julie Wolfe opened her eyes, expecting to be somewhere in the forest. It was dark and silent. Panic gripped her. Where was she? What had happened? The terrifying knowledge that the plane was going to crash had come from the frantic shouts from the pilot. He told them all to hug their knees as visibility was zero and he'd try and put the aircraft down somewhere. Terrible memories spun around in her head and she moaned, holding up her hands. "Help me. Someone, help me."

A light poured over her and she made out a small room. She started at the sight of a huge man filling the doorway. Hope filled her. "Is that you, Dave?"

"No, my name is Johnny Raven." The man came into the room and looked down at her. "What's your name?"

Head spinning, fear caught in Julie's throat. Cool sheets pressed into her back. Where the heck was she and how did she get here with this stranger? For now she'd cooperate because she had no choice. With effort, she pushed words out of her dry throat. "Julie Wolfe."

"Do you remember what happened?" Raven sat beside her

and flicked a flashlight across her pupils. "I can't find any head injuries. How do you feel?"

This man was acting like a doctor, but if he had been, wouldn't he have said so from the get-go? Gritting her teeth, Julie moved her head and went through a self-check. "My leg hurts and I was in a plane crash. I recall the pilot telling us to brace for impact and then waking up here."

"Do you need something for the pain?" He indicated behind him. "I have morphine or pain meds."

As if she'd trust a stranger to drug her. No one was that stupid, but she did need something for the pain shooting up her leg. She dragged her dry tongue over cracked lips. "Not morphine and I'll want to see the bottle before I take anything. I've no reason to trust you and I need to ask questions. Where am I and how long have I been here?" She looked around the tidy log-built room and then lifted the covers. She swallowed hard at the sight of her PJ's. One leg was split to the knee and she made out a heavy bandage. "Where are my clothes?"

"You were soaked through." Raven's eyes narrowed. "I needed to get you warm before you died."

I need to get out of here. She touched her ear, searching for her earring but it was missing. One squeeze and it would activate a tracker and her dad would come. A shiver of fear ran down her spine. Had Raven removed it to stop her escaping? Heart racing, she looked at him. "Did you remove my earrings?"

"You have one on the left." Raven narrowed his gaze at her. "Why would I remove it? You must have lost it in the wreck."

Reason washed over her. He'd have no knowledge of her tracker. She nodded. "I need to call my dad. Have you got my purse? My phone is in there. It has a satellite sleeve."

"I brought a set of pink luggage with us, but I didn't find a purse. You were covered with snow." Raven frowned. "It was bad up there. You were the only survivor."

Horrified, Julie burst into tears. "Are you sure? That can't be possible."

"I checked everyone." Raven frowned and shook his head. "The plane hit the mountain and broke in half. The first half caught fire. The tail section, where you were sitting, broke off and was stuck in a snowdrift. You're lucky to be alive." He placed a box of tissues on the bed beside her. "I'll get word out as soon as I can get through to the next cabin. There's a CB radio inside. My truck and snowmobile are there as well." He sighed. "Avalanches have blocked many of the trails. We were lucky to make it here."

Blowing her nose and tossing the tissues into a bin he held out for her. She blinked through tears. "I want my dad. He'll be able to fix me."

"I'm doing my best and I can't get your dad right now. Even if we could reach him, there's no way around the avalanche to my cabin from the closest road." Raven gave her a long searching look. "You've been through a very traumatic experience and you're injured. Please don't get upset. I'll do everything in my power to get word to your father."

Shaky and unsure, Julie took another tissue and dabbed her eyes. Right now she had little choice but to try and get her head on straight and then decide what to do. "Okay."

"I'll get the bottle of meds. There's water beside you but would you like a hot drink?" Raven turned away and then paused at the open door. "Is coffee okay? How do you like it?"

Blowing out a breath and trying to calm down, Julie nodded. This man was only trying to be kind and hadn't acted threatening. "Yes, thank you. Cream and sugar, but first I need to use the bathroom."

"Oh." Raven nodded. "That door leads to the bathroom. It's a Jack and Jill, so lock your side when you're using it, okay? For now, I'll need to carry you and support your weight. I don't have any crutches, but I'll make you a stick as soon as possible. I figure your tibia is broken or at least cracked. I've straightened it and it's splinted, but you'll need to get to the hospital for X-rays. The problem is, we're snowed in and I'm all you've got right now, but you're in good hands. I served in the US Army Medical Corps and I'll take care of you for the time being."

She understood and looked at him. "You're a medical doctor? My dad served as well. He's the medical examiner out at Black Rock Falls."

"Then you'll know I'm competent at treating injuries like yours." Raven's lips flattened into a thin line. "Ready?"

When he tossed back the covers and scooped her into his arms, she cried out in pain. As her leg hung down, intense agony shot through her and she trembled and grit her teeth. "Oh, that hurts so bad."

"It will get better." He carried her into the bathroom and stood her before the toilet. "Hold on to my shoulders and I'll close my eyes."

Julie shook her head and glared at him. "I'll manage. Is there anyone else here? Do you have a wife who can help me? Who changed my clothes?"

"No wife. I undressed you, washed you, and put you in your PJ's." Raven shook his head. "You haven't got anything I haven't seen before. I'm a medical doctor. I took an oath to do no harm."

Her cheeks grew hot as embarrassment rushed over her. Doctor or not—if she could believe him—she didn't feel comfortable with him touching her especially when she'd been unconscious. She didn't trust him even with looks most women would melt over. He was tall like Dave but younger. As he bent closer, to steady her, she caught the smell of woodsmoke and soap. His clothes were clean and dark wavy hair flowed to his collar. His broad shoulders and arms were as hard as rocks. When his soft brown eyes settled on her and he scratched his short beard, she shook her head. "I don't know you. You could be a serial killer for all I know."

"Okay, it's going to be tough love or a wet bed." He pulled down her PJ's and lowered her onto the toilet. "You can do the paperwork. I'll get the coffee. Call me when you need a hand to get up." He turned and walked away.

Face burning, Julie did the necessary and managed to stand on one leg. Dizzy with pain, she gripped the edge of the basin and struggled to pull up her PJ's. Pivoting on one leg as waves of agony shot through her, she tried the faucet, glad to see running water even during a freeze. The hot water surprised her. This cabin was well equipped and from the spotless bathroom, Raven took pride in his home. She washed her hands and face and dried them on a towel beside the sink. "I'm done."

"I don't want you to put any weight on that leg." Raven lifted her with gentle care and carried her back into the bedroom.

The room had changed. Light flooded in through a frosted window. Wood had been added to the fire, giving the room a toasty glow. The pillows were piled up, so she had no problem sitting up. Beside the bed was a steaming cup of coffee in a huge ceramic mug. As Raven adjusted her pillows and made sure she could reach the coffee and water bottle beside the bed, he handed her a bottle of meds to examine. She recognized the label. "Those are fine, thank you."

"Two every six hours." He removed two from the bottle and dropped them into her palm. "I'll give them to you when necessary."

She looked at him. "Thank you. I do appreciate you helping me. It's been such a shock."

"It was fortunate I was out checking my traplines." He smiled and sat down in an easy chair facing her. "I have a meat locker stocked for winter, but I need extra food for my dogs, so I trap critters. The dogs pulled the sled that brought you here. I'd have never gotten you here without them. The dog in the house is called Ben. He's a military K-9 but he won't hurt you."

Concerned for the other dogs outside in the blizzard she could still see raging outside the window, she frowned. "Are your other dogs out there in the cold?"

"No." Raven chuckled deep in his chest. "They have very warm kennels in the barn. They're all rescue dogs and get along just fine. I was able to set the barn up same as the cabin. Solar panels and large-capacity storage batteries. We have a wealth of sunshine here. It powers everything I need, but I use wood fires in the rooms. There's never a shortage of dead trees to use in the forest."

Sipping her coffee, Julie met his gaze. "So in the winter when it snows, the solar panels would be covered. What happens then?"

"They're on a tilt, which in itself is self-cleaning, but once it stops snowing, I get up on the roof and clean off the snow." Raven took a cup of coffee from the nightstand. "When it's snowing, I'm careful with the power, and the wood fires heat the water. Power is used for lighting and appliances. So not so much really." He gave her a long look. "Tell me about you. I don't have many visitors. In fact, you're the first person to see my cabin."

Julie explained about moving to Black Rock Falls after her mom died and her uneventful life. "I've changed my mind about my career so many times it's driving my dad insane. I love kids so was thinking pediatrics, but then I've seen so many terrible things happen to kids. I'm not sure I could cope with it."

"Having a father who is a medical examiner wouldn't help." Raven's brow crinkled into a frown. "He must deal with many of the children caught up in serial killer homicides."

Finding Raven's conversation soothing, she relaxed. The pain was easing and hunger gnawed at her belly. Her stomach rumbled and she pressed a hand to it. "Tell me about how you came to be here all alone in the forest."

"It's a long story." He stood, gathered the cups and checked his watch. "It's a little after one. I'll get us something to eat." He smiled at her. "I found you about five hours ago. I figure the plane crash was about seven this morning."

Recalling the early flight time, Julie nodded. "Yeah, I managed to get onto a cargo flight. Mostly medical supplies and canned goods I believe. We left around six."

"Yeah, I collected the medical supplies and as much of the canned goods as I could carry on the first trip and then went back for the rest. Then an avalanche blocked the trail and now I doubt anyone will get to the wreck until after the melt. Once everything is frozen it's useless. I'll keep it here. If the owners want it back, they can collect it from me." He gave her a long look. "I took the first aid kit as well. The medical supplies had a variety of pain meds and antibiotics. I needed pain meds for you. It wasn't looting. It was a necessity. I left all the luggage but yours in the cargo hold. As you were the only woman on board, I figured it belonged to you."

Julie thought for a beat. "Thanks, and to be honest, I doubt anyone will worry about the supplies. They'll be more interested in collecting the remains and personal items of the victims. The cargo will be insured. I don't honestly believe anyone will be too concerned about a few cans of beans." She leaned back in the pillows. "When my dad comes to get me, you can give him the medical supplies. He'll know what to do with them. Although, I gather you'd put them to good use. Do you treat many people here in the mountains?"

"A few. Some hunting accidents if I come across them." Raven stood, filling the doorway, two cups in his hands. "I don't have any communication with the outside world apart from the CB radio I mentioned. If Breda gives me the heads-up about someone ailing, I'll go and help out. My license is current. I could start up a practice in town, but right now I'm enjoying the solitude. I live off the land, sell dogs I train, and have an Army pension. I don't really need to go back to nine-to-five."

Wondering what had happened to make him want to live a solitary lifestyle, Julie's mind went to Agent Ty Carter. He'd suffered PTSD and taken himself off the grid for three years, preferring to live alone in the forest than being with people and memories. Maybe something real bad had happened to Raven in the Army? She nodded. "It sounds like bliss, although I'd miss TV."

"Oh, I have a dish but I rarely watch the news. I prefer movies or documentaries." Raven grinned at her. "I need mental stimulation or I get restless and howl at the moon." He chuckled and turned to go. "When you feel better and the blizzard has passed, I'll carry you out into the family room. With luck, I'll be able to clear the snow from the dish and you can watch TV."

Julie watched him go, leaving the scent of woodsmoke behind him. Maybe it was his bedside manner, but even doctors weren't that friendly. Well, not any she'd met. He seemed so nice. Maybe a little too nice. Her mind conjured up a series of weird scenarios and she blamed it on having just finished reading behavioral analyst Jo Wells' series on the mind of a serial killer. A shiver of concern slid down her spine. Charismatic, tick. Lives alone in the forest, tick. Single white male, tick. Did he show empathy for the other victims? He'd checked them and they were all dead, but all still lying out for the wildlife to devour. So lack of empathy, tick. As panic gripped her, she recalled how some serial killers cared for others. Some even married and had double lives. Not everyone fit their fantasy. Maybe she'd be lucky. So far, he hadn't hurt her. If he was a serial killer, just how long would that last if she accidentally pulled his trigger?

SEVEN

Even bundled up against the cold wearing her snow goggles, a hat, a scarf, and a hood, icy shards bit into Jenna's exposed flesh as they headed along narrow trails in the direction of Bear Peak. Rowley led the way. Having roamed the forest since he was a boy, he could find his way to most areas. When he slowed and held up a hand, Jenna leaned in closer to Kane's wide back. "What's happening?"

"I'm not sure. Rowley is off his snowmobile and looking at something." Kane wiped snow from his visor. "He wants us. It looks like he's found something."

Concern gripped Jenna as she climbed from the seat and waited for Kane and then followed Rio with Wolfe and Emily behind them. As they reached the place where Rowley had abruptly stopped, Jenna gaped in horror at the body of a young naked woman gaffer-taped to a tree. Her hair had been hacked off with a knife and was scattered over a pile of snow-covered clothes. Small cuts had bled in glittering crimson rivulets against her bald skull. She was frozen solid, and what was left of the young woman's hair stood in small tufts and looked as if it had been draped with diamonds. Her cloudy and frozen eyes appeared doll-like as she peered ahead from under exaggeratedly long false eyelashes, as if searching the view. Dark tears, from where her mascara had run, tracked down both cheeks. She'd been placed as if to look through the trees to the river beyond and across the valley. On her forehead a red smiley face peeked through the ice.

Jenna's gaze slid over the woman. She couldn't make out any obvious cause of death. No marks marred the woman's smooth flesh. No blood spotted the snow at her feet. "I wonder how long she's been here?"

"It's hard to tell until we thaw her and then it will be a guess." Wolfe frowned. "This is very disturbing. We'll take down the coordinates, secure the scene with tape, and deal with her later. Nothing will change here in the next twenty-four hours or more. Our priority is reaching the victims of the plane crash. Every second counts in this weather."

"Copy that." Kane took the coordinates as Rio and Rowley wrapped crime scene tape around trees, cordoning off the immediate areas. He looked at Jenna. "We need to get to Julie's plane. There will be people there who need our help. This woman is past helping right now."

Nodding, Jenna walked back to the snowmobile. "If it's not bad enough trying to find a missing plane, now we have a killer on the loose. I can't win."

Ten minutes later Rowley slowed again and waved his arms frantically. Jenna poked Kane in the back. "Ride to where he is. We can't keep stopping all the time."

"Okay." Kane shot past Rio and slowed beside Rowley's snowmobile.

Stunned, Jenna stared at another body. This one's once long dark hair littered the snow-covered pile of shredded clothes at her feet. It was the same MO right down to the hacked-off hair and the smiley face on the forehead. "Okay, make a note of the coordinates and keep moving. Seems we have a serial killer roaming the forest decorating the trees with his victims. Heaven knows how many more he has out here."

It was the very first time in her life Jenna had walked away from a crime scene. Leaving the victims behind played on her mind. It seemed callous and mean-spirited. They needed her help to bring their killer to justice but the people on the plane needed her too. She bit down on her bottom lip, torn between giving the victims respect and her need to find Julie. Maybe she should split the team? Dismissing the idea, she shook her head. In all cases, the living took priority. Moving on was the right decision. She sent up a silent prayer. *Please let Julie and the other passengers be safe.*

Another ten minutes passed, they were moving faster along hiking trails, the way was wider, and it was easier to see obstacles in their path. Each of Rio's and Rowley's and Wolfe's snowmobiles had trailers attached that were suitable to carry any injured to safety and extra medical equipment and body bags. Again ahead, Rowley waved and Kane flashed to his side. Jenna's heart missed a beat at the sight of the twisted burned wreckage. She could see charred limbs poking out of the snow. The front half of the aircraft was still smoking. Choking back a sob of despair, she climbed off the snowmobile and looked at Kane, lowering her voice so that Wolfe wouldn't overhear. "We're too late. They're all dead."

"Maybe not. The tail part of the aircraft is still intact." Kane waited for Wolfe to climb from his snowmobile and walk to their side. He pointed to the rear of the plane. "That might be a positive sign as I recall Julie saying that she always preferred to travel in the back of the aircraft. It looks like the snowdrift buffered the impact."

"We'll check the remains, and if we can't locate her, then get someone to search the outlying areas around the aircraft." Wolfe turned in a half circle. "The way it broke in half on impact, it could have thrown people out as it landed. There were six souls on board and the pilot." Wolfe tuned to Emily. "You gonna be okay?"

"I've been thinking about finding her dead all the way here." Emily straightened and glanced at Jenna. "I'm sure Jenna has too, but I'm sure if Julie is out there in the snow, she'd want me to find her. She knows I'll take care of her."

"Okay, but if it gets too much for you, tell me." Wolfe gave her a hug. "I'm hoping we'll find her alive. If she was in the tail, she'd have a fighting chance." He walked from one charred remains to another and shook his head. "Dave, she's not here. Check the tail section."

"Copy that." Kane trudged through the snow.

"Okay, I'll place markers on any bodies or parts I find." Emily gathered what she needed and walked toward the mangled burned bodies.

Surveying the crash scene with trepidation, Jenna dragged her professional persona around her. Falling to bits wasn't an option. "Rio, Rowley, search the perimeter for survivors. I'll contact search and rescue and give them our coordinates. As soon as the weather clears, they might be able to land a chopper." She turned to Wolfe. "Will they be able to land a chopper on that slope?"

"That's doubtful. It's little more than a sheet of ice and with the low visibility it's not worth the risk." Wolfe headed toward the tail of the aircraft sticking up in the air. "Unless the weather gets worse, they'll be able to send a team by snowmobile to help search the area."

Jenna made the call and followed Kane and Wolfe to the broken tail section. Sharp metal fragments, body parts, carry-on luggage, cans of soda, and garbage stuck out from the snow. She stepped in Kane's footprints and cupped her mouth. "Sheriff's department. Is anyone here? Call out."

Not a sound other than the creak of metal and branches moving in the wind came through the forest. She listened and searched the trees and reached the plane as Kane pulled himself over the ragged edge and disappeared inside. The next moment the door swung open and hung moving back and forth in the wind before closing again. She turned to Wolfe. "Someone has been here. Look how the luggage has been piled up."

"It sure looks like that, which could be a good sign, if they helped survivors. Worst-case scenario, someone living close by has looted the plane." Wolfe climbed up onto the luggage and pulled open the door to peer inside. "The seats at the back look okay and the cargo door is open."

"The cargo has been tampered with." Kane stuck his head over the edge of the plane. "I found this. It's Julie's purse and her phone and ID are inside." He frowned and held up an earring. "This is why she hasn't contacted you. This is her tracker, isn't it?"

"Yeah, dammit. Can you see pink luggage?" Wolfe took the purse, tucked the earring inside, and handed it to Jenna. "It's not with the others."

Confused, Jenna searched around and found nothing. She waved to Emily. "Can you see Julie's luggage?"

"Nope." Emily placed another flag in the snow and turned her attention to Wolfe. "I can't find a trace of her, Dad. Are you sure she took this flight?"

"Yeah, for one, I tracked her to this general location, although the signal was sketchy, but now we have her purse. She also called me to give me the flight number just before she boarded." Wolfe scanned the clearing from his perch on top of the luggage. "It was an hour before the regular flight and she managed to get a seat on a cargo plane. She didn't want me and Norrell waiting around the airport for hours."

"That's kind and considerate Julie for you." Emily sighed and stared at the victims. "I figure all these bodies are men. They're big-boned even with the burns. They didn't stand a chance. Maybe Julie got out alive?"

"How many bodies do you make it? I counted six." Wolfe jumped down and headed toward Emily.

"Yeah, I counted six too. That would be five passengers and the pilot, Julie was number six on the passenger list." Emily's gray eyes brimmed with tears. "If her purse was here, she was here. Where is she now? There's nowhere to go and she knows to stay with the wreck. It offered her shelter inside the cargo hold. Why would she leave? It makes no sense."

"I'll check the bodies again. Keep looking under any lumps in the snow." Wolfe moved around, bending over. He looked up when Rio and Rowley arrived back from their search, shaking their heads. "Rio, can you take pictures and then we'll bag these bodies. Our time here is limited. We have no shelter and we'll freeze to death before the sun goes down." He blew out a puff of steam. "We'll come back tomorrow."

Horrified, Jenna picked her way through the carnage. "No, we can't leave, we must keep looking. If someone was here and left with her, they would have left a clue."

"Doubtful, all tracks would be covered by the snow." Kane bent over, brushing snow from lumps and moving to the next possibility. "If her luggage is gone, I figure someone came by to help and took her with them, but why didn't she take her purse?"

"Y'all assuming she was conscious?" Wolfe's eyes narrowed. "If she was in the tail, she'd have taken the window seat. Part of the wing pierced that part of the fuselage. Chances are she's injured. I can't see any blood but that doesn't mean she didn't sustain head and neck injuries or leg injuries. Anything can happen during a wreck, but it gives me hope someone cared enough to haul her out."

"Well, whoever riffled through the cargo, took medical supplies and canned goods. But left her purse, although it was under the seat and there is snow all over in there. Maybe he missed it?" Kane held up a clipboard with paper attached. "This is a cargo inventory. Just a minute." He thrust the clipboard into Wolfe's hands, leapt up onto the luggage, and peered inside the tail section of the plane. "The first aid box has been ripped from the wall. This tells me Julie was alive and taken somewhere."

Panic gripped Jenna. She stared through the snow-laden pines. "Where is she?" *Oh, sweet Jesus, don't tell me she's been rescued by a serial killer.*

EIGHT

Moving his field glasses across the frozen landscape he cursed under his breath at the sight of the sheriff and her team. How had they managed to find the downed aircraft and miss his line of frozen fakes? He took in the preparation to leave. Each body was carefully slid into a body bag along with an evidence bag filled with possessions he assumed belonged to each victim of the air crash. The way they were heading led right to the two bodies he'd left close by, but he didn't worry about the sheriff finding him as his tracks were covered by thick layers of snow. He smiled to himself. She didn't know the extent of his line of fakes but maybe with all the attention on the air crash, teams would be coming in from different directions before too long.

His mind went back to Carolyn Stubbs waiting for him in the cabin. Living in the forest had its advantages. Most people would leave their cabins vacant over the winter, preferring not to risk being snowed in for months on end. It gave him the opportunity to use the cabins for his own use. When the women were found, an investigation would commence, and by selecting a different one each time, he would throw suspicion across all the cabin owners. The forest was vast and he had come to know it like the back of his hand. The protected trails during snowfall made it easy for him to move around using his snowmobile. Dense forest offered a canopy to lessen the snowfall and allowed him to move freely to many of the fire roads, which in turn gave him access to the highway. He'd made his home in two cabins but never took a woman that he planned to murder there. The one on the edge of the forest housed his truck and snowmobile, the other, deep in the forest, he used as his secret hideout. Protected by dogs, and signposted, no one came by. He'd become the recluse, the man nobody approached because they figured he'd shoot them dead. It was a great place to hide.

In someone else's cabin, Carolyn Stubbs waited for him. Waited to die. He chuckled. Excitement bubbled over at the idea of tying her to a tree while the sheriff was in the forest. The sheriff would no doubt be back with other officials as there was no way they had completed their examination of the crash site. He would wait until they left the area and then take Carolyn to look at the crash site and leave her somewhere close by for them to find on their return. Thrilled by his ingenious plan, he tipped back his head, allowing the snowflakes to touch his face like butterfly kisses. The chilled air didn't worry him. In fact, the snow was his friend. It took the lives of the self-important women he loathed and covered all traces of his existence. It gave him time to walk his line and see them all caught like vermin in his traps. All staring sightless ice sculptures of gargoyles. It was as if they'd grown from the trees like parasitic plants sucking the life out of them, but in his experience, high-maintenance women did that to a man. The women in his collection had spent all their waking hours touching hair framed around a face a surgeon had given them. The sight of their oversized breasts and huge ugly lips made him shudder. At first, he'd laughed at the way their eyebrows reached almost to their hairlines and the thick false eyelashes made them look like freaky dolls, but it was the hair that drove him to distraction. It was always long, usually colored, and then they tossed their heads and moved it over one shoulder and then back, tucked it behind one ear, and milliseconds later did the same thing over. Watching them preen was like a macabre *Groundhog Day*.

Nothing soothed him like cutting off all their hair and showing them what they looked like. He couldn't shoot, stab, or strangle them. No, all that blood and mess wasn't his style and it was just too quick for them. They owed him for annoying him for so long, and freezing them to death made everyone see them for what they truly were: fakes. When all the layers of fine clothes were peeled back, the surgical scars laid bare, and the hair removed, the world would see them as they truly were. He pushed his field glasses back into the case hanging around his neck and trudged back to the cabin. Carolyn would be waiting for him by the fire. Her fat red lips would spread to show her new snow-white veneers. Not one wrinkle marred her filled swollen cheeks and then she'd start to play with her hair. He shuddered and stood for a few minutes, allowing calmness to float down over him. He was a nice guy—well, at first at least. He grinned. The women saw him in the persona he portrayed, but just like them, inside a different person lurked. They wore their masks on the outside, but he hid his true self until it was too late to run.

NINE

Trying not to allow his concern for Julie to outweigh his common sense, Kane checked his watch. Taking into account the time it would take to return to the highway, load the snowmobiles, and go and collect Tauri from Wolfe's home, he figured they had approximately one hour to search the immediate area for any sign of life. He went to Jenna as she watched Wolfe go through the motions of collecting and labeling body parts, his face grim with determination. Even though Emily was as professional as usual, tears streamed down her face. Kane turned to Jenna. "If somebody took Julie with them, they must have a cabin close by."

"Close by could be two miles away." Jenna turned tragic eyes to him. "It makes sense they must have had a snowmobile or some form of transport because no one would be carrying her and all that luggage on their back." She hugged her chest and shivered. "What direction should we take? We need more boots on the ground and aerial assistance." She shook snow from her hood. "This snow is endless. It won't give up."

Hearing voices, Kane looked into the distance and spotted

Blackhawk heading toward them leading a group of snowmobiles. "Atohi has made it through. That's a good sign. There must be a clear stretch between here and the rez."

"Any survivors?" Blackhawk climbed from the snowmobile and stared at the wreckage. "Julie?"

"She's missing." Jenna leaned against Kane. "Everyone was killed in the crash."

"That's bad news. You all look exhausted." Blackhawk went to his trailer. "I have hot coffee and sandwiches. Eat and then we'll search the area. All of my friends know Bear Peak. We've hunted here many times."

Relieved to see him, Kane nodded. "Am I glad to see you." He gave him the details of everything they'd found. "So we're looking for cabins in the area and any more bodies. It's unlikely he stopped at two."

"This is a very sick mind." Blackhawk handed out cups and filled them from Thermoses. "No one will fly in this weather. The visibility is bad and the wind blowing through the pass would push a chopper into the mountain, just like the aircraft. The way we came through was difficult, but the forest provided cover and the snowdrifts weren't too deep for now. One more day and we'll be unable to get here."

Sipping the hot brew, Kane nodded to Blackhawk's friends, all he knew well. "Thank you all for coming. I need your knowledge. How many cabins would be around here in, say, a two-mile radius?"

"Too many." Blackhawk frowned and pointed to the west. "Two in that direction, hunting cabins. I didn't see smoke when I came down the mountain and I don't smell any. If someone is staying close by, we'd smell smoke. Whoever has taken Julie is outside the perimeter you've considered. When you return to collect the murder victims, maybe bring a drone or two. Look for smoke and you'll find your cabin." He frowned and filled a cup for Wolfe and pushed it into his hands. "I know you are worried but think about what you have told me. Julie is gone, so are her things. Someone rescued her and thought enough to take her luggage and medical supplies. If they meant to do her harm, they'd have done it and tied her to a tree also."

"That's logical." Wolfe took a bite from a sandwich and ate mechanically. "We don't have a clue where to start looking. I figure we take the remains back to the morgue and get a list of next of kin for DNA samples. None of those poor souls are recognizable. We know we can get through from town. We'll bring the snowmobile team from search and rescue with us at first light."

"We can get into town." Blackhawk looked from one to the other. "We'll meet you on the fire road at Bear Peak at first light. Bring the drones." He handed out coffee and sandwiches to Rio, Rowley, and Emily. "We'll scout around on the way back to the rez and see if we can find any tracks but it's doubtful. Look, our tracks are almost covered already. You must keep hope that Julie is in safe hands. We'll find her but not this afternoon."

"What worries me is that we haven't had a call." Rio looked from one to the other. "We all have satellite phones. If someone had called 911 and told Maggie they'd found Julie, she'd have called."

"Not everyone has a satellite phone or even a phone." Rowley looked around. "This is off-the-grid country. People who come here don't want to communicate with others." He leaned against a tree and met Kane's gaze. "My thoughts are, if someone has her, they'll wait for a break in the weather and then get to someone they know has a phone. The cabins on the edge of the forest are all dwellings. People have lived there, rain, hail, or shine. Most would have phones or CB radios for sure."

"Okay." Wolfe looked at the pile of body bags. "We can fit the murder victims on the trailers. All the victims will take days to thaw. Norrell can watch them. She's in charge at the morgue in my absence." He looked at Kane. "Can you ask Maggie to send out a call on the office CB to ask about Julie?"

Handing the cup back to Blackhawk, Kane turned to Wolfe. "I'll call her now. She'll contact everyone she knows. Atohi has a point. Whoever has taken her means to care for her or they wouldn't have taken her things. We must think positive and get back here as soon as possible to search for her. Right now, we have little time to get home before the temperature drops again. I'm just hoping the mayor had the snowplow guys out all day clearing the highway, or we'll be bunking at your house tonight."

"The roads through town and out to our ranch will be okay." Jenna looked at him. "I spoke to the mayor personally and he gave me his word." She stared at the sky. "The search-and-rescue snowmobile team obviously didn't get through, so they can follow us in the morning. The wider the circle we can cover the better." She turned to Blackhawk. "The highway from the top of Bear Peak and into the mountains should be clear. The mayor mentioned keeping a way out of Glacial Heights Ski Resort in case of an emergency."

"That's good news." Blackhawk collected the cups and tossed them into a bag on his trailer. "We will scout around the area for as long as possible and then head home. I'll call if we find anything and we'll see you in the morning." He climbed on his ride and led his team back along the trail.

Worry still curled in Kane's belly but there was little he could do right now. He scanned the area one last time, seeing Blackhawk's team heading opposite to where Rio and Rowley had searched. He took Jenna's hand. "You need to get out of the weather." He led Jenna to the snowmobile. She was blue with cold and had gone past shivering. He needed to get her home. He left her there and went to speak to Wolfe. "Can you manage with the murder victims if we leave Rowley and Rio with you? I'd like to get Jenna back to the office."

"Yeah, we'll be close behind." Wolfe leaned in closer and looked at the team. "We're all cold and heartsore. I feel like tearing out trees to find Julie. Going home and leaving her here is like ripping out my heart but we are doing the right thing." He slapped Kane on the shoulder. "We'll all get through this horrible day. It's tomorrow we should be worrying about."

TEN

Darkness pressed against the window and shadows had crept into the room when Julie woke. Pain shot up her leg in burning agony the second she tried to move. The only light in the room was from the log burning in the fireplace. It had been huge when Raven had added it at lunchtime. She reached for the bedside lamp and switched it on. Beside the bed was a Thermos, two pills, and three energy bars. The house was completely silent and previously she had heard Raven moving around the house with Ben close behind. The dog's claws tapped across the wooden floors each time he moved. Perhaps it was the middle of the night? She had no idea how long she'd been sleeping. Dragging herself into a sitting position, she cried out in pain. Sweat formed on her brow and trickled down her face and yet the room was cool. If the fire went out completely, it would be freezing inside.

With shaking hands she reached for the Thermos and poured a cup of coffee. Lukewarm liquid poured down her throat as she took a sip to swallow the pills. She peeled an energy bar and took small bites. If Raven had prepared dinner, she wondered why he hadn't woken her. It seemed strange for him to leave coffee, pills, and snacks if he was at home. Her attention moved to the bedside table, pushed between it and the bed was a long stick that resembled the figure seven. The bark had been stripped from it and the top of the seven before the bend had bandages wrapped around it. It was a crude but serviceable crutch. She looked around, noticing her spare pajamas on the nightstand and her pink fleece bathrobe draped over the end of the bed. Raven had unpacked her bags or taken out a few necessities. Should she call out? Maybe not if the man was asleep.

Needing to use the bathroom, she eased to the edge of the bed. Her injured leg dropped down and with it a wave of pain so intense, Julie cried out and tears ran down her cheeks. She sat on the edge of the bed sucking in deep breaths just trying to live through the pain. As the agony slowly subsided to a throb, she grabbed the crutch and using it as a hook, grabbed her bathrobe. Getting it on wasn't a problem although moving caused pain in places she didn't know existed. Her ribs hurt, her shoulder stiff and painful, and one of her arms was black and blue right down to her wrist and fingers. Using her good leg, she stood slowly, tucking the crutch under her arm. The moment she tried to take a step, giddiness engulfed her. She pressed one hand against the wall. The bathroom seemed a mile away. She pressed her lips together and moved the crutch, swinging her good leg forward. It took forever to make the few steps into the bathroom and turning around was a nightmare, but she made it. Using one leg to stand wasn't so bad, but when she hobbled to the basin, she noticed her personal things laid out. She swallowed hard and stared at the other door. It was closed but not locked. She desperately needed to wash. Her face felt stiff and needed moisturizer. She removed her garments the best she could, filled the sink with hot water, and using one of the washcloths in a pile on the shelf, went about making herself feel better. Once done, she brushed her hair and applied moisturizer to her face. She had a bruise on her forehead. In fact, she had bruises all over.

Moving had come easier since the initial rush of intense pain. She made her way slowly to the open bedroom door and peered outside. It was a short passageway that led to a cozy family room at one end and kitchen at the other. The cabin was large enough to be comfortable for two people and it was empty. In the fireplace, red embers glowed, but cold was creeping under the door. Moving slowly, Julie made it to the fire, pulled back the guard, and dropped two logs into the grate. The effort made her pant and every movement hurt but staying warm was necessary for survival. She edged her way back along the passageway, intending to peer into Raven's room. He might be asleep. If not, why was he out in the wilderness? Where would he go for so long? Going out in the middle of the night in below-freezing temperatures wasn't normal. What was he doing that was so secret that he needed to hide it from her?

Without as much as a sound, the front door flew open, wind scattered snowflakes across the pristine floor, and Raven stepped inside. Suddenly afraid, Julie's heart raced at the sight of him and she took a few painful involuntary steps backward. She must have been gaping at him as he stamped his feet on the old mat and stared at her with a quizzical expression. Beside him, Ben sat staring at her as if waiting for a command. Uncertain, she froze on the spot. Cold surrounded him and ice had formed on his short beard and eyebrows. "You look chilled to the bone."

"That's because I am." Raven removed his boots and stood them by the door and then grabbed a towel hanging nearby and dried Ben's legs. The dog wore a coat and he removed it before his own. "I tried to get back to the wreckage to see if anyone had come by but there's been another avalanche cutting off the trail. It was difficult to find a way back here. I've dried the dogs and settled them for the night." He glanced at his watch. "You must be hungry. It's five after nine. I figured I'd be out for two hours." He looked her over. "It's good to see you up and moving around. How much pain are you in right now on a scale of one to ten, ten being the worst pain you've experienced?"

Julie leaned against the wall as he removed hat, gloves, and coat. "Ten when I tried to get off the bed. Not so bad when I'm standing, maybe a six. Why is that?"

"Probably nerve sensitivity." Raven headed for the kitchen and splashed water over his face and dried it on a towel hanging beside the sink on a nail. "The pain will ease when you rest and then hurt when you move it. I'm not sure it's broken, a crack maybe. Which is just as painful and often they take longer to heal than a fracture."

Julie hobbled closer and made it all the way into the kitchen. "Anything I can do to help?"

"Ah, no." Raven grinned at her. "You might fall down and hurt yourself. Your bruises are coming out already. Any blurred vision, bad headaches?"

Shaking her head, Julie stared at a man used to caring for himself. She'd known many men in the military and most had spotless homes, could care for themselves, and cook meals from scratch. Many, like Carter, preferred the forest to living in town. "I have bruises all over and my leg hurts, but apart from that I'm okay." Her mind went to her dad and sisters. "My dad will be frantic. He'll be out searching for me. How do we let him know I'm okay?"

"I took a sign and planned to leave it at the crash site giving the approximate coordinates of my cabin, but like I said, the way back there is blocked." He took a casserole dish from the fridge and pushed it into the oven. "It's elk casserole. I prepare a ton of it and freeze it for winter. I left it to thaw when I went out. I hope you like mashed potatoes. I baked a ton in the fire, scooped out the centers, and added butter. They reheat well and I can fry the leftovers in the morning with vegetables." He met her gaze. "Carbs are good in this weather."

Heart sinking, Julie nodded. "I like that fine, but it sounds like I'm going to be here for a long time." She waved a hand toward the snow pelting the window. "I don't figure the snow is going to let up anytime soon." She sighed.

"I'll enjoy the company, but I won't be here all the time." Raven filled the coffee pot and added the ground beans to the filter. "I check my traps daily and will be looking for a way through to the old man's cabin. If at any time, I don't come back, there's plenty of food and the pipes won't freeze. Water flows from an underground stream, directly below the cabin. I designed a way to heat the water before it reaches the pipes to the house. It's filtered as well."

Julie raised both eyebrows. "How did you know to do that?"

"When I decided living off the grid was what I needed, I read many survivalist books and searched the internet for ways to live without power. I do have a generator for emergencies and a truck, which is parked in the barn of the old man's cabin. From there, I can get to the highway via the fire roads if I need to get into town." He shrugged. "The problem is, right now, we're snowed in. I'm afraid you're stuck with me."

Horrified at having to spend a moment longer with him, Julie bit her lip. Why did he act so nonchalant, as if everything was turning out as planned? She'd read about smooth-talking serial killers. One second, they were as nice as pie, but say the wrong thing to trigger them, and she'd become his next victim. Sifting through all the information he'd given her, every excuse could have been a lie. Sure, it was snowing but people moved through the forest all through winter on snowmobiles. Had there really been an avalanche or was that another excuse? Was he planning on keeping her prisoner in the cabin forever? Right now, she had no way of telling. Helpless and alone, she had no choice but she'd never trust him—not ever.

ELEVEN

SUNDAY

"Jenna."

Jenna dragged herself from a dream at Kane's voice and blinked at his face. It was so good to wake up and just see him there. She reached out to touch him. Yes, he was really there and it hadn't all been a dream. "Morning. Did I miss the alarm?"

"Nope." He smiled at her. "Sit up nice and slow." He pushed a pillow behind her. "Now sip this ginger beer. Wolfe insists it helps with the morning sickness and there are crackers. Sit still for a time and see if we can beat this thing."

Grinning, Jenna patted his arm but took the soda and sipped. "Okay but it's just my body adapting to the baby. It won't last forever."

"This I understand but we're meeting Blackhawk in the mountains at daybreak." Kane frowned. "He called last night and his friends searched for a good radius around the crash site, but they didn't find Julie or any tracks. He made it to a couple of cabins close by as well. They're shut up tight for winter." He stood slowly and rubbed the back of his neck as if he didn't want to tell her something.

Sipping and feeling okay, Jenna met his gaze. "Spit it out. I know you have something to tell me and don't want to. I'm pregnant, not dying of some terrible disease." She tugged at his sweater. "Look, I know you worry about me all the time. Yes, I seem to be a little more tired than usual. Wolfe said that's fine and he's checking my blood work in case I need a supplement. You trust him, don't you?"

"Yeah, with my life, but shouldn't you have an obstetrician?" Kane shook his head. "I don't really want our baby delivered in the medical examiner's office."

Frowning, Jenna shook her head. "Neither do I, but don't worry, Wolfe will be using all the facilities at the hospital, including the ultrasound. There is a delivery suite there and I trust him to deliver our baby. Him and Norrell."

"So you want a forensic anthropologist and a medical examiner rather than a specialist obstetrician?" Kane ran a hand down his face. "Okay, but I'm not leaving your side."

Giggling, Jenna nibbled on crackers, so far feeling fine. "I'd expect no less, Dave. Now stop making excuses and tell me what Blackhawk told you last night."

"It was a little puzzling." Kane scratched his chin. "They did a sweep of the area and then met up back at the crash site before leaving and found another body attached to a tree. Same MO as before." A nerve twitched in his cheek. "It's not far from the crime scene tape we used to mark out the crash site. I'm not sure how Rio and Rowley missed it, but Blackhawk did say it was well hidden by bushes covered in snow."

Swallowing a mouthful of crackers, Jenna gaped at him. "Did you tell him to travel in numbers until we catch this killer?"

"Yeah, he knows the deal. His group will be joining search and rescue, so about ten guys on snowmobiles. When we get there, we can spread out and start searching all the trails we can find passable. Right now, everyone is trying to find where someone took Julie."

Concerned for the people walking into a serial killer, Jenna frowned. "I'll brief them when we get there. Most of them will be carrying rifles and satellite phones. I'm surprised the killer decided to dump another body near the crash site. It's like he is thumbing his nose at us. It's a 'catch me if you can' scenario. He thinks he's untouchable."

"The snow is nonstop, which makes him just about invisible." Kane took a woolen cap from the chest of drawers and pulled it on. "You sit for a while and see how you go. I'll go and tend the horses." He smiled at her. "It feels strange with Tauri away. I know letting him sleep over at Wolfe's last night was the right thing to do, but seeing his bed empty this morning made me feel sad."

Jenna nodded. "He was so excited to sleep over with Anna and I didn't want to drag him out in the cold last night and again early this morning. He's having fun, and right now, he's a distraction for Anna. She'll be so worried about Julie it's better they're together. We'll see him this morning and bring him home tonight." She looked down at Duke's head resting on the bed and rubbed his soft ears. "We'll leave Duke with him as well. He'll love being with the kids."

"That's a good idea. He misses Tauri as well. Okay, now I want you to relax, sip the soda, and nibble on the crackers." Kane backed out of the room. "Wolfe said that ginger beer is brewed in Texas and he swears it will help. I'll be back soon."

Feeling fine, Jenna leaned back on the pillows. Her mind was fixed on Julie. She must find her, but who was killing the women and how come the wildlife hadn't eaten them? In the middle of winter food was scarce. Who was killing people in the forest? She needed to know more about the cabins in the crash site area. Who owned them and how many empty hunting cabins existed? Many bad things had happened at Bear Peak. It was known as the local killing field. Remote until the fire roads had cut through the forest. Later hikers and hunters had found graves all over. She wondered why anyone would live there and not be concerned about the morbid history of the place, but then maybe that's the reason they chose it, because no one would drop by.

She reached for her tablet beside the bed and made notes. She might not be in the office, but she had an ally in the FBI, computer whiz kid Bobby Kalo. He lived in an apartment in the FBI field office in Snakeskin Gully, where he worked with her good friends, agent Ty Carter and behavioral analyst Jo Wells. He was a young man who spent his downtime online gaming and never minded a challenge no matter what day of the week. She shot him an email explaining what she needed and why. With everyone involved with the search, he was her best choice for tracking down the owners of the cabins around Bear Peak. He'd also be able to tell her who had been hunting in the area. All kills must be recorded by the forest wardens, and he would be able to access those records. Being FBI opened doors she would usually find locked. She swung her legs off the bed and stood slowly. So far so good. This was the best she'd felt in days. Two steps inside the bathroom, she clasped a hand over her mouth, dashed to the toilet, and spewed. *So much for Wolfe's wonder cure.*

TWELVE

Warm inside from seeing Tauri happy and contented at Wolfe's house, Kane ignored the icy chill biting into his exposed flesh and gripped the handlebars of the snowmobile. His fleece-lined leather gloves protected his hands most times, but in these temperatures his fingers were going numb. At least his back was warm with Jenna snuggled close behind him. She seemed fine, recovering faster this morning and eating breakfast. He'd packed a large carrier with sandwiches and filled all the Thermos flasks with hot coffee and chocolate, then tossed in a box of energy bars just in case. He'd even packed a change of coats, jeans, gloves, and boots for both of them. He'd loaded his covered trailer with everything he could think they might need. The weather could turn again in a second. Right now, the snow was light, but the weather report mentioned another blizzard on the way and temperatures dropping again. Nothing could prepare him for the extreme and unexpected changes in climate. He'd just take every precaution. If they became stuck out overnight, their chances of making it through the night were minimal. Up ahead, Blackhawk and his friends led the way through trails they'd discovered, pointing out the cabins they'd found along the way. At each one they stopped, hammered on the doors, and looked around for any sign of habitation. Most people would have a fire going all winter long, so the lack of smoke told them no one was at home.

When they arrived at the location of the body, Wolfe dismounted along with Emily, and they walked around searching the ground for clues. Kane walked to his side with Jenna, and they waited for him to examine the victim. "Is it the same MO?"

"It sure looks the same." Jenna moved closer. "Why do you figure he cuts off their hair like that?"

"I examined the bodies of the other women this morning. They'll still take a long time to thaw but there are no apparent injuries. They've had extensive cosmetic surgery: face and breasts, as far as I could tell. Teeth are porcelain caps on both victims. The nails are false too. These women were high-maintenance. From the amount of hair at the scene, both had long hair, neither appear to be natural color, but I'll confirm once I get back to the lab." Wolfe frowned at them. "I figure he tied them to the tree alive and left them to freeze to death. Talk to Jo Wells. What's happened here is significant. The extensive cosmetic alterations, being naked, with the hair hacked off and left to die means something, and she'll know." He sighed. "We'll photograph the scene and get her bagged and tagged before the wildlife do any more damage. It looks as if something nibbled at her ankles, is all."

Kane took in the figure before him. The usual smell of death was missing. The body must have frozen in a short time. Death would have come quickly in such low temperatures, but would it have been painful? He turned to Wolfe. "She looks like a sad statue. Did she suffer?"

"At first, the constriction of the blood vessels due to the sudden drop in body temperature causes pain, but as the process continues the body becomes numb, organs start to shut down, and at the end, no, there's no pain." Wolfe met his gaze. "My fingers are numb and painful, so I guess yours are as well. It's much the same but it gets worse before it gets better."

"She looks like the others, as if she can't believe what's happened to her." Jenna shook her head slowly. "Why would a woman come out here in the middle of winter with someone she just met?" She flicked a glance at Kane. "It would be very difficult to bring someone here against their will on a snowmobile or dogsled."

"Yeah, it would." Wolfe pulled a scarf back over his nose and slapped his hands together. "When I do the blood work, I'll check for drugs, but she was awake and alive when her hair was cut off with a knife or she wouldn't have bled."

Taking in the crime scene, Kane bent and peered at the shredded garments. "The damage to the clothes is the same as the others too." He straightened. "This hasn't been done by a critter, these were cut from the body first. See how the hair is scattered on top? The eye makeup on all three was running down their faces as if they were crying when he was doing this to them. I figure they knew him."

"I agree and I'll talk to Jo but, right now our main concern is finding Julie. By all means help Wolfe get the body bagged, but then we keep searching." Jenna frowned. "Blackhawk mentioned one of the trails is blocked by an avalanche. It's getting dangerous to be moving alongside the mountain looking for cabins. I wish we could use the drones but they're useless in this visibility."

"I'm done taking pictures." Rio pushed his phone back inside his pocket and pulled on a glove. "Man, my fingers are frozen solid."

"We'll get her into a bag and onto the trailer." Wolfe bent to cut through the gaffer tape. "Take the weight. I don't want her hitting the ground. Rowley, get ready to assist. We lift and carry her to the open bag."

Taking in Rowley's troubled expression, he shook his head. Rowley had a weak stomach when it came to homicide and the idea of him spewing at a crime scene wasn't an option. "I can manage alone. The less people contaminating her body the better." He looked at Rowley. "Scoop up the clothes and hair and bag them. You know the drill for collecting evidence. Note the time and weather on the label as well as the date."

"Copy." Rowley let out a stream of steam as he exhaled. "Thanks." He collected evidence bags and a pen from the back of Wolfe's trailer.

With little effort, Kane carried the slight figure to the body bag. It was fortunate the victim stood upright. He couldn't imagine the trouble they'd have fitting a frozen bent figure inside the bag. He looked at Emily, as she assisted Rowley. She concealed worry and frustration like her father. He'd very rarely seen Wolfe show emotion unless it concerned his daughters, yet at the moment he was eerily calm, as if finding her dead was inevitable, and Emily was echoing his mood. He turned as Jenna went to Wolfe's side.

"We'll find her." Jenna squeezed Wolfe's arm. "Someone came and helped her. She's probably in front of a warm fire recuperating and doesn't have a satellite phone to call you." She looked at him, her face upturned and pale against the hood of her sheepskin-lined parka. "Looking at these women, she isn't his type."

"This is my concern." Wolfe frowned. "She is slightly built like these women, and has natural beauty, long blonde hair, and long dark eyelashes. Her lips are naturally full like her mother's. She's my daughter but I'm not blind. I know her looks are what these woman pay a surgeon to achieve. It's even more so with Emily. To the animal who tortured these women, my daughters would be like magnets."

Kane rested one hand on his shoulder. "Julie would have been bundled up, right? She would have been wearing so many clothes and a scarf. No one would have seen her face. Look at Jenna and Emily, only their stature would make someone assume they are women. Whoever rescued her would have found a bundled-up woman." He blew out a breath filling the air around them with steam. "We'll keep searching until we find her. She must be out here somewhere. If not, she's in town. They might have taken her to the hospital. If she was unconscious with no ID on her, they're not going to call you, are they?"

"Em, call the hospital and make sure if anyone fitting your sister's description is brought in, they're to call me immediately." Wolfe climbed onto his snowmobile. "Let's keep searching."

"I'll call Maggie and ask her to contact the medical centers in town in case they've seen her." Jenna pulled out her phone and made the call.

The next moment, Blackhawk came hurtling toward them. "We can smell smoke. There must be a cabin ahead. Follow me."

THIRTEEN

Hope gripped Jenna and she clung to Kane as they headed along the winding trail, the vibration of the snowmobiles causing great clods of snow to slip from the surrounding tree branches and slap into them. It was as if the forest was bombarding them with giant snowballs. After a time, they came out in a clearing alongside a frozen creek. Set against the mountain and covered with snow sat a small cabin. The smell of woodsmoke hung in the air but no smoke curled from the chimney, but there wasn't a vehicle in sight. As they came to a halt beside Blackhawk's team, she looked around at everyone. "Leave this to us. We don't know who is inside and they have every right to protect their property. We can't act as a threat, so stay back and wait for my signal." She climbed from the back of the vehicle and turned to Kane. "You call out. Your voice is louder than mine."

"Sheriff's department. Is anyone inside? We need to talk to you about a plane crash." Kane's voice echoed against the rocky outcrop above the cabin, but no sound came from inside. He repeated the message and then looked at Jenna. "I guess we take a look."

With Wolfe on one side and Kane on the other, Rio and Rowley close behind, they headed for the cabin. Jenna pounded on the door and stood to one side and listened. Not a sound came from inside. "This is Sheriff Alton. Please come to the door."

Nothing.

Beside her, Kane tried the doorknob and the door swung open with a grinding creak. Heart pounding, Jenna drew her weapon and gave him a nod. They'd done this move a thousand times before. Kane went high and she went low as they moved inside. Above her head, Kane's M18 pistol swept the room. He moved inside and peered behind a kitchen counter and then headed down to a small bedroom.

"Clear, but someone has been here recently." Kane indicated toward the bedroom. "I smell perfume and the bed is mussed up."

"From the ash in the fireplace, I'd say that fire is at least three days old." Wolfe was bending down staring in the grate. He stood. "Check the kitchen."

"Wood stove, used recently, and a coffee pot with coffee that smells okay." Kane checked the garbage. "Food wrappers. Cheese and crackers and an empty bottle of red wine." He pulled an evidence bag from his pocket and bagged the garbage.

Jenna moved to the kitchen. "Two glasses, washed and left on the sink. A romantic getaway?"

"I'll check the stomach contents of the victims." Wolfe moved around the cabin. "I'll take the bed linen as well. They'll have left trace evidence behind." He moved to the door and called in the deputies and Emily. "We haven't got much time. Help Emily strip the bed and bag the linen and pillows. I'll swab the bathroom."

"I'll check for prints." Kane pulled out a fingerprint scanner. "I noticed a few in the bathroom."

Pulling out her phone, Jenna called Kalo. "Morning, Bobby,

sorry to wake you on a Sunday. I sent some requests to you last night but I'd like to add another."

"I just checked my emails. I'm working now. What else do you need?" Kalo sounded wide awake.

Jenna smiled to herself; she could always rely on Kalo to run information at light speed. "I'm sending you the coordinates of a cabin out at Bear Peak. I need to know who owns this one in particular. There's no street address. It's alongside the mountain."

"Okay, the coordinates make it easier. Many are owned by the Forest Service. I do have a few names already but nothing at those coordinates. I'll do a search now. Is this to do with Julie missing?"

Jenna closed her eyes as grief welled up and rushed over her. "No, there's no sign of Julie at the crash site. We believe someone rescued her but we don't know who. We've found three homicide victims along the trail to the crash site. As we're searching for Julie, we came across this place. It's been used recently but now it's empty. I need to know who owns it. This person is a suspect in the murder inquiry."

"Gotcha." Kalo's chair squeaked across the tile as he moved from one computer to the next. *"I'm on it. I'll call as soon as I have a result."* He disconnected.

She walked out of the front door and waved to Blackhawk. As he came toward the cabin, carrying a cup of coffee in one hand and a sandwich in the other, her stomach growled with hunger. Pushing the need to sit down for a few minutes to one side, she walked out to meet him, her feet sinking into the ever deepening snow. "Someone was here but it looks more like a romantic interlude than a murder scene. No signs of the use of medical supplies. We have a few items to collect here and then we'll keep moving."

"Okay." Blackhawk nodded, tipping snow from the brim of his hat. "We'll scout ahead and call you if we find anything. My cousin recalls a cabin closer to the edge of Bison Ridge Canyon. Follow our tracks. They should be visible for a time, although the fall is getting heavier. We all might need to head home before it's too deep to get through."

"Jenna." Kane came through the front door. "I've checked the kitchen for fingerprints and Wolfe has finished with the kitchen and family room. We're all freezing and hungry. Sit for five minutes out of the cold. Just long enough to eat a sandwich and drink a cup of hot chocolate." He gave her a long look. "We'll all be able to keep going longer if we keep up our calories." He smiled at her. "Blackhawk and his friends were eating while they waited. They'll scout around and keep us advised if they find anything." He indicated to the sofa. "Sit down, I'll grab the food."

Leaning into him and welcoming his arms around her, she nodded. "I thought you'd never ask."

With the door closed, Kane added a few small logs and soon had a small fire burning in the grate. It didn't take long before the cabin warmed. Exhausted, Jenna removed her coat and gloves and sank into the sofa before the fire. Warmth crawled into her freezing feet and she pulled off her boots to wiggle her toes in front of the fire. She leaned back and relaxed as Kane and Rowley collected sandwiches and Thermos flasks from the trailer. Her team welcomed a respite from the bitter cold and they all sat around the fire, eating in silence. Most just stared into the flames as if in deep contemplation. Beside her, Kane pushed food and drinks into her hands. On the other side of the sofa, Emily leaned back, eyes closed, food untouched in her hands. Jenna placed her cup of hot chocolate onto the coffee table. "It will be okay, Em. We'll find her. The fact we haven't found a trace of her, is a good thing. It means someone has taken her somewhere safe and warm. She's not wandering around the forest on her own."

"I don't feel like she's dead. It's like we have a connection. I always wake at night if she's sick." Emily sat up slowly and stared at her sandwich as if she'd just realized she held it. "When my mom died, I had this hollow feeling in my chest, an emptiness, like a deep void. I'm not feeling that with Julie. Maybe it's just hope filling the hole in my heart, but I keep placing myself in her shoes. What would I do if I were injured and with a stranger?"

"What would you do?" Rio perched on the arm of the chair beside her.

"I figure I'd get strong again and then insist he or she takes me to a phone." Emily took a small bite of the sandwich and washed it down with coffee. "I would imagine a man has her because it would take someone pretty strong to lift her from the tail of the plane. She wouldn't leave without her phone—she knows how important a phone is out in the forest—so she's hurt. He had transport, a snowmobile, and a trailer to carry all the stuff he took from the plane because moving someone unconscious on a snowmobile would be near impossible." She thought for a beat. "I keep thinking, Why was he in the area? Hunting or just passing through? Was he trying to get home before the weather closed in? Is this why he's now isolated and can't get a message out?"

"There are survivalists and ex-military guys all through the mountains." Rowley's red hands closed around his coffee cup. "Most are here to escape civilization. The mountain men as well, they all keep to themselves and live off the land. There could be thousands of them in Stanton Forest. This place goes on forever."

"The thing is, if she has been picked up by one of these guys, he should have a radio. Most of them communicate by CB radios." Kane shrugged. "It makes no sense that no one has contacted Shane."

"Like I've said all along, but y'all aren't listening." Wolfe sank into a chair by the fire. "Julie is sensible. She'd make contact if she was able but she could have suffered a head injury and be unconscious. She might have suffered amnesia. There are so many options apart from the fact this guy might not have a way to communicate with the outside world. It might be a choice to be incommunicado. If y'all think about it, we know Carter was off the grid for three years. He needed time alone to deal with his problems but he didn't hide his whereabouts. The FBI had the local sheriff and priest drop by every so often to check on him. He was totally self-sufficient for all that time. He hunted and fished for food for him and his dog. The only time he communicated with anyone for more than a few minutes was when Jo Wells insisted he return to work. We could be dealing with any of the above reasons, and this is why Julie hasn't contacted us."

Concerned, Jenna stared at him. "That's possible but surely Julie would insist a message be sent to you?"

"She would and signs tell me, she's injured but alive. Maybe she can't communicate or she's unconscious." Wolfe met her gaze. "Not knowing where she is right now is eating me alive. I can only hope someone has her holed up somewhere warm and is caring for her."

Heartsore for Wolfe, Jenna stared at his carved stone expression. He'd never give up searching and neither would she. "Well, let's hope we find her soon."

"We will." Kane squeezed her leg. "There's only so far someone can travel in this weather."

They finished up and packed everything back into the trailer. Jenna headed out to the snowmobile and climbed on behind Kane. The next minute, Wolfe dismounted and ran past her and headed back toward the cabin. "What's up?"

"I didn't collect the trash. It might contain evidence, if I can link it to the murders." Wolfe gave them a wave. "Emily, ride with Rio for a time. Keep going, I'll catch up to y'all." He ran back along the trail with evidence bags gripped in one hand and disappeared inside the cabin.

"Mind if I ride with you?" Emily looked at Rio, hands on hips.

"Yeah, sure." Rio's expression was hidden behind his sunglasses.

Jenna frowned. "What's up with the two of them?"

"I have no idea and it's none of my concern." Kane shrugged.

Jenna sighed, blowing out a stream of steam. "Emily usually talks to me if she has any problems, but like you say, it's none of our concern."

"I'd rather wait for Wolfe." Kane looked over one shoulder at the cabin. "There's a serial killer close by and he's alone."

Scanning the wall of white, it was difficult to make out the others in front of them. "Then go slowly. I'll watch out behind for him."

"Okay." Kane pushed the snowmobile forward and the noise shattered the silence in the forest.

As they followed the disappearing procession, Jenna leaned into Kane. "It's so cold. I wonder how far ahead Blackhawk and his team have searched?"

Before Kane could reply, a slow rumbling came in the distance, like a roll of thunder. Jenna couldn't distinguish which direction the sound had come from. She looked up at the sky but the same heavy clouds poured snow down on them. "What's that noise?"

"Avalanche." Kane waved everyone forward. "Head away from the mountain, any trail that goes toward the falls."

As they drove away Rio slowed, behind him Emily turned in her seat searching behind them. Jenna waved them on. "Keep moving."

"What about Wolfe?" Rio swiped at the snow on his visor. "We can't just leave him behind."

"I'm going back for my dad." Emily stared at Rio. "Turn this thing around."

"No! Rio keep going. That's an order. Rowley, take Jenna with you. I'll go back for Wolfe." Kane turned his head to look at Jenna. "Go. Now. No arguments. Think of the baby. Get yourself to safety. You must go now!"

Reluctant to leave him, Jenna complied and swung behind Rowley. He took off at high speed. Jenna turned to stare after Kane. As he disappeared along the trail, the trailer bumping up and down behind him, fear gripped Jenna. A cloud of white was billowing toward them. Kane was heading for certain death in a crazy attempt to save his best friend's life.

FOURTEEN

A roar like a tornado broke the silence as Wolfe removed his examination gloves. The floorboards under his feet shook and rocks pinged off the bare roof as snow ran down the sloped sides and plopped to the ground. Glass smashed as a tree speared through a window like a deadly green dart, pushing the sofa across the room in a grinding screech. Wolfe stared in disbelief for two seconds before survival instinct took over. Dragging on his gloves, he grabbed the evidence bags and, clambering over the pine sapling, headed for the door. In a rush of wind, a cloud of white billowed through the opening in a surge so intense it knocked him back a few steps. Ice needles bounced off his cheeks, like an attack of angry bees. *Avalanche.*

Outside, chaos reigned as the fury of nature's aggression took hold and shook the earth. Of two minds to risk going outside, he glanced around for a safe place, but when the roof creaked and the building leaned sideways under the pressure of the snow, he dashed out of the door. Inside would mean certain death but outside he'd be safer if he could make it to the forest and his snowmobile. A deafening noise greeted him in a wall of swirling white, buffeting him with every stride. The wind elevated him and it was like floating in the ocean in a storm. Behind him snow tumbled down the mountain in ferocious waves of white. As Wolfe ran toward the forest, the first force of rolling snow picked him up and he became one with a swirling wall of death.

Ice-filled air clogged his nose, and helpless, he gasped for each breath. As he tumbled, in the distance he caught sight of the edge of the pine forest. The trees stood like ghostly sentries around the perimeter. He must get there but the speed of the sliding snow was too fast to gain his footing. His feet left the ground and the snow lifted him and then rolled him over again. Slices of ice cut across his cheeks and blood filled his left eye. His mind went to Julie, she was out there alone and needed him. He must survive at all costs.

Chunks of debris, boulders, and broken tree branches surrounded him. Snow swirled around his head in a blanket of white. The evidence bags vanished from his grasp and he lifted his arms to cover his head as the rush of deathly white engulfed him. His back hit something solid expelling the air from his lungs. Struggling to breathe as the white fury rushed past him, he made out dark shapes around him. The wave of snow had carried him to the forest. Blinding snow rushed against his face, chilling him to the bone. He forced opened his eyes as trees, still trailing their roots, flew past. Pinned against a tree, he rolled his shoulders and slowly turned. Muscles screamed as they tore from the exertion but he managed to loop his arms and legs around the trunk. The avalanche tore at his clothes, as if trying to rip him from the tree but he clung tight, using every last ounce of strength to survive.

Trapped in an ice tomb, he forced his head back to make a pocket of air. Snow was all around him, above and below, but the incredible force stopped as fast as it had started. Silence followed as if he'd suddenly gone completely deaf. An icy wall pressed hard against his back but steadied him. He moved one hand from the trunk and punched up alongside the tree. Time was ticking away and he must get air. He dragged himself up inch by inch and punched again. His hand burst into open space. Air rushed in and he drank in each painful lung-burning breath. Cold seeped into him, as if his clothes had been ripped from his back, but that sliver of light above him was like a beacon. Slowly, he climbed the tree. His arms screamed in protest, but refusing to give in, he pushed on. The bark tore at his clothes and cheeks, but the small broken branches offered a foothold.

Without warning, the small tunnel above him collapsed over his face, smothering him. Panic gripped him and he dug deep to keep calm. Dammit, he'd been trained to cope in situations like this. Remaining calm was the key to survival. He punched one fist up high in the air and the light and rush of air fell over him like a ray of hope. Dragging in deep painful breaths, he pulled himself higher up the tree. As his head poked through the surface, the sound of a snowmobile engine broke the silence. He climbed up the last few inches to expose his shoulders and then hugged the tree gasping for each breath. A wave of gratitude rolled over him at the sight of Kane riding toward him, standing up on the snowmobile searching all around. He took a deep breath. "Dave. Over here." His voice came out in a tiny squeak.

He tried again but Kane turned around and headed along the edge of the snowfall, obviously searching for the cabin. More noise filled the forest as the other snowmobiles came into sight. He dragged himself higher up the tree, now his shoulders were visible. When they all dismounted, Emily ran toward Kane. He turned to her. "I can't see him."

"Dad, where are you?" Emily ran up and down the edge of the avalanche, stumbling over chunks of ice. "Daddy, call out." Tears streamed down her face as she pushed into the snow and started digging.

"Look." Jenna pointed toward something and they all ran forward.

With effort they uncovered his snowmobile and Rio started it and dragged the trailer out of the snow. He searched around where the snowmobile had been and shook his head. "He's not here and from the debris the cabin was flattened."

Wolfe stared at them in disbelief. "I'm here. Over here." He waved one hand when Jenna turned and looked in his direction. "I'm here."

His heart sank when she turned away, but he kept on yelling, his voice not more than a croak. Why couldn't they hear him? He swallowed hard. *Maybe, I'm dead.*

FIFTEEN

Kane pulled Emily from the snow and turned her to face him. "Emily, look at me. I want you to calm down, okay? With everyone making a noise, we'll never be able to find him."

"Okay." Emily sucked in deep breaths and swiped at the tears streaming down her cheeks.

"Shane keeps his phone inside his jacket, right?" Jenna stared at him. "Call him."

Kane pulled out his phone and called Wolfe. "Quiet everyone and listen for the phone."

He turned slowly in a full circle listening. All he could hear was his own phone.

"Over there." Beside him Jenna pointed. "In that pile of snow. Hurry."

Bounding over fallen saplings and boulders that the avalanche had pushed into the forest, Kane ran with Rowley and Rio close behind toward Wolfe's distinctive ringtone. He waded waist-high in snow to peer up a tree surrounded by snow. Relief flooded over him at the sight of Wolfe, waving frantically. He frowned and turned to Rio and Rowley. "He's hurt. There's blood all over his face. We'll need to dig him out."

"I'll grab the shovels from the trailers." Rowley took off at a run.

Kane and Rio scooped snow away with their hands, making a path toward the tree. As they got closer Kane looked up at Wolfe and grinned. "I can't leave you alone for a second, can I?"

"Just get me the heck out of here." Wolfe gave him a stare to freeze Black Rock Falls. He coughed and wheezed.

Concerned, Kane lowered his voice and turned to Rio. "I hope he hasn't broken his ribs. He doesn't sound too good." He kept digging.

"We're coming, Dad." Emily was up to her knees in snow, digging with both hands.

"I'll go and get the first aid kit and Wolfe's spare clothes. We'll need to get him warm." Jenna stared at Wolfe. "I'll call Blackhawk and see if he's found a cabin close by. I know there are a few Forest Service cabins in this area. We'll need to hole up there until we assess your condition." She hurried away.

After Rowley arrived with the shovels, it took them twenty minutes to clear a path to the tree. The snow had been holding Wolfe against the trunk and Kane climbed up to help him down. Concerned by Wolfe's ashen face and blue lips, he lowered him gently to the ground and into Rio's arms. When Wolfe leaned heavily on Rio, Kane jumped down beside them. "We need to get you warm."

"I have your spare coat and the foil blankets." Jenna ran toward Wolfe. "Where are you hurt?"

"I'll know more when I thaw out. Help me remove the coat. It's ripped to shreds." Wolfe moved one gray eye toward Kane; the other was stuck shut with blood. "I'll put on the dry one and we can place the old one over the top. It's dry inside and will keep in the heat. The foil blankets will help." He took a deep breath and let it out on a groan. "I'm okay, no broken ribs. I figure I've cut my head with the blood and all but it's frozen right now."

"Blackhawk says there's a Forest Service cabin alongside the river. It's empty with no signs of life, so he moved on, but I told him to go back and light a fire." Jenna had driven Kane's snowmobile as close as possible to where they'd found Wolfe. "Get into the trailer and we'll cover you with blankets. Have a hot drink and then we'll head for the cabin and get you warm." She pulled out a Thermos and nodded at Kane and Rio, who supported him under each arm. "In our trailer not with the corpse." She glared at Rio, who smothered a grin.

Kane helped Wolfe remove his jacket and had his dry one on in a few seconds. He instructed Rowley to remove the cover. They lifted him into the back of the trailer and then reattached the top. Emily went to crawl in beside her father, and he patted her cheek and insisted she drive his snowmobile. It wasn't too difficult to see that Wolfe didn't appreciate anyone making a fuss. Kane bent his head to peer inside. "You look like a foil-wrapped potato ready for the oven. How are you feeling?" He sighed. "It's not going to be a smooth ride. You sure you'll be okay?"

"The thawing out will hurt and then the wound will bleed." Wolfe shrugged. "I look worse than I feel." He handed Kane a cup. "Best we keep moving. The temperature is dropping and the wind has picked up again, I figure another blizzard is coming. We need to get off this mountain ASAP."

Kane pushed the cup back onto the top of the Thermos and stored it away. "We will as soon as you're ready to travel. If we go now, you'll die of hypothermia before we get out of the forest. I'll drive as fast as I can, just hold on tight." He frowned. "One thing, why didn't you phone me and tell me where you were?"

"I couldn't risk falling off the tree." Wolfe met his gaze. "I knew you'd find me. You never give up or leave a man behind, dead or alive." He waved him away. "Get moving, before we all freeze to death."

Following Blackhawk's disappearing tracks troubled Kane until he came to a fork in the trail and discovered that Blackhawk had marked the way with crime scene tape. The snowscape was blinding and everything in the forest appeared identical. In this weather, it would be easy to get turned around and be wandering hopelessly lost for a long time without the GPS on his phone. As they drove through the forest, huge wedges of snow dropped down from the vibration of the snowmobiles. The forest for as far as the eye could see was deserted—not one species of wildlife had ventured out after the avalanche. He took another fork and the trail opened up to a small clearing beside a frozen river. The cabin looked like something out of a horror movie. It leaned to one side and there were holes in the porch floor. All around thick icicles hung like huge daggers over two feet long. Just one breaking off could do a lot of damage to someone walking by.

He parked beside the snowmobiles belonging to Blackhawk's team and in a few seconds the others all came in behind him. With care, Kane, with Rio's help, lifted Wolfe out of the back of the trailer and carried him into the cabin. A wave of warmth hit him, and Blackhawk grinned and dropped another log on the fire. Kane lowered Wolfe onto a battered sofa beside the hearth. "Thanks, you're a lifesaver."

"How bad?" Blackhawk frowned at Wolfe. "Do you have internal injuries?"

"I'm going to be fine." Wolfe leaned back in the chair with exhaustion written all over his bloodstained face. "Any sign of Julie?"

"No, we found nothing, not one trace of anyone else moving through the forest." Blackhawk frowned. "The snow is falling so fast it is covering all trace of her. All we can do is to keep searching, but I don't know how long we can get through the drifts; they are six feet high in some places."

The door opened and Rowley came in carrying supplies.

Emily had Wolfe's medical kit and the moment she entered the cabin she ran to Wolfe's side. Tears streamed from her eyes and ran down her cheeks. As she was the only other person with medical experience, Kane needed her to remain calm. "What do you need, Em?"

"I have everything I need in the medical kit." Emily dragged a small packet of tissues from her pocket and mopped at her face. She went about examining Wolfe's head. "I can't feel or see any injuries on the back of your skull, Dad, but that cut on your forehead will need sutures." She paused as if not sure what to do. "Any other injuries?"

"I'm bruised all over but I'm sure nothing's broken. I can breathe better here in the warm." Wolfe met her gaze. "The blood in my eye is a problem. We'll need to deal with the cut ASAP."

"I've only stitched cadavers." Emily took a shuddering breath. "You'll need to talk me through administering the local anesthetic."

"Sure." Wolfe smiled at her. "You know how to stitch a wound. You've done it a hundred times in the lab. This is no different, apart from I'll bleed some, but that's okay."

"I don't want to hurt you." Emily's face paled as she stared at him.

"You won't and we'll laugh about this when you've completed your residency at the hospital. You'll be stitching up people all day." Wolfe patted her arm. "Grab one of the suture kits. Clean the wound and as much blood as you can from my face. Use the saline to clean the blood from my eye and the pink antiseptic for the wound. Remove any debris with the plastic tweezers. Use the two-percent lidocaine and inject a small amount through the wound and into the superficial fascia. Then stitch it up." He squeezed her arm. "You'll do just fine."

Kane turned and went to grab bags from Jenna. "You're frozen. Get closer to the fire."

"I'm good. We need to get the stove going. It will add heat and we can cook and refill the Thermoses for the ride home." Jenna looked at Blackhawk. "We have coffee and hot chocolate, canned goods, and utensils in Kane's trailer. If you can light the stove, we can all have a hot meal."

"That sounds like a plan." Blackhawk indicated to his friends and they moved around the cabin. "We'll hunt down some blankets as well, these cabins usually have the essentials."

"I'll grab the supplies." Rowley headed for the door.

"I'll help." Rio followed after him.

"You find something for us all to eat and I'll help Emily clean up Shane." Jenna lowered her voice to just above a whisper and leaned into Kane. "She's really upset. She was convinced we'd find Julie today and now this. To her, Wolfe is indestructible. She is shattered seeing him injured."

Kane nodded. "She'll drop into professional mode soon. It's her dad. She's going to be upset. That's normal." He glanced at his watch. "We have two hours at the very most before we must return home. The snow will soon block our way to the fire road. As it is, we'll likely be digging out our vehicles." He pulled her close. "If it were possible to remain here until we found Julie, I'd never give up searching, but the truth is we'll die without shelter and food. We have no choice but to leave and come back when we can. As we've found no trace of her, we must consider that she's safe in someone's cabin and they're like us, unable to move around. Atohi has come across avalanches blocking the regular trails. I figure Julie would have gotten through before they slipped. My guess is she's where we can't get to her just now. Once it stops snowing, we'll get choppers up searching. Right now, leaving while we can is our only option."

"I don't like it but I understand." Jenna's eyes held a deep sorrow. "Julie is very sensible. If she could hole up somewhere safe, she would, and I can't imagine her expecting everyone to risk their lives trying to get to her." She checked her watch.

"Okay, let's get warm and fed and then head home. We'll call Carter. The moment the weather clears, I want him out there alongside search and rescue. We'll go with him. I'm going to find her. I'll never give up."

SIXTEEN

MONDAY

Julie woke muddle-headed in the dark again and came to the conclusion that the medication that Raven had given to her was stronger than she imagined. If she lay still in bed, her leg pain was tolerable, but the moment she tried to stand up it hurt so bad it brought tears to her eyes. She needed to go to the bathroom and, sliding carefully to the edge of the bed, lowered her foot to the floor slowly. Searing pain shot up to her knee and she gasped and swayed with dizziness. Raven had made her a pair of crutches. Standing on one leg she reached for them and, slipping one under each arm, made her way to the bathroom. As she washed her hands, she noticed the door to Raven's bedroom stood slightly ajar as if he'd forgotten to close it properly. Curiosity got the better of her and she opened it slowly and peered into his bedroom. The bathroom light spilled over the empty bed. She limped inside and the smell of men's cologne drifted toward her. A bottle stood on the nightstand and she couldn't resist going to sniff it. A strange feeling crept over her. Why did a man living alone in the forest use cologne? Had a woman lived here before? If so, where was she now? Or did he use his good looks to lure women to his cabin and then murder them?

She needed to know more about this mysterious man living alone in the forest with his dogs. Julie scanned the room and her gaze alighted on a small desk in the corner. She hobbled across the floor toward it and turned on the lamp. The top of the desk was clear apart from a small tin containing pens. Although Raven wasn't home, she looked over one shoulder before sliding open the drawers. In the top one she found a neat pile of folders, each with a name written on the top. She peeked inside and discovered medical records of the people he had treated. Another drawer had detailed notes of each dog he'd trained, along with any problems he'd encountered and how he dealt with them.

Guilty, she kept searching the room. She wanted more information but found nothing of interest. This guy may be treating people and training dogs as he had informed her, but any past life had been erased. Not one photograph or personal identification of any type whatsoever in his room. She found a small envelope stuffed with receipts, but apart from that, it seemed that Raven had no identity prior to moving into the cabin. How much of what he had told her was fabrication? Was he living a lie?

The smell of his cologne curled toward her nose. There must be a woman in his life. She ran his conversation back through her mind. He'd mentioned a woman he visited when he wanted to sell or rescue a dog, but he'd told her repeatedly that at the moment there was no way through to the next cabin, let alone all the way into town. If what he was telling her was true, where was he? She had no idea how long he had been missing and couldn't imagine why he'd want to go out in the freezing cold during a snowstorm in the middle of the night. She tried to recall how long after dinner she'd fallen asleep. They'd eaten around six and she'd taken the medication with her dinner. She recalled yawning halfway through her meal and the effort it took for her to clean her teeth before she went to lie down. That was the last thing she remembered, so she'd been asleep since around six-thirty.

If Raven had gone out after dinner to tend his dogs, he should be back by now. If something had happened to him, surely his dog Ben would have been going ballistic by now? She hobbled to his bedside table and lifted the alarm clock, turning it so she could see the face in the light from the bathroom. She had been asleep for twelve hours. Panic gripped her. What would happen to her if he didn't return? She had no idea of her location in the forest even if she had a telephone. Trying to get through the snow with a broken leg would be suicide. She would just have to try and survive until the melt. A trickle of anxiety crawled up her spine at the thought of Raven lying out in the open injured or, worse, dead. Then there was Ben. Shouldn't he be here inside the warm house? Her mind went to the dogs in the barn that he mentioned pulled his sled. She couldn't just leave them out there to die locked in their kennels. Perhaps when it stopped snowing, she could figure out how to attach them to the sled and then try and find her way home. Her stomach tied in knots at the thought of being alone in the freezing cold in the middle of the forest. Surely once the snow stopped falling, the choppers would be out looking for the crashed aircraft. If she could get back to the crash site when she heard choppers overhead, she would have a slim chance of being seen.

She went back into her bedroom. Raven had unpacked her things and put them in the chest of drawers and the closet. It took her so long to get dressed. By the time she'd maneuvered her cut-up jeans over the splint, sweat trickled down her back and her heart pounded with overexertion. The agony shooting up her leg made her nauseous and she sat on the bed and sipped water until her head stopped spinning. Outside the sun was creeping into the sky, but even in the dark, with so much snow it was surprisingly light. She dragged on her coat, hat, and gloves and using her crutches made her way to the front door. It was like a Christmas card and even the barn had a wintery charm about it. The forest wore a mantle of white that extended to the black mountains. From her position she could make out Bear Peak with its distinctive bear's head rock formation. She shivered recalling all the terrible stories Emily had told her about the graves at Bear Peak. It was called a killing field by the townsfolks, and it was very close to the cabin. She could hear water and gathered the river that Jenna had fallen into when out with Atohi looking at old gravesites last year would be close by. She recalled flying over Bear Peak and through the canyon when the blizzard hit with force.

She hobbled along the porch and stared at the barn. No lumps lay along the cleared pathway. Piles of snow each side told her Raven cleared it daily. She stared at the barn. It seemed a mile away but in truth it was less than fifty yards. She hobbled down the steps, gasping and spilling great gusts of steam into the air. So very slowly she made her way to the barn. At the front was a sliding door, and to one side a regular door. She made for the regular door and turned the knob. It opened with oiled ease and she peered inside. The barn smelled of dogs but not in an unpleasant way, more like the smell of puppies. No barking greeted a stranger in their midst. She moved toward the kennels, noticing the furnace pushing out the heat. She stood gaping at the empty pens. Wherever Raven had gone, he'd taken his dogs. Suddenly very alone, Julie made her way painfully back to the house.

In the kitchen the wood stove still had red embers glowing inside. Julie added more wood and moved painfully along the cabinets, searching for food. The coffee pot sat on the counter, filled and ready to turn on. She flicked the switch, glad to see it spring into action. From what she discovered searching the kitchen, Raven froze everything. He must have gone into town every six months or so and purchased a ton of bread. The freezer was filled with it, along with butter. He used powdered milk but a jug had been prepared and sat in the fridge along with half a loaf of bread. She made toast and coffee and sat at the kitchen table. Before she'd finished eating, she heard dogs barking. Relief and suspicion rolled over her in equal measure at the sound of Raven returning. It wasn't the first time he'd vanished for hours. It was getting difficult to get her head around the fact that he insisted there was no way out and yet he managed to move around without any trouble at all. She poured a second cup of coffee and added more bread to the toaster. The cold made her hungry and she wanted an excuse to be sitting there. She couldn't wait to see his expression when he walked into the cabin.

Half an hour later, the door opened slowly. Raven removed his coat, shook the snow from it at the door and then walked inside. He at once dried Ben before removing his hat, gloves, and boots. When he straightened, he still hadn't noticed her. He went to the hearth and added more logs to the fire and stood for a time warming his hands. His dog flopped on the rug before the fire and yawned. When he eventually turned, he started at seeing her. Julie smiled. "Good morning. Where have you been all night?"

SEVENTEEN

Unaccustomed to having someone living in the house with him, Raven blinked at the sight of Julie sitting at the kitchen table. She was indeed a beautiful young woman and reminded him of a Nordic ice maiden. Her long blonde hair hung past her shoulders like a silk scarf. It never seemed to be untidy and it framed a face that could have been made from porcelain. The look was accentuated by the high color in her cheeks and her remarkable gray eyes. He'd never seen anyone with large expressive gray eyes like that before. *She's too young for you.* He gave himself a mental shake. The high color in her cheeks might be a fever. Infection in her injured leg could be fatal. He noticed she'd dressed and frowned. The jeans must be uncomfortable pressed against her leg. "You should be resting. Moving around all the time on that leg won't help."

"First you tell me to move to avoid blood clots and then you tell me not to move." Julie waved a slice of toast at him. "I woke up and you were gone. Your bed hasn't been slept in and Ben was missing. I figured you might have fallen and went to make sure you were okay." She stood and poured him a cup of coffee and dropped more bread in the toaster. "Did you find a way of contacting my dad? Or anyone to tell them where I am?"

Rubbing freezing hands together, he shook his head. "I tried a few more trails but they're either blocked or too narrow for the dogsled. I'm trying, Julie, but the weather is making it impossible."

"Okay, but I need to let my dad know I'm okay. He'll be going nuts. You don't know him. He'll never stop searching for me." Julie eased into a chair and her eyes resembled a trapped animal. "I have a family out there. Friends who care about me. I need to get them word. You need to keep trying."

Raven moved into the kitchen, washed his hands, and then went to the fridge. "I'm going out every day, Julie, and that's good your dad will never give up. Maybe he'll see the smoke from my chimney and head this way. If he has a snowmobile, it would be easier to find a way through the deep snow." He sighed. "Try not to worry too much. You need to recover and then we can both go out and search for a way back to civilization. Right now, I'll make us some eggs. I collected them yesterday. I have my chicken pen split up for winter. One half gets light from six until six; the other pen gets natural winter light. Halfway through winter I switch. It means I get eggs all through winter and the chickens get a rest from laying."

"You have chickens?" Julie's gaze followed him. "I didn't see any chickens."

Breaking eggs into a bowl, Raven looked at her over one shoulder. "You went outside?"

"Yeah, to see if you were lying in the snow." Julie shrugged. "I saw the kennels. You sure take care of the dogs. Do they all like living together like that? I figured they'd be locked in pens like horses."

Shaking his head, Raven poured eggs into a pan with a dollop of butter. "They're all neutered and social, so they have a nice area to run around and places where they can sleep. They are all rescue dogs. I only took social breeds that are strong and willing to work. My dogs enjoy pulling the sled. They're not hunters, so when the snow melts they'll spend most of their time lying around. They don't venture too far and understand that bears are best left alone." He divided the eggs onto two plates and pushed one toward her followed by a fork.

The walking outside would account for the flushed cheeks, but he needed to be sure. "Do you feel okay?"

"Apart from the pain, yeah." Julie buttered the toast, pushed a plate in his direction, and sucked the butter from her fingers.

He took the toast and pushed a forkful of eggs into his mouth. "No shivers, hot and cold feelings? Does your leg hurt or does it burn?"

"You sound like my dad." She leaned back in her chair. "I don't have a fever, but I'd sure like to take a shower. You have hot water, don't you?"

Nodding, Raven sipped his coffee. "Yeah, the furnace heats the water and the house. It keeps the pipes from freezing as well. When I set this place up for long term, I made sure it covered all my needs." He frowned. "Are you sure? I'll need to remove the splint from your leg. I don't have anything to replace it with if it gets wet."

"There are handrails all over the bathroom and in the shower." Julie gave him a direct stare. "Why is that?"

Not wanting to reveal his secrets, Raven shrugged. "I was injured at one time and it was necessary."

"Which brings me to where you go all night." Julie ate slowly. "You said there was no way out of this place and no other cabins close by. So where did you go?"

He looked down at his plate and chuckled. "Did you miss me?"

"No, I figured you were dead." Julie glared at him. "It's not funny. It hurt like heck, going to the barn looking for your sorry ass."

Raven finished his eggs. "I went out just before five. I always make my bed. It's a leftover from the Army, and I like being neat and tidy. I checked the traps, collected the critters, and then went along a few trails to search for a way through to the fire road. Unfortunately, avalanches have blocked the trails. I could have tried a few tracks unknown to me but staying out in the cold is limited and I can't expect my dogs to keep going for hours at a time." He met her gaze. "Right now, we're stuck here." He sighed. "I can't even get back to the crash site. I had planned on leaving a message that you were safe here with me. I should have thought of leaving a message before, but getting you to safety was my priority."

"So you haven't been away all night?" Julie nibbled on a slice of toast, her gray eyes examining his face as if seeing right through him.

He shook his head. "No and when I plan on leaving for an extended time to find a way out of here, I'll tell you."

"I can't stay here. If you're planning on leaving, I'm going with you." Julie's stare remained fixed on him. "Promise me you won't disappear again without telling me and you'll get me back to my family." She hadn't as much as blinked.

Stroking his short beard, Raven leaned back in his chair. He didn't trust people, not now. Making promises had never been an option he'd considered. His word was good enough—well, it had been when there was anyone left who had actually known him. The problem was a small part of him deep down didn't want him to return her to her family. Had this intelligent woman picked up on that? He sighed. What the heck? She'd be a nice memory soon enough, a passing ship in the night to haunt his dreams. He shrugged. "Sure. I promise."

EIGHTEEN

The persistent blizzard stacked snow against the window as Jenna paced up and down her office. They'd followed the snow-plow into town this morning and would follow it back home this afternoon. The snowfall was relentless and the chances of searching for Julie became more remote by the hour. She desperately needed to go out and hunt for her, but after speaking to a bruised and battered Wolfe, who had insisted on working on the bodies of the victims for clues, she'd reluctantly conceded on two counts. The first being if Julie had survived the crash and was alone in the mountains, she couldn't possibly have survived two nights without food and warmth. The second was the hope she glimpsed in Wolfe's eyes that a Good Samaritan had come by, taken her to safety, then been isolated by the rolling blizzards bombarding the state. It made sense, after seeing the medical supplies and canned goods missing, that someone with transport had been by. She'd needed time to think. So many important things were taking her attention right now. She'd issued orders to her deputies to get an investigation underway and sent them to the conference room to discuss the murders.

She'd coped well dividing her and Kane's time between work and caring for Tauri, but a new baby would need all her attention. If she planned to remain as sheriff and care for her family, she must put the plans into action they'd made the day she'd married Kane.

Since experiencing the power of the mothering instinct from the moment Tauri came into her life, it was obvious their lives would change even more dramatically when their baby arrived. She had always vowed that her family would come first. They had Nanny Raya, a Native American ex-FBI agent with the highest clearance, as Tauri's nanny. She stepped in daily to collect him from kindergarten and was there for him in emergencies. but after speaking to Jo Wells about being a mother and an FBI agent, it was obvious she'd need a live-in nanny for the baby. After speaking with Wolfe, he'd explained that a nanny needed separate quarters.

Plans had been drawn up and passed by the local council for an extension to the ranch house. The reluctance not to do this before was that Kane's position in the military was so sensitive the risk had been too great. He'd spoken to Wolfe, and after waiting for him to discuss the problems with POTUS, they'd agreed that Nanny Raya would move into the ranch once the extensions were finished. She'd care for Tauri as before and be there when the baby came along, should the need arise. It was a safe and practical solution. After the birth Jenna would take six months' leave. After that she would work remotely unless working on a case. It wasn't a perfect solution, but her other option was handing over the reins to a new sheriff. When she'd discussed this with the mayor, he'd been quite adamant that she had a fine team to work the day-to-day problems and should concentrate on the big cases and not to sweat the small stuff. He'd advised her to make one of her deputies her chief deputy. As Kane was deputy sheriff, having been elected to that position at the same time she'd been reelected as sheriff, this would leave the general running of the office to the chief deputy and the homicides and other high-profile cases to her and Kane. This would mean she'd be free to spend more time with her children.

There was enough in the budget for two more deputies and a criminal consultant should they need more boots on the ground. They also had Jo Wells and Ty Carter, Beth Katz, and Dax Styles a phone call away. It could actually work as Jenna preferred working on the criminal cases rather than issuing speeding tickets and dealing with lost property. Everything was falling into place. An hour earlier she'd attended a meeting with the mayor for the results of the budget Jenna had put forward for the following year. It included a substantial pay raise for the deputies and upgrading of equipment and weapons. After discussing with Kane which deputy would be the best option for the position of chief, they'd both agreed on Rio. Although Jenna's heart ruled it should go to Rowley, Rio's gold shield detective background, his exemplary work in the field, and retentive memory made him the best option. She headed for the door to find Kane leaning against the wall outside. He'd given her time alone to think things through. She smiled at him. "Okay, set the plans in action for the extension to the ranch house. I know you have a secured team ready to go." She sucked in a breath. "The chief deputy is the best option. It will give us time with our kids. This means we can do the work we love, and they'll be safe and well cared for in their own home." She frowned. "Unless, as deputy sheriff, you want to take over the office?"

"Nope." Kane shook his head. "I'm taking paternity leave. I'm not missing out on the time with our baby. Should a serial killer decide to start up here over that time, well, I guess the plans you have set in place will cover any situation."

Anxiety rolled over her. Not being there left her deputies vulnerable. "Are you sure they'll be able to cope without us?"

"Truthfully?" Kane met her gaze. "Either is capable of being sheriff. They're grown men, well trained, and proficient. We're lucky they've stuck around and haven't moved away to get promotions. They have the skills."

Nodding, Jenna chewed on her bottom lip. "That's true. We're lucky to have them."

"You're doing the right thing." Kane put an arm around her. "You know you can't walk away from this job. I've watched you work your time around caring for Tauri so he never misses out on family time. This way you'll have more time to spare. The baby should be settled in the six months you take on maternity leave. They'll know Nanny Raya and should be contented. You'll be at home more than on the job. We can afford to take less hours. It's the best move."

Jenna hugged him. "It's a big decision and our family comes first, but I'll still be sheriff and calling the shots. It's a win-win." She straightened. "Okay, let's tell the team our decision and see how they're going with the investigation."

Excitement mingled with nerves gripped Jenna as she walked into the conference room and stood at the head of the table. Rowley was working on his laptop and Rio was busy writing on the whiteboard. She waited for them both to turn and look at her and then took her seat. "Sit down for a minute, Rio. I've just come back from a meeting with the mayor about next year's budget. I need to discuss a few things with you both." She waited for Rio to sit down at the long conference table littered with laptops, papers, maps, and crime scene photographs. "First, I'm happy to inform you that you'll both be getting a substantial raise from the end of the month, also that when our baby arrives, we'll be taking six months' leave. After speaking to the mayor today, we've decided to promote Rio to chief deputy to run the office. When we return from leave, I'll be overseeing remotely from home, and Kane and I will only be dealing with homicide and criminal cases, everything else will be handled by you. I have room in the budget for another deputy if necessary and a consultant."

"Do you mean, for instance, a deputy with a K-9?" Rio smiled at Kane. "Not that Duke isn't the best tracker around, but something more aggressive, like Agent Styles' dog? He was a military K-9 bomb squad but after some extra training he can bring down a perp."

"That's a good idea." Kane smiled. "Duke isn't aggressive and a dog is very useful bringing down perpetrators that decide to run. It does save shooting them. They train the dogs to scent for drugs as well. Finding someone willing to work here would be a problem. The dogs are usually trained with a handler who is part of the deal."

Thinking it through, Jenna nodded. "I agree. We wanted to take Duke with us when we searched for Julie but he's getting too old to be dragged out for days in the snow. K-9s are trained in response, detection, and obedience. They will attack. Yeah, that's a great idea. Having one on standby would be very useful. It would be a part-time consultant type of job. Someone like Styles, who retired from the military, would be perfect but the FBI already has him."

"You seem to have gotten on well with Styles." Kane gave her a side-eye.

Jenna chuckled. "He's certainly different. He carries this huge revolver in a shoulder holster and is one man you should never play cards with because he never allows his emotions to show. I'm not sure what the military does to men, but he's got that cyborg quality to him when he's on the job."

"That's good to know." Kane smiled and looked at Rio. "We need to find someone like that, ex-military with a K-9. Whatever other skills he has would come in handy. We have plenty of time before the baby is due, but maybe we should start advertising the position in the next three months or so?"

"Sure." Rio frowned. "If he's ex-military, the chances are the dog would be retired. I'll look into it. Maybe we can purchase a suitable dog, I'd be happy to train with it."

"Yeah, but that's defeating the aim." Kane reached for a pen from a container on the table. "We need boots on the ground and someone who can defend themselves. Man or woman, it makes no difference. It's all about the skill." He glanced at him. "Maybe hunt down someone who trains dogs for protection. We can buy a dog and employ a military ex-dog handler. I figure that would be the best option. You can specify the qualifications we require and hopefully we'll find someone who'll fit our needs."

"Gotcha." Rio nodded. "I'll start researching as soon as we've solved this case."

Jenna looked at Rowley. "As Rio will be running the office, I'll be looking at you to supervise any new deputies we employ. Any work you do with our new recruits, as in weapons, fitness, and the like, you'll get paid triple time. I have that in writing from the mayor."

"Neat." Rowley grinned.

Turning to stare at the whiteboard, Jenna cleared her throat. "Now, back to the case. What have you got for me?"

NINETEEN

The list of evidence, or lack of it, on the whiteboard concerned Jenna. Her deputies had found a few people of interest but they had nothing on the victims and no evidence or a possible motive. She turned to her deputies and waited for them to bring her up to speed.

"I have good and bad news." Rio stood and went to the whiteboard. "We all know that there are cabins littered all through the forest. Only a very few of them are owned by the Forest Service. Some of these old Forest Service dwellings have been sold over the years as the forest wardens were moved to improved premises. Others have been left as hunting cabins for people caught in the forest overnight or needing assistance. The cabins that we found near the crash site were Forestry Service cabins. There are others in the area within a mile or so that had been sold and are currently owned by people either living in town or hunters who use them for vacations. Kalo sent a list of the ones that are legitimate owners of cabins in the immediate area, but a check of the vehicle records tells us another story. There are many people, as in hundreds of people, who list their address as somewhere in Stanton Forest." He rubbed his chin.

"This is where we pulled up possible suspects. Kalo found six men who listed their address as Bear Peak, Stanton Forest. We can only assume that these are scratch-made cabins. There are another three that were part of a parcel of land that was sold and divided as a recreational area near the river. Cabins were built but the business collapsed. This was some thirty years ago. People have moved in and made improvements since. Two years ago, someone claimed three of the cabins. They went through the legal process and the entire complex now belongs to them legally. They allow the other people to live there. Some are off-the-grid survivalists."

"Do we have any names?" Kane frowned. "The whereabouts of the off-the-grid survivalists might be useful in finding Julie."

"I have a list of names of everyone living out at Bear Peak but none have an actual address as such." Rio indicated to the whiteboard. "This is where we hit the wall."

Jenna leaned forward. "How so? We must start somewhere."

"This is why we looked at the problem from a different angle." Rowley twirled a pen through his fingers. "We contacted the forest wardens and asked them to check their records for people hunting around Bear Peak during the last hunting season. Usually some of these people use the forestry hunting cabins overnight, and some book them for a short stay. So in other words, we have their details." He smiled. "I got a list of names and called as many of them as I could find. I managed to create a rough map with the location of the cabins they used for shelter during the hunting season."

Raising both eyebrows, Jenna stared at him. "I figured that they just left early each morning, hunted during the day, and left by sunset as per the rules."

"Nah, as they are not allowed to hunt between dusk and dawn, they stay at the cabins so they can leave early in the morning. Not everyone wants to go home and travel all the way back to the forest each day during hunting season. It makes sense to stay in a cabin and leave from there. They can move from one cabin to another during the course of their visit." Rowley leaned back in his chair. "Some of these cabins I didn't know existed. The problem is, we can't access any of them at the moment. When I spoke to the forest warden, he said that the current avalanches are making it difficult to move around the forest. Many of the main trails are blocked."

Pushing her hair from her face, Jenna blew out a long breath. "I don't recall so may avalanches in the past. The snow is great for Glacial Heights Ski Resort but an avalanche there would ruin everything."

"Yeah, it's caused by increased seismic activity in the area." Rio frowned and rubbed his chin. "There have been tremors all winter and they're increasing. Anywhere on the mountain in this weather is dangerous right now. The snowfall is heavier this year as well. It came late and made up for it. I know we have the snowmobiles but getting around the blocked trails is going to be murder."

"So what do you know about these guys?" Kane pointed to the whiteboard. "Why have you chosen Steven Oberg, Luke Sierra, Davis Davidson, and Dan D. Williams? The other name, John Raven, why is he underlined? Is he a prime suspect?"

"Nope, he is the guy who owns the group of cabins we mentioned earlier." Rio smiled. "I've discovered some information on him. When his name came up, I received a call from Carter. He figures he met him at one time. He goes by Johnny Raven. If it's the same guy, he's ex-military medical core, went off the grid after his entire team was wiped out in a chopper crash. He survived and left with a Purple Heart and other bravery medals. Although, as Carter said, he has no idea what mental health issues the man has now, but apparently, he kept his medical license current. He owns properties in the mountains. He did work with K-9s for a time. He spent his rehabilitation working with the dog trainers. As far as Carter is aware, he trains dogs for personal protection. He selects suitable dogs from the animal shelter and makes sure they end up in good homes. That's how he makes his living, selling dogs and doctoring the locals." He shrugged. "He must live in one of the cabins alongside the river. He could be one or two miles from the crash site. The only map we found is thirty years old from the land claim and it covers a ten-mile stretch of land from Bear Peak to Bison Hump Bridge." He drummed his fingers on the table. "Before you ask, I have no idea how people communicate with him. He doesn't have a phone or a CB radio as far as we know."

"If Carter knows him and he's not a threat, take him off the list." Kane pushed a hand through his hair. "We have enough people to chase down. If he found Julie, she'd be in good hands and likely this guy does have a communication device or how would he sell his dogs? Maybe he only sells dogs through a contact in town?"

Jenna rubbed both hands down her face. "What about the other guys on the list?"

"We've narrowed it down to the men on the list." Rowley looked up from his laptop. "Steven Oberg and Luke Sierra are survivalists who live somewhere in the Bear Peak area. The other two men, Dan D Williams and Davis Davidson, live in town and hold hunting licenses. They were all hunting last elk season at Bear Peak. We found them through the DMV."

Relieved they had a starting point, Jenna nodded. "Okay, conducting interviews will be a problem until the blizzard stops, but we'll need to get background info on the men who live in town. Dave, I'll get you to work on that for now. Run them all through the databases and see what comes up. Include

John Raven. Military men go bad same as everyone else. Being known by Carter isn't a reference."

"Okay." Kane went to work. "But you're wasting my time. I know Carter. He'd have run his name before he called us, but I'll hunt him down if you insist."

Jenna thought for a beat. "It won't hurt, will it?" She shrugged. "Right now, Wolfe has nothing to assist us in discovering the identity of the frozen victims. We need to do a state-by-state search for missing women. There's no one missing locally but I'll extend my search to the entire state. Rio, I want you and Rowley to send out the information we have so far on the victims and see if we get a callback. We have hair and eye color, approximate height. Put their age between twenty-five and forty as they've had extensive cosmetic surgery."

"So they could be tourists?" Rowley leaned back in his chair and stared into space. "The ski resort is very busy at this time of the year. Maybe I should call them and ask them if they have any missing guests?"

"Follow your instincts. We have three dead women, no clues to who they are or how they came here. Check everywhere in town where they might have been staying." Kane glanced at him over his screen. "It would be strange for a woman to be arriving in town alone, so the killer came with her."

Jenna shook her head. "Not necessarily. Many people make friends online and become attached just as if they had met in real life. It wouldn't be unusual for a person to travel somewhere to meet someone they'd met online."

"It's a normal thing to do now." Rio grinned at Kane. "Technology is great, isn't it?"

"Maybe, but you'll never take the old-school values out of me." Kane shook his head ruefully. "If we have a little girl, when she's grown, I'll want to meet any boy who plans on dating her."

Grinning, Jenna nodded. "No doubt by then all the kids will be microchipped so you won't have to worry."

"That is so not gonna happen on my watch." Kane's face was deadly serious.

Recalling the time when Wolfe dug the tracker from Kane's back, Jenna nodded. "Mine either. Okay let's get back to work."

TWENTY

Muttering under her breath, Carolyn Stubbs huddled in front of the fire. She'd have it out with him the moment he walked through that door. How dare he just walk out and leave her alone in this old cabin. He'd promised a vacation at the Glacial Heights Ski Resort not in this rat-infested hole. The excuse that the road was blocked and he needed to find his way back to the highway was no excuse for dumping her here. Plus, the fact he'd promised—promised—he'd only be gone forty-five minutes max. It had been at least three hours and she'd gotten bored and hungry. It was too cold and dark to move away from the fire and she'd dozed on the carpet for a time. The old cushion pressed to her cheek smelled musty and she sneezed. Pushing herself up, she stared into the glowing embers. He should have been back by now to take care of her. The fire needed more fuel, but she'd break her nails digging into the pile of wood. As darkness surrounded her and a cold chill sneaked under the blanket, she reached for a log from the basket beside the fire and tossed it onto the hearth. Sparks flew out everywhere, spilling across the rug. Carolyn gaped at the flaming embers in disbelief and then jumped to her feet to stomp on them before they caught the rug on fire.

Hugging a ratty old blanket around her, she braved the chill to search through the backpack he'd left on the table. It held cans of food, an opener, and a spoon. Bottles of water stood in a row beside it. No coffee or anything decent to eat. She stared at the cans: beans and chili. It might as well have been dog food. How hungry would she need to get before she opened a can? Anger rose up and she brushed the cans and water from the table and watched satisfied as they rolled around the floor. She'd make him pick them up when he returned and give him a piece of her mind. She hadn't spent a fortune on new jeans and boots to spend the night in a filthy cabin in wherever this place was, but as sure as heck if it wasn't the end of the earth, no doubt she could see it from here. They hadn't seen another soul since leaving the truck on the fire road.

Unsettled, she ran her last conversation with him through her mind. His reason to bring her into the forest had sounded wonderful. He'd wanted to show her the scenery and when he'd left had mumbled something about making sure they could drive the truck along the backroad to the ski resort. A worry crawled into her belly. What if he didn't come back? What if he'd died out in the blizzard?

Carolyn went to her purse to get her phone. Calling him was her only option. She stared inside her purse in disbelief. The phone was gone. Panic gripped her and, frantic, she searched each small pocket. She scanned the area around the coffee table and then, kneeled on the sofa and pushed her hands between the dusty cushions. Nothing. She stood and tossed the cushions onto the floor. Where was her phone?

Moving around the cabin, she searched every space. Darkness filled the tiny bedroom and she dragged the drapes from the window and tossed them onto the floor. Outside, the snow offered a glimmer of light. She stood panting and staring at the barren room furnished with one bed and a small nightstand. She collected the flashlight he'd left on the coffee table and went back into the bedroom. The cobweb-filled drawers were empty. She searched the bed, tearing the linen from the moldy mattress and found nothing. Frightened, she leaned against the wall. Realization gripped her. He'd taken her phone and abandoned her in the middle of a forest in a blizzard. Why had he done this to her? Carolyn stared at her reflection in the dust-covered mirror above the nightstand. She'd spent so much time and money making herself beautiful. She could have any man she wanted but she'd wanted him. Had she made a terrible mistake?

TWENTY-ONE

Darkness pressed against the windows in the conference room as Jenna took a sip of cold coffee and grimaced. She checked her watch. "It's ten after six and the snowplow guy is due to leave town by six-thirty. We need to go, now." She looked at Kane. "Go and collect Tauri from Nanny Raya's and I'll meet you downstairs." She closed her laptop and gathered her things before looking at Rio and Rowley. "We'll discuss what we've found in the morning unless it's significant. I want to hunt down the suspects before anyone else is found bound to a tree."

"I'll call you after supper." Rio stood and rolled his shoulders. "I'll chase down a few more details from home. We all need to take advantage of following the snowplows this afternoon. My guy heads in the direction of my ranch around seven."

"I'll be right behind you." Rowley picked up his laptop and grabbed his hat from the table.

Jenna headed back to her office to collect her coat and pull on her boots. She attached Duke's coat and he yawned and stretched before shaking his big head and making his ears pinwheel. She patted him. "Ready to go home and go back to sleep?"

Duke barked and leaned against her leg. Jenna rubbed his soft muzzle and smiled. "You are such a good dog."

As she headed downstairs Maggie the receptionist, or administrative assistant as her new job role was explained by the mayor, glanced up at her. "Time to go home, Maggie. It's getting dangerous out there. Will you be okay getting home?"

"I'll be fine." Maggie smiled and reached for her coat. "My truck has new snow tires and it's only a five-minute drive. You stay safe now." She waved her toward the door.

Glad to see Tauri, Jenna pulled open the door to give him a hug before settling Duke beside him. Tauri was dressed for bed and hugged his dinosaur. "Have you had dinner?"

"Yes." Tauri smiled. "Meat, and I ate the greens and had apple pie. I am full up to here." He indicated to his chin. "I brushed my teeth too." He gave her an exaggerated grin.

"That's good." Kane turned to look at him. "We're sorry we're late tonight."

"I know you've been looking for Julie." Tauri's face was serious. "You must find her, Daddy."

"We'll find her." Kane started the engine and headed along Main negotiating the piles of snow each side of the road left from the snowplow. He indicated ahead. "There's the snowplow guy. It's going to be a slow ride home tonight. Best you pull that blanket up to your chin."

During the long slow drive home, Jenna listened to Tauri's day with Nanny Raya. When she heard that Atohi Blackhawk had dropped by to spend some time with him, she smiled. "How lovely. Did he tell you stories?"

"Yes, and he taught me how to say more neat things." Tauri yawned and put one arm around Duke. "We talked about feathers and what they mean." His eyes fluttered and he dropped to sleep.

Jenna smiled at Kane. "He's all tuckered out. I figure the cold weather has us all exhausted. Did you discover anything interesting on our suspects?" She sighed. "I have sent the information on our victims all over but had no replies as yet. I concentrated on the names we have and where we could find them. None of them have professions listed, and most itinerant workers head to local ranches, bars, and food outlets where they can get work as cleaners. Some get work with the landscaping business as unskilled workers. I discovered a few places where they've done a couple of days' work, but they all move around. It will be hard to pin them down."

"Apart from John Raven, who is clean, I found they all have rap sheets. Most are misdemeanors, so I extended my search." Kane sighed. "My results aren't all in yet but so far they all fall into the interesting box because three of them have arrests for assaults against women."

Frowning, Jenna stared out at the dark landscape. The snow pelted down, filling the wipers and dragging an icy film across the windshield with each swipe. Snow flattened landmarks, and at night everything turned blue and gray, it was like being on the moon. "It's strange. In most of our cases we don't have a motive and no clue as to why the killers murdered, but suddenly, everyone we look at has a dark past. It's going to make it difficult to single out one as the potential killer."

"Until I know otherwise, they're all potential killers." Kane hunched as melting snowflakes sneaked under the collar of his jacket. "We need a timeline and their whereabouts."

Nodding, Jenna tapped her bottom lip, recalling the frozen corpses. "It would help if we knew a time of death. It's been below freezing for weeks. He could have been killing for a month by now. We have no idea. When they died is crucial evidence."

"When you spoke to Wolfe this afternoon, did he have any information on the victims?" Kane flicked her a glance and then returned his attention to the snowplow moving slowly along the road in front of them.

Wiping condensation from her window, Jenna shook her head. "Only they are all the same type of woman. Not hair color, but as in all have had extensive cosmetic surgery. He managed to get fingerprints and Kalo is currently feeding them through the databases. The victims will take time to thaw before Wolfe can make a time-of-death determination and then it will only be a guess. The last time we had frozen corpses they'd been frozen for a year."

"That doesn't apply in this case." Kane shrugged. "The animals would have eaten them if they'd been dumped before winter."

She leaned back in her seat. "Agreed, oh, and I spoke to Carter this afternoon as well and brought him up to date. He is anxious to be out searching for Julie and said his chopper can fly fine in the snow but the visibility is an issue, especially traveling along and through mountain ranges." She sighed. "It looks like we have no choice but to wait and hope Julie is somewhere safe."

"She's sensible." Kane heaved a sigh of relief as they pushed slowly along their driveway, the snowplow fitting on the front of the Beast cutting a path through the snow. "Wolfe and I taught the girls how to survive in the forest in all climates. Blackhawk instructed them on what to eat if they were stranded. If someone found her and is a survivalist, her chances are good. It depends on her injuries. We must hope she's making out okay, because right now, there's nothing more we can do. The snowmobile team has been searching all over as far as they can for as long as they can. Same with search and rescue and Blackhawk's friends. It's all we can do right now."

Without warning hot tears ran down Jenna's cheeks. She buried her face in her gloves and gave in to the emotions slamming into her. The chances of Julie being rescued by someone nice was hit and miss. She could be with a man who abused or raped women, a serial killer, or anything in between. The odds she was safe was way less than fifty-fifty. Who knows what she could be going through? The idea of not being able to help her was eating her up inside. The Beast stopped and Kane clicked off his seatbelt and hers and pulled her into his arms. He held her close and rubbed her back. She let it all go then, safe in his arms. The pressure of the job crushing down on her with such force she broke. Julie was missing, likely dead or in serious peril, and she could do absolutely nothing. Her reputation of a tough get-the-job-done sheriff with the best team in the West meant nothing. Inside, she screamed to get out and keep looking for Julie, but after one day in the freezing temperatures, zero visibility, and avalanches, she had to concede that Kane and Wolfe knew best.

The mayor had deployed organized teams of well-equipped and trained people to search the forest. For a time, she leaned into Kane, absorbing his strength. Until she'd married him, she'd never believed the possibilities couples could achieve, but leaning into his solid strength and inhaling his scent was better than any medication. He never rushed her or pushed her away when she needed him. It was as if he knew just the right time to offer his support. His hugs were priceless to her wellbeing. She lifted her head, seeing the wet patch on Kane's chest and took the tissues he offered and blew her nose. "I'm sorry."

"Don't be." Kane pushed hair from her face. "We're all worried about Julie, but the work we're doing hunting down cabins and people in the area will help us to find her. You need to trust the system, Jenna. You can't fix everything on your own. We fight crime. Leave the search and rescue and the snowmobile team to do their job. I know they're grid-searching on both sides of the avalanches. They have enough people to work in shifts. The mayor has the snowplows opening up the fire roads to give them access. I've been watching the snow reports and usually we get thirty-five inches of snow and Glacial Heights recorded eighty inches just this morning. The constant blizzard conditions and now earth tremors are making everyone's job harder."

Unable to understand why she couldn't control her emotions, Jenna swiped at her eyes. "I feel so useless. Julie and those poor women. Why do serial killers choose our county all the time? Are they challenging us to catch them?"

"Who can fathom the mind of a psychopath?" Kane shrugged, snapped on his seatbelt, and started the Beast. "I'll get you home. You need a nice hot shower, a good meal, and a long sleep." He waited for their gate to slide open and drove to the house. "Don't worry, Jenna, we'll work together and take it one day at a time as always. We'll find her and solve this case."

With Kane by her side, Jenna could climb mountains. Strengthened by his presence, she dabbed at her eyes. "I know we will." She squeezed his arm. "I'm so lucky to have you, Dave."

TWENTY-TWO

TUESDAY

Lying awake waiting for sunup, Julie heard Raven leave the house. She'd seen the glow of lights out in the barn and heard the barking dogs as he headed off. The previous evening had been interesting, to say the least. She guessed living alone could go two ways: either a person would be craving conversation or would shut down communication completely. Raven employed both options and last evening he'd taken the latter when it came to her. It was as if she'd suddenly become a burden or that unwelcome visitor who drops by unannounced and refuses to leave. Although he ignored her, he talked to his dog and had quite amusing conversations with Ben. The dog seemed to understand every word he said and could fetch objects from around the house and bring them to him. Last night, rather than being hospitable, he'd spent most of his time checking his watch and glancing toward the door. Why?

Last evening after returning late he'd been on edge and when she'd asked where he had been, he'd shut down communication with her after supper. As it was too late for him to go outside and remove the snow from the satellite dish, the promise of watching the news was a nonevent. She wanted to know what was happening. Had rescue teams found the aircraft? Was anyone looking for her? Not knowing was driving her insane. After trying to strike up a few conversations with him and failing, she'd hobbled into bed. She'd not taken the meds he'd handed her and dropped them inside a drawer. Why was he drugging her each night? What was he doing when she fell asleep? The need to know gnawed at her. Something wasn't right and she'd connect the dots soon enough.

As light streamed through the window, Julie sat up in bed and pushed back the blankets. She bent and unbandaged her leg. Under the bandages, blue bruising marred her flesh. The dark inky mark ran across her shin and matched a similar lighter mark on the other leg. She wiggled her toes. Her leg hurt but the agony was lessening. Sucking in a breath against the pain as she dropped her feet to the floor, she grabbed her crutches and made her way into the bathroom. The light flickered but then filled the small room with light. She needed a shower and the thought of being supervised by Raven unnerved her. He'd be gone for a time and as there was the luxury of hot water, she'd wash her hair. Being careful not to use too much water, she managed to get everything done in a few minutes. Although she'd have loved to stand under the hot flow, she'd never been inconsiderate. She used the rough but clean towels and managed to get back into the bedroom without mishap. After rebinding her leg without the splint, she dressed and, grabbing her hairbrush, hobbled into the family room. She poked at the fire and then sat beside it, hanging her hair over her face and brushing it so close to the flames the water dripping from the ends hissed in the embers.

After drying her hair, she stared at the front door. She wanted to know more about Johnny Raven. He spent a good deal of his time in the barn. What was there apart from the dogs and chickens that kept him so busy? She dragged on her coat and carefully pushed her thick socks into the rubber boots by the door. Her feet swam in them but her own boots were still drying out beside the fire from her last excursion into the snow. Wearing gloves and a woolen hat pulled down low over her ears, she swung her way outside on the homemade crutches. Cold seeped into her toes, and snowflakes coated her jacket in seconds. The forest was a sea of white with only the blackened trunks of the trees as a contrast. The path had been cleared but her boots sunk in deep as she swung her leg along. Panting out great clouds of steam, she'd made it only halfway to the barn when she heard the dogs barking. Ahead was a shed, set some distance from the barn but she could hide there. She glanced behind her. No doubt he would see her tracks unless the dog team obscured them when they arrived. A shiver of apprehension slithered through her. She'd take her chances.

She slid inside the shed, surprised to see it neat and clean. Since arriving in Black Rock Falls, she'd worked alongside her dad fixing things. He might be a medical examiner but also had field training to fix just about anything on the fly. She recognized spare parts for a snowmobile and the full cans of gas. Why was he using a dogsled when he had a snowmobile? She searched the shed. Under tarps she found plastic-wrapped bags of dog kibble and boxes of supplies, some no doubt taken from the aircraft. He had enough food to last him a year. A meat locker sat in one corner with a padlock. Metal boxes along one wall all had locks attached. What the heck was going on here?

Out back of the barn, she'd noticed two meat lockers, the kind used in winter to store frozen meat. Some people she knew would store an entire elk in one and eat it right through winter. With Raven lurking around outside, Julie couldn't remain inside the shed. Raven would be through settling the dogs and would find her missing. She needed to move while he was busy. Slipping out the door wasn't easy on crutches and balancing on one leg. She listened at the door for any movement, opened the door a crack to peer outside, and then froze. In a cloud of mist,

Raven was dragging something wrapped in a tarp alongside the barn. Her heart pounded as he unlocked a meat locker and lifted the wrapped bundle onto the edge. He pulled back the tarp and rolled the contents into the locker. As he stepped to one side to push it over the edge, fear gripped Julie's throat, stealing her breath at the sight of pink skin.

Panic gripped her, and she stepped back inside the shed, heart pounding so fast she couldn't think straight. Had he murdered someone? Where was the snowmobile and why wasn't he using it to get her out of here? Had she become his prisoner? Pressing her eye to the crack in the door, every muscle froze as he turned slowly to look in her direction. He couldn't know she'd seen him. What could she do? She hobbled over to the boxes piled high and scanned the labels. Finding a stack of powdered milk in cans, she pulled one out of the plastic wrapper and then found a stash of ground coffee. Would her excuse for being here fly? As muffled footsteps came toward the door, she held her breath.

The door opened slowly, and she turned to see Raven filling the entrance. "Oh, you're back."

"What the heck are you doing out here?" Raven's steady gaze settled on her face. "If you keep doing this, I figure I'll need to start locking you in the cabin."

You can't reason with a serial killer. Jo Wells' words hit Julie like a sledgehammer. Acting frightened could trigger an attack. She straightened her spine. "I figured I'd make breakfast but I couldn't find the powdered milk. You told me you'd collected supplies from the crash site, so I came out to hunt them down."

"How did you plan on carrying those cans and using your crutches? You'd have fallen and I'd have come home to find you frozen." Raven leaned against the doorframe staring at her. "Don't you want to get better?"

Nodding, Julie clamped her jaw shut to stop her teeth chattering. She met his bewildered gaze. "I figured I'd put them under my coat and inside the top of my sweatpants." She kept her chin high and shrugged. "I feel much better today and planned on doing two trips. I made it here okay and figured I could manage it."

"Sure you could." Raven took the cans from her and placed them back under the tarps. He handed her the crutches. "Hold them in one hand."

Pulse thundering in her ears, Julie did as he asked. What did he have planned for her? The next moment he took her arm and ushered her from the door. He slid the bolt across the shed door and then swung her into his arms. Julie's nose wrinkled at the smell of fresh blood. Trying hard not to panic, she forced her muscles to relax. He was so strong, fighting him would be just plain stupid. "Where are we going?"

"Back to the cabin. Where else? You didn't figure I was going to bunk you in the kennels, did you?" He whistled to Ben and the dog came tearing out of the forest.

Shrugging, Julie swung one arm around his neck. Being held like a baby disconcerted her. "You have places here you've never mentioned and a snowmobile. Where is it?"

"I own a few dilapidated cabins around here." He carried her toward the cabin. "I use them for storage. Nobody goes near them. They're all signposted with TRESPASSERS WILL BE SHOT signs. No one has touched anything yet. I built safe places for my dogs there, so I can use them as outposts. As in, I can leave the dogs there with food, water, and shelter and take the snowmobile in an emergency or when the going is too difficult for the sled. Before you ask, the reason I don't use it all the time is the gas. The dogs are renewable energy. Sure I have kibble, but every day I collect fresh meat for them by trapping critters. Gas means I need to drive into town. FYI, I have a trail bike and an old truck on the other side of the avalanche, plus another decent cabin. It was owned by an old man who died. I claimed it."

Interested, Julie clung to him as he climbed onto the stoop.

"So once we can get through the avalanche, we can drive into town?" She clung to her crutches. "Don't worry about the gas. My dad will make sure you have a full tank before you leave."

"That's good to know." He shouldered open the door and lowered her gently to the ground, supporting her as she removed her boots and coat. "You mentioned something about cooking breakfast? The dry milk is on the counter along with the coffee." He snorted and grabbed a towel from a peg to rub down Ben. He gave her a side-eye as he worked. "You don't need to head outside the moment my back is turned, Julie. I'd be happy to show you around—but not today. I'll be heading out again as soon as the dogs are rested. I have things to take care of."

Gripped by terror, Julie shuddered. *I just bet you do.*

TWENTY-THREE

The last few days had been more stressful than Wolfe could have imagined possible. With Julie lost in the blizzard, he'd spent restless nights imagining a wide variety of scenarios. The possibilities of what had happened to her were endless. Convinced she had been injured in the crash, the only saving grace was the fact that someone had taken medical supplies from the aircraft. The amount missing from the manifesto was too great for one person to carry, so whoever rescued her must have had a snowmobile with a trailer or another form of transport to get her away from the crash site. Although he knew that Jenna and Kane were doing everything possible to discover who owned cabins in the immediate area of the crash site, it didn't help with his feeling of total uselessness when it came to looking for his daughter.

It had been Norrell who'd come to his assistance when they'd arrived back at the morgue with the bodies from the crash. Although devastated about Julie's disappearance, she had given him and his girls emotional support. Without asking, she'd taken it upon herself to work with the burn victims, to match their identities to the list of passengers on the aircraft. The pilot had been in situ when they'd discovered his body and part of his uniform was still identifiable. Apart from one man, who'd been thrown from the back section of the aircraft, the others were damaged beyond recognition. Unlike the victims of crime, thawing the crash victims was undertaken at a faster speed. DNA swabs were taken and where possible, impressions of the teeth to check against dental records. All the victims, apart from the pilot were residents of Black Rock Falls and the local dentist had arrived at the morgue to assist Norrell with comparing them with the X-rays of the victims he had on record.

Wolfe had worked alongside Emily with the homicide victims, doing whatever was possible, but as they were frozen solid, they had to thaw in a controlled environment to avoid contamination. He'd contacted Rio earlier in the day to ask him to issue a media report to request that families of any woman between the ages of twenty-five and forty traveling to Black Rock Falls over the last month should contact them to ensure their safety as three women had been found deceased during the blizzard. As none of the women had been identified as Black Rock Falls residents, their only hope was that their families would report them missing once they couldn't be located. He could only imagine, as they were not from the local area and hadn't shown up as missing anywhere in the US, they must be on vacation. Right now, he had general descriptions of each woman.

After examining cells from each of the bodies he determined by the deterioration due to freezing that they must have been frozen within the last four weeks. In fact, around the time of the first snowfall in the mountains. Unfortunately, using frozen cells, deterioration as a time-of-death method was extremely unreliable, and if the area had been constantly below freezing, he could have stretched that time of death to more than a year. He had completely discounted the fact that these women might have been kept in a freezer or similar as the cell deterioration was variable, which meant the temperature went up and down during the time they were exposed to the elements. This result wouldn't occur if they were held at a constant temperature, as in a freezer, for instance.

He assisted Emily laying damp sheets across the bodies of the victims. Frozen bodies tended to dry out as they thawed and needed to be maintained at a constant temperature. As they covered the last of the three bodies, he looked at Emily. "That's all for today. I'm going to check on the weather report so we can find out when we can get back out to the crash site. The moment I get the chance I'm going to fly around the area searching for any cabins on either side of the avalanches. It makes sense to me that whoever rescued Julie took her to one of the cabins. Searching for them from the ground will be difficult at the moment as everything looks the same. From the air we at least have a chance of seeing a spiral of smoke."

"Will you be involving Carter in the search?" Emily had been despondent since her sister had gone missing. "I know Jenna has her mind on the homicides. Since that first day when we all went out searching for Julie, no one apart from Blackhawk has set foot in the forest." She pressed the release on the door and it whooshed open. "Have they given up searching for her?"

Shaking his head, Wolfe followed her through the door. He removed his PPE and tossed the gown into the receptacle and his mask and gloves into the garbage. "The mayor has experienced people working out in the field, Em. Search and rescue and a team of snowmobile riders who know the area. Blackhawk and his friends have been trying to discover trails that are passable and searching for any cabins in the local area. The problem is it's so darn cold no one can stay out for extended periods of time. Until I can get the chopper up to start searching for her myself, my job is to be here for the victims of crime. When the blizzard blows itself out, Carter, I, Styles, and the search-and-rescue helicopter will be out looking for her." He stood hands on hips and stared at her. "Do you honestly believe that I would be here when I could be out searching for my daughter? I know for a fact that Jenna wanted to keep on looking no matter what the cost. Having Julie missing is tearing her apart just like the rest of us." He waved a hand absently toward the window where the snow was a constant flow of white. "Right now, there's nothing we can do. I'm sure someone rescued her from the crash site. All the evidence points in that direction. We must assume she is safe and in a cabin with one of the locals who can't contact us for one reason or another. You know as well as I do that people live off the grid for a reason. They don't communicate with the outside world and live off the land. The simple fact that this person collected all the medical supplies on the aircraft and boxes of canned goods tells me that he made more than one trip. I figure he must be in a one-mile radius of the crash site and right now is hemmed in by the avalanches. We don't know if his communication was knocked out by the storm. Maybe he didn't have time to get the word out."

"I hope you're right." Emily stripped off her PPE and stared at him. "Do you want me to go next door and assist Norrell?"

Wolfe took in Emily's distraught expression and slipped one arm around her shoulder. As an independent young woman, she rarely came to him for a hug anymore, but he needed to let her know he was there for her. "Why don't you give Rio a call and ask him to meet you down at Aunt Betty's for lunch? They usually take a break around this time."

"Did you know that Rio has been promoted to chief deputy?" Emily raised one eyebrow. "I figure it's gone to his head. When I called him yesterday, all we talked about was his future. When I said I'd be staying here to finish my internship at the hospital and then be working with you, his attitude toward me was as if I'd asked him to sell his house and give me his life savings." She leaned into him. "His ambition is to be sheriff one day, which will mean moving to another town. Jenna is never going to retire and I doubt she'll ever lose an election in Black Rock Falls." She stepped away and leaned against the wall looking sheepish.

Raising both eyebrows, Wolfe met her gaze. "If Jenna did retire, Kane would take her place. Rio wouldn't win an election against him." He frowned. "He works so well with the team, I figured he was happy here. What else did he say?"

"That I should consider applying for an internship in another town." She rolled her eyes. "He mentioned a few backwoods towns where they were looking for a new sheriff, and with his credentials, he'd have a good chance of the mayor giving him an interim position. Once he was there, his reelection would be in the bag. I told him I wouldn't leave Black Rock Falls. My hopes and dreams are here working alongside you." She let out a long sigh. "He said he has his family to think about, and in a year or so, if the chance comes up to take over from a retiring sheriff, they'll move to that town. He plans to get himself known to the townsfolk so he'll be elected."

Concerned, Wolfe straightened. "You won't be through your internship by then and his siblings are adults. He doesn't need to provide for them." He rubbed the back of his neck. "Has the spark gone out of your relationship because, as sure as heck, I wouldn't be planning on walking out on Norrell for a darn promotion."

"I don't think he's being cruel." Emily frowned and crossed her arms over her chest. "He's a young man who is looking toward a future, I guess."

Staring at her, he didn't see a woman falling to pieces because the man she loved was planning to abandon her. "Do you love him?"

"After seeing how Norrell looks at you, and how she is when you're around, I figure Rio is more of a close friend. I've kept him at a distance for a long time and he is fine with that. I mean, we don't kiss other than a peck on the cheek. He doesn't cheat on me, but I don't think we'll ever have what you and Norrell have or Jenna and Dave. We'll be friends. I'm not sure that's enough. I was more concerned about losing a friend than a potential husband. I have the horrible feeling we've just become habits, as in we're there for each other when we want to go to a dance or out for a meal, but the hot romance thing is missing."

Wolfe took her arm and led her to his office. "I'll tell Webber to watch the shop. We'll head down to Aunt Betty's. Do you want to run this past Norrell or Jenna?"

"Jenna is my closest friend, and although Norrell is wonderful, she is not my mom. I need an outside opinion, but I won't mention Rio might leave some day because maybe he won't." She waited for him to pick up his phone. "I'm wondering if he's saying this to break up in a nice way. I could understand that. It's a long wait until I get my ME license, even though we could marry when I start my internship, I'm not sure I really want to marry him now."

Finding the conversation difficult because, in truth, no one was good enough for his girls, he tried to be as honest as possible. "When it comes to getting married, you don't marry someone out of obligation or because they've become a comfortable habit." He gave her a long look. "You marry them because your heart would break without them and because every second away from them is an eternity."

"Does everyone feel that way?" Emily blinked a few times and swallowed hard. "I'm starting to think he's just a friend." She ran her hands down her arms. "Oh, Dad. What am I going to do?"

Wolfe called Jenna. "Mind if I steal you for half an hour? Aunt Betty's in fifteen minutes? No, not about the case. It's personal. Yeah, Dave can come." He disconnected and looked at her. "Grab your things. They're on their way."

TWENTY-FOUR

At the sound of the snowmobile, Carolyn got to her feet and stood hands on hips, chin raised, and stared at the front door. She had a few things to say to him for leaving her alone all night and then having water and cold beans for breakfast. She heard a key turn in the lock and a blast of freezing air rushed across the room along with a flurry of snowflakes. "Where the heck have you been all darn night?" She smoothed her hair and brought it over one shoulder.

"We need some rules." The man of her dreams removed his coat and shook out the snow before hanging it on a hall tree beside the door. He sat down on the small bench seat below and dragged off his boots. "First, don't ever raise your voice to me again or swear in my presence. It's not ladylike." His dark gaze hardened as he straightened and walked toward her. "I expected a more welcoming response from you when I arrived. I figured you might have been concerned about my welfare out in the snow all night, but no, all you care about is yourself."

Carolyn ran her hands through her hair, arranged it over one shoulder, and then curled the ends around her index finger. The move usually made men forget their names. She smiled and wet her lips. "I don't follow rules. If I did, I wouldn't have come out here with you, would I? Doesn't every girl's mother tell her not to get into a car with a stranger, and yet here I am, in a cabin in the woods with somebody I hardly know." Her thoughts went to how they'd met as it had only been a week and he'd swept her off her feet. He was everything she wanted in a man and, with money to burn, he was perfect. She walked toward him. "I missed you. Are you okay? Where did you stay last night?"

"Don't touch me." A sneer crossed his mouth as he held up both hands like a traffic cop and glared at her. "Look at this place. Is this how you live? Stop touching your hair and get this place cleaned up." He picked up a bag he'd dropped on the floor when he came in and tossed it onto the kitchen counter. "I'll get the stove going. You can cook, right?"

Annoyed, Carolyn glared at him. Was he joking? "I don't cook or clean. We have people to do that where I come from." She looked around the dust-laden cabin. "Look at me. Do I look like a cleaning woman?" She tossed her hair and rearranged it again, smoothing it on her shoulder.

"You look like a spoiled brat." He shook his head slowly. "I bet if I go into the bedroom, you will have cleaned a space in the dust on the mirror to look at yourself."

Shocked by his ice-cold expression, she took a step back when he came around the kitchen counter. He stood a few inches from her, glaring down at her. It was as if he'd changed into a different person overnight. She lifted her chin, refusing to cower before him. "Don't be a dumbass. You know I like to make myself look good for you. That's why I'm here, isn't it, so you can show me off to your friends like a darn trophy?" She snorted. "Don't concern yourself on my behalf. I'm used to it."

The open-hand slap came from nowhere. Carolyn rocked back and sat down hard on the floor. No one had ever hit her before. She lunged forward and grabbed him by the leg and sank in her teeth. When he howled and grabbed her hair, she bit harder. He had handfuls of her hair. The extensions were coming off in his hands as he dragged her from him. Pain shot through her scalp as he twisted his fists, she needed to let go but had tasted blood. When she spat the blood from her mouth, he lifted her up by her hair. Screaming, she went for his face, but he moved so fast, twisting her around and grabbing both her hands. Forcing her to her knees, he pressed one knee in her back. The weight of him pushed the air from her lungs. Agony tore through tendons stretched well over their limit as he wrenched her arms high up behind her. "Stop it, you're hurting me."

"Oh, I haven't started hurting you yet." Viciously, he dragged her to her feet and marched her into the kitchen. He went into his bag and took out gaffer tape and wrapped it around her wrists. "Get into the bedroom. Now." He shoved her hard in the back.

Sobbing with terror, Carolyn stumbled forward. Was he planning on raping her? She stared at him over one shoulder. She could twist guys around her little finger. She just needed to give him what he wanted. "Look, I'm sorry, all right? I'll clean the cabin if that's what you want. There's no need to get violent."

"Shut up. That's just become another rule. You don't speak unless I ask you a question. I can't stand the sound of your baby voice any longer. You sound like a two-year-old." He stared around the room and growled deep in his chest. "Move and I'll make you sorry."

Trembling, Carolyn stood in the corner. She caught sight of her reflection in the mirror over the nightstand and gaped at her swollen red eyes. Her hair was standing up all over and mascara tracked lines down her cheeks. She turned as he heaved the mattress back onto the bed, tossed on the linen, and then stared at her as if deciding what to do next. Without warning, he grabbed her and pushed her into the tiny bathroom and secured her hands to the towel rail. She stared at him. "I said I was sorry and I'd clean the house. Stop acting like a blockhead and untie me... unless this is your kinky side? If it is, I can deal with it."

"Really." He shook his head slowly. "We'll see, shall we?" He took a hunting knife from a sheath at his waist and cut her free from the towel rail. "Get onto the bed. Face down arms and legs spread like a starfish."

Convinced she'd won him over, she gave him a coy smile and climbed awkwardly onto the bed, falling flat on her face. "You can untie my hands now."

Instead, he grabbed each ankle and secured them to the old metal bed ends. He climbed onto the bed and sitting on her back, cut her hands free before attaching them to the head of the bed. Carolyn turned her head to look at him. He stood looking down at her, a faraway look in his eyes, then he turned away.

"Think about the rules, Carolyn." He stood in the doorway staring at her. "It's going to get cold, but as I'm a nice guy, I'll add more wood to the fire, but I might not be back for hours, maybe not until tomorrow. I'll see if you are ready to comply. When you've cleaned the house and cooked me a meal, I'll reward you by taking you out to look at a beautiful view."

Panic had her by the throat. She could hardly move and her face pressed into the filthy mattress. "You can't just leave me here like this. What if I need to use the bathroom?"

"I'm sure one more stain on that old mattress won't make any difference." He turned and walked away, stopping to collect his bag, put on his coat and boots, before opening the door. A freezing wind rushed into the room. "Don't die before I get back. You'll spoil all the fun."

TWENTY-FIVE

Needing to make a decision on the fly, Jenna looked from Rio to Rowley. The weather hadn't changed and the wind was now buffeting the snow against the windows at an alarming rate. Her deputies had located Steven Oberg and Luke Sierra. Both men lived in Stanton Forest, with access to their cabins by fire roads. The fire roads should be passable using snowmobiles and the terrain in the immediate area of both cabins shouldn't be subject to avalanches. Rio had suggested going there right away. As both men had eaten lunch and could take supplies with them, Jenna considered Rio's request. She glanced out the window. Snow swirled and danced like a thousand brides on their wedding day. Going anywhere in this weather, even through town, was dangerous. The snowplows and salt spreaders had been at work twenty-four hours a day keeping the roads around Black Rock Falls clear and safe, but visibility was poor and reports of fender benders on Main were coming in hourly.

"With all the collisions in town at the moment, I really need you both here." Jenna frowned. "I'll go with Dave."

"Jenna." Kane looked at her with a troubled expression on

his face. "They would be able to move much faster than us, and to be perfectly blunt, they have more experience than you do in these conditions if you plan on going it alone on a snowmobile, which would be the only way we'd be able to make it there and back before nightfall." He leaned forward on the desk and met her gaze. "It's your call."

Drumming her fingers on the desk, Jenna recognized Kane's advice for what it was, a practical solution to a problem, and not being overprotective of her. She nodded. "You're right, I'm not experienced on a snowmobile like these two." She turned to Rio and Rowley. "Okay, make sure you take your satellite sleeves and check in with Maggie on arrival and when you leave. These men are both criminals, so don't trust them. And remember to announce yourself when you arrive. I don't want to come out and find your frozen bodies riddled with gunshot wounds."

"Don't worry, we'll take due care." Rio stood and gave her a small smile. "We'll get the job done, don't worry. If either of these men had anything to do with the murders, we'll flush them out."

"From what I've read on their rap sheets, both these guys have been round the block a few times." Kane stood and gathered the papers together on his desk and tapped them into a pile. "You're the enemy. Play it like you're going door to door looking for a lost woman from the plane wreck, which to some extent you are. Be careful not to ask any leading questions that might cause them to get jumpy and run. I'm sure you are both experienced enough to know if you're speaking to someone capable of murder. If you do get into trouble, I can be there with Wolfe before you know it, so don't hesitate to call."

"Thanks." Rowley slapped Kane on the back. "Catch you later." He followed Rio out of the door.

"What did Wolfe want?" Kane pushed documents into the filing cabinet and then turned to look at her.

Jenna pushed all thoughts of the investigation from her

mind and stood, closing her laptop. "He wants to meet us at Aunt Betty's to discuss something personal over lunch. He didn't say exactly what it was he wanted to speak to us about, but he did say it wasn't about the case."

"Okay, I'll put Duke's coat on." He headed for the door.

Jenna smiled. The dog had already climbed out of his basket and was wagging his tail at the mention of Aunt Betty's Café before scampering after Kane. She followed. "Are we walking?"

"In this weather?" Kane raised one eyebrow. "Taking Duke outside for a potty break was enough for me. That's why I parked outside the back door this morning. We get an undercover walk inside and the Beast stays moderately snow free."

Jenna pulled on her coat and then changed her shoes for boots. "So that's why you didn't want to interview the suspects. Arthritis playing up, old man?" She poked him in the ribs and giggled.

"Not quite yet." Kane pulled on his woolen cap and then added his Stetson. "Sometimes you forget you have a team around you to support you. Trying to carry the entire load of an investigation by yourself is counterproductive. You know this deep down in your heart or you wouldn't have agreed to make Rio chief deputy. If we're going to make this work with you as sheriff and a mother, you must start delegating now." He looked deep into her eyes. "By the time the baby comes along, you will feel more confident in their ability to handle things when we're not around. We both need that time to bond with our children. It will be a difficult time for Tauri. He needs to know absolutely that he is equal in every way to the baby."

Jenna smiled at him. "Oh, I agree. Since I discovered we were having this baby, I've been speaking to many working mothers. Trust me, I'm not the only working mother. In fact, most women with young children work. We have everything covered. I am more fortunate than most as I have you there twenty-four/seven and we've agreed to work only on the homicide cases or criminal cases going forward. Trust me, our kids will see us so often they won't even know we work at all."

"Okay." Kane took her hand and led her to the stairs. "I wonder what Wolfe wants. Maybe to ask me to be his best man?"

Jenna laughed. "That's a given. I know they're postponing the wedding until after the baby is born. Shane said that if he went away on his honeymoon, something would happen. This way, he can guarantee I have a safe delivery."

"Worst-case scenario, I can deliver our baby." Kane squeezed her hand. "I know what to do."

Jenna rolled her eyes. "Oh, won't that be fun? One thing: why don't you want to know the sex?"

"Oh, I know what sex it is." Kane grinned at her. "I just want it to be a surprise after all your hard work."

Speechless, she stared at him. "Trust me, holding a live healthy baby is all the reward I need."

TWENTY-SIX

Locating a place to park the Beast was proving difficult as they slowed outside Aunt Betty's Café. It seemed to Jenna that everyone had taken advantage of the local cuisine. She'd noticed the number of people packed inside the surf-and-turf restaurant, and also the pizzeria had people lining up outside in the freezing cold. Everything outside was so white she was glad of her sunglasses and pushed them up her nose as she climbed out of the Beast. Stepping carefully over mounds of frozen snow alongside the curb, she negotiated her way to the sidewalk, glad of Kane's hand under her elbow to steady her.

"What do you think this is all about?" Kane stood to one side as a young mother walked by pulling a small sled filled with children behind her.

Staring down at the rosy cheeks on the children, all dressed in the same knitted hats with bright yellow bobbles on the top, her stomach squeezed. The mother of the children smiled as she walked past, seemingly oblivious to the noise behind her and the snowflakes dashing at her face. Jenna smiled back and followed Kane along the well-salted footpath to Aunt Betty's. The ash and salt mix crunched under her boots as she walked, breathing in the mixture of wonderful aromas escaping from the front door. "Wolfe didn't say what it was about, only that it was personal. By meeting here, I would say he doesn't want the conversation overheard by anyone in either of the offices."

"Hmm." Kane scanned the room. "He's sitting at our usual table with Emily, so it can't be anything to worry about. Maybe he's just making plans for the wedding."

Shaking her head, Jenna followed him to the counter. "If that had been the case, Norrell would have been with him. He wouldn't be bringing Emily with him to discuss the wedding. I'm sure Norrell will be making most of the decisions. She made it clear what she expects. Her family will be arriving from overseas and be staying for a few weeks on vacation. I'm sure she'll want everything perfect. She's very organized and will likely handle everything herself."

"Wolfe has spoken to her parents. They share video calls and he gets along with them." Kane raised both eyebrows. "Her father is a cosmetic surgeon and insisted on paying for everything, so I figure it will be a lavish affair." He stared at the specials menu and sighed, one hand rubbing his belly. "Hey, Susie, I'll have the pulled pork with all the trimmings, apple crumble, and ice cream."

Suddenly ravenous, Jenna smiled at Susie, the manager. "I'll have the same and a glass of milk. The cold makes me so hungry."

"Yes, it's affecting everybody at the moment. We've been rushed off our feet since five this morning. It seems everyone wants a hot breakfast before starting work, so we've changed the opening hours to accommodate the townsfolk." She glanced down at Duke, sitting and watching her every move. "I have sausages left over from yesterday for Duke. I'll send Wendy with them and get your order to the chef. We've hired three extra line chefs just this week. The town is flocking with visitors." She took the order and turned to pass it back to the kitchen.

They made their way through the packed restaurant filled with the appetizing aromas of great dishes. A low hum of conversation buzzed in the room along with the clinking of silverware. There was something special about Aunt Betty's Café, almost magical. It had a feel-good quality, like being embraced the moment she walked inside. The smells of amazing food were one thing, but Jenna always believed it was the years of contentment baked into the restaurant that seemed to hang around. If happiness and contentment could be shared among a group of people, it was in this place. It was like the safe hug of a grandma, something her children would never have, but they would have Aunt Betty's Café and would make memories there just like she had with Kane.

Removing her coat, Jenna looked at Wolfe's strained expression and was immediately concerned about Emily's health. Always calm unless seriously provoked, nothing upset him unless it was something to do with his children or, of course, Norrell. "Have you ordered?" she slipped her coat around the back of the chair and removed her hat, gloves, and sunglasses before sitting down at the table.

"Yeah, Emily needs your advice. I can give her guidance as her dad, but she needs to speak to you, Jenna, and maybe Dave as well." Wolfe's arms rested on the table, his hands clenched as he watched Kane remove his coat. "Y'all don't mind, do you?"

"Not unless it makes me want to break someone's nose." Kane raised both eyebrows and sat down, making the chair groan. He looked straight at Emily. "Rio isn't being an ass, is he? If he is, I'll dig the hole and Shane can fill it."

When Emily paled, Jenna reached out to pat her hand. "Oh, don't take any notice of Dave's trash-talking. You know what he's like. He is so old-school. If anyone crosses the line, he's gonna be the first person to push them back over it. I figure if we have a little girl, he'll be going to the prom to make sure nobody acts inappropriately toward her."

"I was considering going to school with her as well." Kane gave them both a wide grin. "I'm not that bad, am I?"

Not amused, Jenna gave him a long look and nodded in unison with Emily. She cleared her throat. "You are both a little overprotective, and although it's good to be caring, smothering people with love only leads to rebellion."

"Okay." Kane held up both hands. "I see your point." He leaned toward Wolfe and lowered his voice. "You dig the hole, and I'll fill it in."

Seeing Emily's fraught expression, Jenna leaned closer. "What is it, Em? Would you rather chat in the restroom?"

"No." Emily rolled her eyes toward the ceiling. "Dad is making such a big deal. I just needed your advice as a woman and Dave's for the masculine side of things. Not having any brothers to grow up with, I have no idea how men think. I know how my dad thinks, but he doesn't believe anyone's good enough for me or Julie, so he doesn't count." She sucked in a deep breath. "Zac is a good friend, the best I could ever imagine to have for a guy, but I'm not in love with him. He asked me if he ever decided to move away from town, would I give up my career as an ME to go with him. I realized then, if he left, I'd miss him as a friend, but my heart wouldn't break. I'd be happy to see him during vacations, but like if I had a brother, not like someone I would want to marry."

As Rio was extremely smart, Jenna wondered if this was his way of finding out Emily's true feelings toward him. They had a very casual relationship and did act more like best friends. She doubted that he'd ever kissed her as they'd never intended the relationship to escalate while Emily was studying. "I believe you've answered your own question, Em." She met her gaze. "When Dave went missing, it was as if my heart was wrenched from my body. It was physical pain. I would walk over hot coals to be with him. Nothing or no one could stop me. If he left town for any reason, I wouldn't hesitate to follow."

"If you want my opinion"—Kane leaned back in his chair and swiped one hand down his face—"as a male, we can be kinda stupid sometimes. We take relationships for granted, forget to say the things women need to hear. Rio might be blissfully unaware that you consider him more than just a friend. Some men are happy with that, they might value a long friendship over a short burst of passion that might not last the test of time."

"So what about you and Jenna?" Emily's gray eyes moved from one to the other. "You took an eternity to decide you cared enough to marry."

"No, that's not the case at all." Kane leaned forward and cupped his hands on the table. "I had strong feelings for Jenna from the start and the attraction between us was electric. I would have been starting a relationship maybe a few weeks after I arrived, but I carried a ton of baggage. I had someone I cared about dearly who'd just died, and I'd been seriously injured on the job. I wasn't able to consider committing to a relationship until I had my head straight. In the meantime, we became very close friends, and I figure that first rush of attraction just grew until I realized it was time to tell Jenna everything." He sighed. "I needed her to know, I carried baggage."

"Do you carry it now?" Emily's eyes had filled with tears. "I'm so sorry for your loss."

"It's a fond memory, rather than a gaping hole in my heart." Kane squeezed Jenna's hand. "That is overflowing with love for Jenna and Tauri now."

"That's why it took Dad so long to find someone else." Emily glanced at Wolfe. "He loved my mom."

"I still do." Wolfe nodded slowly. "It doesn't go away. It's like a warm memory. It's just when I met Norrell, it was like a burst of sunlight banishing the shadows. When you've had one great love, you never consider the chance of another. I've never looked for anyone else. I figured it was being unfaithful to your mom's memory. Trust me, no one was more surprised than me when I met Norrell. We fit together as if we were meant to be. This is how you should be with Rio. If not, it will lead to unhappiness, because if either of you meet that special someone, things will go sideways real fast."

Not having suffered a bad breakup or intense relationship before meeting Kane, Jenna didn't have the experience to give advice. She had learned more listening to Kane and Wolfe in those few minutes than in her lifetime. It was common sense. "Em, you're both adults, sit down and talk with him. As friends, you have that trust between you. Tell him the truth."

"There is one thing you should avoid." Kane scratched his cheek and gave his head a little shake. "Maybe don't say, 'Can we still be friends?' Maybe say, 'We've been friends for some time but is that enough basis to get married?' It's not so dismissive and hurtful if you want to break up with him."

"I figure whatever I say will hurt him." She pushed both hands into her hair, holding her head and staring at the table. "Maybe I'll say I need time alone to study and concentrate on my career. I don't want him to wait because, when I'm done, I might not want to marry. I know he wants a ton of kids and that's not for me. I want a career first, and when I have all that out of my system, I might or might not want to settle down."

"The first thing he'll ask you is if you've met someone else." Kane eyed her critically. "Is that what this is all about?"

"No." Emily looked up at him. "I haven't met anyone who makes my toes curl and my heart race. This is the problem." She leaned back in her chair. "I'll be honest with him and see how it goes. I appreciate everyone's help. I know what I need to do." She looked up as Wendy came to the table with a tray carrying pots of coffee, a tall glass of milk for Jenna, and a big pile of sausages on a paper plate for Duke.

"Your meals will be right along." Wendy arranged the cups and silverware. "Enjoy." She turned and headed back to the kitchen.

After checking her phone, Jenna's heart sank. She'd messaged everyone involved with the search for Julie and all her replies had been negative.

"Bad news?" Kane squeezed her hand.

The concern over Julie was eating away at all of them, this meal was a moment's respite and she didn't want to spoil it, but she nodded. "I asked for updates on the search for Julie just before and no one has found a trace of her." She wiped a hand down her face as Wolfe winced. She needed to change the subject smashing into them every waking second, even for a few minutes.

Jenna blew out a long breath and turned to Wolfe. "Any updates on the victims?"

"Norrell has most of the crash victims identified." Wolfe frowned and poured coffee. "They had next of kin waiting for them to arrive, so she was able to identify them using personal effects, but the provisional identifications will be backed by DNA or dental evidence." He added the fixings to his cup and stirred slowly. "The homicide victims, nothing so far. I asked Rio to put out a media release. I figure the women were here on vacation. This is why they're not showing on any missing persons files. No one knows they're missing."

Jenna sipped her milk. "Well, that makes sense." She placed the glass on the table. "The town doesn't need a reputation for killing visitors. Tourism means a thriving town."

"I wouldn't worry too much." Kane smiled at her. "Going on the influx of visitors at Halloween, I figure at least half of them come here to rub shoulders with serial killers. I'm expecting a T-shirt with I SURVIVED BLACK ROCK FALLS to show in one of the stores soon."

TWENTY-SEVEN

Rio climbed from the snowmobile and waited for Rowley to join him. They'd found a cabin in the general area of where they believed the suspects were living. It was some distance from the fire road but accessible using the snowmobiles along an old hiking trail. He'd decided to part with the snowmobiles and walk toward the cottage to look like less of a threat to the occupants. He had no idea if either of the suspects resided here. He glanced at Rowley as they crunched through the ice-covered snow. "It's not signposted, so maybe the people living here are okay with visitors."

"I'm not planning on risking my life on that assumption." Rowley looked at him. "What's up with you today? Your mind is miles away. If you have a problem, spit it out. I'm not planning on getting shot anytime soon."

Rio snorted. "That obvious, huh?" He stopped walking and turned to him. "It's not working out between Em and me." He blew out a cloud of steam. "We want different things. I want a house full of kids and she wants to play with dead bodies until she's in her thirties. If a position comes up for sheriff in the future in a different town, I might spend some time there as a deputy and then throw my hat into the ring."

"You don't like it here?" Rowley's eyes widened. "What, is Serial Killer Central not exciting enough for you?" He scratched his head. "You just made chief deputy. Do you figure being a small-town sheriff will satisfy you after living here? You'll be bored shitless." He gave him a long look. "Or is it the long wait to have Emily at home surrounded by kids that's the problem?"

Shrugging, Rio met his gaze. "Yeah, that and I don't believe she's in love with me. We're great friends. Heck, she won't even make out with me. She said she promised her dad and she never breaks a promise."

"That's fair enough." Rowley pushed back his hat and stared at him. "Sandy was much the same. The thing is, are you in love with her?"

Rio shook his head. "Infatuated at first, but no, we're just close friends. I haven't looked at another woman, but right now my relationship with Emily doesn't exist. I can't see a future with her. We're heading in different directions. If I stay here, it still won't work. We want different lives and have different ambitions. The thing is, how do I tell her?"

"Easy." Rowley turned back to the trail. "Be honest with her and tell her what you've told me. She'll understand. I've never seen you or her looking like lovesick puppies. Maybe it's time for you both to call it a day. You can still be friends. It's better parting while you are, rather than ending it in a fight. Life is far too short to be angry, and working together would be a nightmare."

The cold seeped through Rio's clothes and he straightened. "Thanks for the advice. The cabin is just ahead. I'll call out. You hang back and cover me, just in case the occupant decides to draw down on me."

Ratta-tat-tat. Ratta-tat-tat. Ratta-tat-tat.

Automatic weapon fire blasted Rio's hat from his head and disintegrated the trees beside him. Bark and splinters exploded into the air in a cloud of brown and green. He hit the ground and rolled, his face ending up buried in the deep snow. He lifted his head an inch, spitting out ice. "Jake, are you okay?"

Nothing.

He raised his voice. "Jake."

Only the whisper of the wind and the patter of overloaded branches creaking under their heavy burden greeted him. Concern overwhelmed him, and determined to find his friend, he crawled on his belly to where he'd last seen Rowley.

Ratta-tat-tat. Ratta-tat-tat.

Snow flew up all around him. Tree branches splintered and pelted him with wood shards, pine needles, and snow. He needed to get to Rowley, but it was pointless trying to return fire against an automatic weapon that could potentially fire up to twelve hundred rounds per minute. He didn't want a war. He'd try and reason with the shooter. "Sheriff's department. Hold your fire. We're not looking for trouble. We're hunting down survivors of the plane crash over at Bear Peak."

Ratta-tat-tat. Ratta-tat-tat.

Not needing to argue the point, Rio dived behind a clump of trees, one of them wide enough to give him cover. He scanned the area and made out the soles of Rowley's boots, tip up in the snow. All around him gunfire had shredded the trees. He pulled out his phone and, after pushing an earbud into one ear, called Jenna. She answered right away. "We're under fire, automatic weapon. One man I figure. Rowley is down. I'm pinned down and can't reach him to see how bad."

"Hold for one second." Jenna was speaking to someone close by in hushed tones. *"Kane and Wolfe are on their way. Send me your coordinates."*

Rio complied and as he sucked in a breath, a thousand ice-cold needles attacked his lungs. "I called out but they shot first.

We're about thirty yards from the front of the cabin and on foot."

"I'm in Aunt Betty's but I'm heading back to the office now." A car door slammed. *"Kane and Wolfe are collecting the trailer with the snowmobiles. They'll make good time in the Beast. Hunker down and wait for backup."*

Rio's attention hadn't drifted from the soles of Rowley's boots. When one foot moved a little, he heaved a sigh of relief. "Copy that. I can see Jake moving. I'll need to get to him to see how bad he's been hurt." He lifted a broken tree branch and hurled it away from his position.

Ratta-tat-tat. Ratta-tat-tat.

As snow flew up all around him, he lunged in the opposite direction and dived behind a tree beside Rowley. His heart sank at the sight of three bullet holes in the front of Rowley's liquid Kevlar vest. Grabbing one of his partner's arms he dragged him behind the trees. "I have him, Jenna. I'm checking for injuries. He's taken three in the vest."

There was no excuse for anyone to shoot at a deputy wearing a vest clearly marked with the bright yellow sheriff's department logo on the front. They hadn't ventured onto a sign-posted property. In fact, all the cabins in this area belonged to the Forest Service. He removed a glove and dragged Rowley's clothes from his pants and slid his hand over his warm flesh searching for wounds. Under his palm, he could feel the rise and fall of Rowley's chest. "I'm checking him for injuries. He's breathing."

"The force of impact could have knocked him out. It hurts. I've been there." Jenna's footsteps echoed on tile. *"Check for broken ribs sticking out. Blood in his mouth."*

When Rio's hand came back clean from under Rowley's shirt, he sighed with relief. He couldn't find any injuries. Bullets hitting a vest could knock a person flat on his back. They stopped penetration but not the force. People had died from the force of the impact. Sometimes the victim suffered a break to the ribs or sternum. He covered Rowley and then examined his face. "No blood. I'm checking his head. Yeah, he has an egg. I figure he's out cold."

He pulled on his glove and grabbed a handful of snow and rubbed it over Rowley's face. "Hey, wake up. Open your eyes, Jake. You're okay. The vest caught the bullets."

After a few moments Rowley groaned and his eyes flickered open. Rio leaned close. "Don't move, we have an active shooter."

"I'm not sure I can move." Rowley took shallow breaths. "I feel like I've been stepped on by a horse."

Rio nodded. "Yeah, after taking three bullets in the vest, I'm not surprised. Take some deep breaths. Jenna is on speaker. Kane and Wolfe are on their way."

"Did you call out and identify yourself?" Rowley wheezed and coughed. "Oh, jeez that hurts."

"Who does the cabin belong to?" Jenna closed the door to her office and her chair squeaked as she sat down.

Rio helped Rowley to sit up and leaned him against a tree. His friend was as white as the landscape. He bent to get a Thermos from his backpack.

Ratta-tat-tat. Ratta-tat-tat. Ratta-tat-tat.

Bullets pinged all around them and great lumps of frozen snow fell like missiles bombarding them. Rio groaned as one as heavy as a brick hit his shoulder. He slid down behind a tree clutching his backpack to his chest. "We're okay. This guy just won't give up. The cabin belongs to Luke Sierra."

"I need to get to my backpack." Rowley's lips had turned blue. "We can't just sit here in the snow. We'll freeze to death."

"You'll need to distract the shooter away from you." Jenna was tapping away at her computer. *"Use the foil blankets to sit on and wrap yourselves in one as well. Drink the hot coffee. Backup is on its way. I can't find anything good about Luke*

Sierra. He's violent. I've found info from a few different counties. Seems he likes causing trouble in small towns. He's been lucky and gotten himself a good lawyer. He's been fined most times or been given community service. He's been behaving himself since he arrived here, until now."

Nodding, Rio held up a hand to Rowley. "Copy that. I'll relay that to Rowley."

After explaining, Rio gathered some clumps of snow and hurled them into the trees to his left. The laden tree branches swayed and snow cascaded down to the forest floor. He threw more and then ducked back behind the tree.

Ratta-tat-tat. Ratta-tat-tat. Ratta-tat-tat.

Running on pure adrenaline, Rio ran back to Rowley, dragged him to his feet, and with one arm supporting his weight, they ran stumbling toward a huge boulder. As bullets rang out, peppering the forest from right to left, they fell behind the wall of granite. Visibility dropped as the blizzard hitched up a notch but the barrel flash from the weapon was visible. The shooter was on the move and hunting them down.

TWENTY-EIGHT

Even in the Beast, driving through a blizzard was a nightmare. Snow piled up on the wipers and ice was forming patterns around the edges of the windshield, visibility was limited but confident that his truck could handle the conditions Kane kept moving. They turned into the fire road. The snowplows had been by recently and cleared the thick crust, but with the relentless snowfall it still had a good coating of snow. Once the snow began to fall it became prolonged and paralyzing to the entire state. The skiers would be overjoyed to have a new powder coating every few hours, but it didn't make traveling any easier, especially through the forest over a snow-laden gravel road. Kane didn't care about the noise of the engine advertising their arrival. He figured it just might give the shooter something else to worry about apart from Rio and Rowley.

Unlike the deputies, Kane and Wolfe had opted to wear tactical gear. With liquid Kevlar vests underneath camouflage jackets, they both wore helmets and would be carrying rifles. Kane's sniper rifle gave him an advantage in the field. He could immobilize anyone from a great distance. Jenna's instructions to take the shooter alive were imperative. She wanted to question him as a suspect in the current murder case. With the last message from Rio saying they were under attack, and knowing he and Rowley were crack shots and would return fire, he wondered just how he'd be able to comply with her orders. Right this second, the future of everyone in the game was in the lap of the gods.

"Rowley says the shooter is heading their way. We'll leave the snowmobiles on the trailer and drive to his front door and then circle around behind him on foot." Wolfe's voice sounded muffled from behind his scarf.

Kane pushed the Beast through the snow, glad of the snowplow attachment and snow tires. "That sounds like a plan. He'll have trouble shooting up the Beast."

"Will you miss the old girl?" Wolfe patted the dashboard. "I was hoping they'd give her to me."

Kane raised one eyebrow. "Yes and no. I do have a sentimental attachment to my truck. It holds a ton of memories, but my family's safety is my priority and the new Beast is incredible. I heard on the grapevine that this one is going to provide safety for diplomats or something, so it will be well cared for." He slowed. "I hear gunshots. I guess we walk from here."

He parked against a clump of trees, gathered his rifle, and slid with Wolfe into the forest. It wasn't often he worked alongside Wolfe on missions like this, but they fit together as if they'd been partners during their tours of duty. They had in one respect, of course, but Wolfe had been in Kane's ear, not beside him in the field. The last five years or so working in Black Rock Falls, Wolfe had proved his worth as a very experienced soldier. It was no wonder he'd been chosen as Kane's handler. Then and now, Wolfe needed to know exactly what danger Kane would be facing and together they made an indestructible team.

Ratta-tat-tat. Ratta-tat-tat.

"Give me your position." Wolfe had lowered his voice to just above a whisper as he spoke to Rowley on the phone.

"We're coming in on the left of the shooter. Stay down. Kane will take him out from here. Do not, I repeat, do not return fire. We will be in your direct line of fire."

Taking silent steps through nature's white blanket, Kane moved through the forest and then held up one hand for Wolfe to stop. He moved to a small clump of trees. "We wait here until I can get a clean shot. Taking down a target in a forest is a nightmare. I can see him heading in their direction, if he keeps moving that way, he'll cross that small clearing just ahead."

"You're the expert." Wolfe blinked away snowflakes. "But make it in the arm or we'll need to carry him back. He looks like a big guy and I'm not as young as I used to be."

As Kane rested his rifle across the branch of a tree, his time as a sniper came back in a rush. It was like a second sense. His body relaxed and everything around him slowed. It was as if the snow fell in slow motion. His heart rate followed and he fell into the zone, where he could complete a shot between a heartbeat. As the shooter stopped to reload, Kane took a breath and let it out slowly. His finger dropped to the trigger. The man walked into the clearing and turned to face them as if sensing they were there. The ammunition clip slid into place and the shooter raised his weapon.

Ratta-tat-tat. Ratta-tat-tat. Ratta-tat-tat.

As the forest exploded around him, without a second's hesitation, Kane squeezed. The shot struck the shooter's right shoulder and went straight through. The automatic weapon in his hand spewed bullets in all directions until it fell to the ground. The man cried out and clamped his hand on his arm and staggered around cursing, his head swiveling around searching for the shooters. From behind him, Rio appeared, weapon drawn.

"Sheriff's department. Get on your knees. Hands on your head." Rio moved forward, his aim not moving from the man's center mass.

Wading through thick snowdrifts, Kane ran forward with Wolfe on his heels. He reached the clearing, picked up and unloaded the automatic rifle as Rio cuffed the shooter and then patted him down. He looked at Wolfe. "I guess you'd better check him. It's a through and through. I didn't plan on messing him up."

"He'll wait. There's little blood loss." Wolfe frowned at Rowley. "I need to check Rowley. If he has a punctured lung, he could die."

"Jake took three in the vest and was out cold for a time. He has an egg on the back of his head." Rio straightened. "He never complains. He's as stubborn as a mule."

"He'll need X-rays and a day or so to recover." Wolfe headed toward Rowley, who leaned against a tree, his face sheet-white. "Can you walk?"

"Yeah, I figure, I'll be black and blue by morning but nothing feels broken. I'm okay. Head hurts a bit, is all, but I can see fine." Rowley walked up stiffly and grimaced as Wolfe checked him out.

"Those liquid Kevlar vests are worth their weight in gold." Wolfe shook his head and removed his examination gloves. You'll be sore for a time but there's nothing to worry about. How is the pain level?"

"It's better since you took your freezing hands out from under my shirt." Rowley's mouth curled into a smile. "I've had worse falling from a horse. I can ride back to Rio's truck, no worries." He turned to stare at the shooter. "What's your name."

"Luke Sierra and I was protecting what's mine." He glared at Kane. "You had no right to shoot me."

Shaking his head, Kane scanned the area and met Sierra's gaze. "Nope, this is part of the state forest. The cabin you are living in belongs to the forestry. Do you pay rent?"

"Nope. I claim squatter's rights." Sierra spat on the ground. "I was defending my property."

Blowing out a stream of steam in a sigh, Kane shrugged. "This is where a little knowledge is a bad thing. I know you moved from Blackwater last year because we've checked you out. To claim an unoccupied property, you need to be living here for fifteen to twenty years before you can make a claim. So that excuse is off the table. Firing at law enforcement officers is an offense. You hit my deputy three times and I'd be telling his wife and kids to start planning his funeral if he hadn't been wearing a vest—a vest clearly marked as sheriff's department. You have no excuse for firing. Not at any time did they discharge their weapons, they identified themselves, and were no threat to you. So I'm afraid you'll be taken back to the sheriff's office and charged." He read him his rights.

"As to duty of care"—Wolfe removed his backpack and pulled out a medical kit—"I'll patch you up and we'll take you to the hospital for X-rays. From then on, you'll be under the care of County."

Once Wolfe was done, Rio and Rowley made it slowly back to their snowmobiles and Kane led Sierra back along the trail to his house. "Is there anyone inside you need to tell? Any livestock that needs tending? You won't be coming back anytime soon."

"No one to tell. My dogs will need tending." Sierra kept his head down and expression guarded.

Being unable to read him was a problem. Kane shot a glance at Wolfe, who gave him a slight nod. "Do you want me to check your dogs? I can feed them and then send someone to care for them in the morning."

"Yeah, sure." Sierra nodded.

Kane pulled out his phone. "I'll need your permission to enter your cabin and barn to feed your dogs, and to confirm I've read you your rights. Do you mind?" He set the phone to record. "Luke Sierra?"

"Yeah, that's my name. You've read me my rights and you've

got permission to enter my house and barn." He spat on the ground again. "That's all I gotta say. I want a lawyer."

Kane turned off the recording. "That's all I need. Get into the back of the truck." He activated the screen between front and back seats and the doors locked. He turned to Wolfe. "There's no way he can escape from there. Let's go and search his house."

TWENTY-NINE

As Kane searched the cabin, Wolfe took a video. The place was small, with one bedroom. In five minutes, it was obvious to Kane that Sierra hadn't kept a woman there. The scent in the house was rank male sweat and he found no trace of anything possibly feminine. The fingerprint scanner showed identical prints all over. Sierra lived here alone. They went outside and found six dogs in half of the barn sectioned off. They appeared well fed and cared for and Kane found a sled and harnesses close by. The other half of the barn held bags of dog kibble, a ten-year-old Ford truck, a snowmobile, and cans of gas, along with tools and other supplies. He filled a trough in the dogs' area with kibble and noted the water supply was drip fed and constant. The dogs would be fine and he'd have animal protection drop by to collect them in the morning. He looked at Wolfe, who dropped his phone and stopped recording. "If he has a sled and a snowmobile, he could be moving around the forest, but I can't see any supplies from the aircraft here or in the house."

"He could be using this place as his base and we have no proof the killer held his murder victims anywhere." Wolfe hunched his shoulders. "This just tells me that he isn't the one who rescued Julie. Search and rescue tried to get to the crash site along this way and the trails are blocked by avalanches."

Kane rubbed his chin. "You mean the killer might be meeting potential victims in town and bringing them to the forest to murder them. Do you figure he drugged them?"

"Unknown at this time." Wolfe removed examination gloves and pulled on his thick sheepskin-lined ones. "I'll do a drug analysis ASAP, but the problem is the freezing. The process of freezing and thawing can degrade drugs. The results aren't usually good enough to convict anyone. I'm hoping we'll discover foreign DNA. I don't believe the victims have been frozen long enough to destroy trace evidence. Well, frozen, thawed, and frozen would have an impact, but from the cell degeneration I've seen so far, these victims were frozen once and not allowed to thaw completely, but it's not conclusive yet. Just an observation."

Kane removed his gloves and rolled them into a ball. "I'll bring Jenna up to date." He made the call.

"If you're not convinced it's him, how far are you from Steven Oberg's cottage? Rio mentioned they were along the same trail." Jenna cleared her throat. *"It would save time if you dropped by. I assume the shooter is stable and Rowley is okay to travel back to town?"*

Leaning against the barn door, Kane nodded. "Yeah, Sierra is angry and would be in pain, but Wolfe filled his shoulder with local anesthetic. He'll be fine for two hours or so. We'll go and check out Oberg. We should be okay. I'll turn on the lights on our approach just in case he decides to open fire at us, but we'll be safe in the Beast."

"Okay, call me when you're done." Jenna paused for a beat. *"Shane. Do I need to insist Rowley goes to the hospital to get checked out?"*

"Yeah, I'll call it in now and they'll be expecting him." Wolfe raised both eyebrows. "He'll complain but make him go."

"I will." Jenna disconnected.

They headed back to the Beast. In the back seat, Sierra was leaning back with his eyes shut. Kane slid behind the wheel. "You okay back there?"

"Oh, I'm just fine." Sierra's mouth turned down and he let out a string of curses. "I won't forget this, Deputy. No, sir. I don't forgive or forget."

Kane shrugged. "Neither do I." He looked at him in the rearview mirror. "I can get you to the hospital faster if you know where we can find Steven Oberg. He's a neighbor of yours, right?"

"Yeah." He indicated ahead with his chin. "He lives up there somewhere. I see him pass by and he drops by here to collect his mail. Seems I get all the mail. His place must be invisible or something." He winced. "I've never had a reason to go there."

Following the dirt road with the thickening snow was slow going. The snowplow attachment on the Beast was handling the drifts for now but not for much longer. Kane sighed with relief when they came to a cabin set deep in the forest with barely enough room out front to turn the truck around. The wig-wag lights sent blue and red flashes across the brilliant white snow. Kane used his loudspeaker. "Sheriff's department. Steven Oberg, are you inside?"

The door opened and a man stepped out, buttoning his coat and then pulling on thick gloves. A large dog slipped out beside him and Oberg bent and pushed him back inside before shutting the door behind him. Kane doubted he was carrying a weapon. He glanced at Wolfe, who nodded and then slid from the truck. "Hi there. We're in the local area searching for survivors of the plane crash at Bear Peak." Behind him Wolfe was out of the truck and making his way toward him.

"Yeah, I saw the smoke and heard the impact." Oberg leaned back against his door, remaining under the porch roof. "I went out to take a looksee but we had an earth tremor and snow was falling down the mountain all over. I haven't seen anyone. I'm sure they'd come to the door if they were in trouble. It's a long way to town from here."

"We're looking for a young woman." Wolfe straightened. "We've spoken to your neighbor and he mentioned often seeing women here. Do you have anyone staying with you at the moment?"

"Not right now." A flash of annoyance crossed Oberg's eyes and then vanished. "It's not a very inviting place to bring a woman in winter but summer, well skinny-dipping in the river is romantic and they love the thrill." He indicated over one shoulder. "You're welcome to take a look inside, but I don't really want you traipsing snow all through my place."

Taking a step forward to gauge his reaction, Kane met a face devoid of expression. Nothing flickered in Oberg's eyes to determine distress. If he had anything to hide, he was keeping it together well, and why would he take the risk of offering to allow them inside? "Can anyone verify your whereabouts over the last month?"

"Nope." Oberg pursed his lips. "I've been into town a few times, did a few odd jobs, but days run into each other in the forest. I can't be specific. Why is this relevant to the air crash?"

"It's not." Wolfe lifted his chin. "There are a few other people we're hunting down in this area, but if you were here all the time, you wouldn't have seen them."

Kane thought for a beat. "Luke Sierra, down the trail a ways. Do you see him often?"

"Nope." Oberg stamped his feet. "We almost done? My feet are numb."

"Do you have a girlfriend?" Wolfe pulled his hat down firmly on his head. "Anyone special in your life that you bring here regular?"

"Nope." Oberg's attention moved to Kane. "I'm not planning on settling down for a time yet. This place here is just a steppingstone. It's cheap to live here and I can do just about what I want, when I want."

"What do you do—when you feel like working?" Wolfe leaned against the Beast but didn't appear to be the least interested in the conversation.

"A variety of things." Oberg shrugged nonchalantly as if he had all the time in the world to chat. "I know the forest, so sometimes I apply to be a guide for the hunters or the hikers. I've held licenses and pay my taxes. Other times, I get work on a ranch. There's always work available on most of them. I can bus tables, clean. You name it and I can set my mind to it." He smiled and indicated to Kane. "Being a big guy like us has its advantages. The bosses know we can work hard and the women fall at our feet. I'm saving to get me a nice place closer to town. I like living here. It's been two years now."

Kane rubbed a hand under his nose. He didn't like this guy. Heck, anyone who laid hands on a woman inappropriately made his hands ball into fists. How any of these guys failed to make the sex offenders lists baffled him. "It's just as well you've changed your ways. The sheriff in this town doesn't tolerate any form of abuse. I've read your sheet, so don't try and deny it." He gave him a long look. "You're on our radar."

"I came here to make a clean start." Oberg gave a great impression of being taken aback. "Hey, man. I've changed. I was young and impulsive. If you've read my files, you'd know I've never been accused of rape. I figure they just got a little scared with my enthusiasm. Now I know better and I'm a real gentleman. They never complain when they leave here. In fact, all of my ex-girlfriends are still close friends. I'm sure they'll sing my praises if you ask them."

"We'll be sure to." Wolfe checked his watch. "The snow is getting heavier. We'd better go."

Kane handed Oberg a card. "If anyone comes by from the

crash, call me. We'll come and get them." He gave him a long look. "The crash site is a crime scene. When you can get through the trail, keep away. The investigations are ongoing due to the weather."

"I understand." Oberg tucked the card into his pocket. "Although, I doubt anyone will come by. There's no way through and it will be like that until the melt. I'm planning on spending the time at home." He placed a hand on the doorknob. "If that's all, I'm going inside."

"Yeah, thanks." Wolfe stamped the snow from his boots and climbed inside the truck.

Opening the door to the truck, Kane looked back as Oberg slid back inside his cabin. He looked at Wolfe. "I'm not too sure about him. I'll keep his name on the list of possible offenders I keep in my daybook. I have a feeling we'll be running into him again someday."

THIRTY

Jenna had made good use of her time in the office waiting for the team to arrive. She'd contacted the DA to request an arrest warrant for Sierra, and prison officers were on their way to collect him. One of the local public defenders, Samuel J. Cross, was standing by. She'd called Rowley and insisted Rio take him to the ER. He'd already been seen and was fine, apart from bruising. She'd sent him home but Rio was busy writing up his report for the DA.

Blackhawk and the head of the search-and-rescue team that were hunting down Julie's whereabouts were due to arrive to give her a rundown of the situation, and Maggie had received calls over the hotline after the media release about the victims discovered in the forest. She'd sent the images to Kalo, along with the shots taken by Wolfe as the bodies thawed. Rather than show the next of kin the gruesome images, Kalo had offered to run the images through his facial recognition software. So far, four women had been reported missing by their families. It had been easy for him to hack into the airport footage for the dates of the arrival of each woman. All had arrived safely in Black Rock Falls and then vanished.

After calling the local hotel, motel, and the ski resort she'd discovered none of the missing women had made a booking. She'd called the forestry about rental vacation cabins and not one had been occupied since the first snowfall. The hairs on the back of her neck lifted to attention. The killer was somehow making his victims come to him. An ingenious idea that would have taken meticulous planning. Women taking a vacation wouldn't be reported missing. No one would be hunting them down. They would make the perfect victims. They'd found three bodies. Jenna pushed both hands through her hair. One other poor soul might be out in the forest tied to a tree and staring into nothingness, but what if the killer had her holed up somewhere waiting for the opportunity to display her like a trophy? What if he had Julie as well? The thought sent goosebumps scattering across her flesh. So long as the blizzard raged, her team was hogtied. The conditions made it impossible to conduct a search from the air. On the ground, the snow and ice obliterated evidence. For once in her time as sheriff, there was nothing she could do.

As she refilled the coffee pot for Kane's return, she checked her watch. The snowscape outside the window was turning blue as the light faded on another day. She'd listened with interest as Kane had given details about the interviews with the potential suspects as he waited at the hospital for Sierra to be examined. She'd crossed Sierra off the list on the whiteboard. They had no evidence against him but added a few notes under Oberg's name. A tap on her door announced Sam Cross and she turned to smile at him. She'd never seen eye to eye with Cross, being on opposite sides of the law, but if ever she'd found herself in trouble, he'd be the one she'd call. Although he presented well in court, he always arrived as if he'd just walked off the rodeo circuit. He was indeed the classic definition of a range-riding, hardworking cowboy, from the worn-down heels of his cowboy boots to his blue jeans and slightly battered cowboy hat.

If this persona was to deflect his true persona away from law enforcement, it probably worked with anyone but her. Under the guise of a good old boy, Cross was often mistaken as an oddball. Nothing could be further from the truth. Jenna needed to ensure her case against Sierra was solid. One crack in the case would be a canyon by the time Cross had read the case file. She turned to him. "I'm sorry to call you out so late with the blizzard and all, but Luke Sierra was shot during arrest. He is on his way back here now from the hospital. I hope we can make this short, so he can be transported to County tonight."

"Or be on his way home." Cross shrugged and leaned against the doorframe. "Deputy Kane shot him, I believe?"

Jenna nodded. "Yes. One shot to disarm him after he put three bullets into Deputy Rowley. All my deputies and Dr. Shane Wolfe were on scene and under automatic weapon fire from your client." She moved toward her desk. "As you are aware, under such circumstances any one of my deputies could have returned fire to take down your client. However, as Deputy Kane has the necessary skills in the field, I was confident he could disarm him. Mr. Sierra has a through-and-through gunshot wound to his right shoulder. He has received treatment and been discharged by the hospital. There is no permanent damage. He'll recover just fine."

"What are the charges?" Cross rubbed his chin and his brow furrowed. "Do you have an arrest warrant?"

Jenna sat behind her desk and rested her elbows on the top, clasping her hands together. "Not in my possession. I've just spoken to the DA. He has the officers' statements, but from our conversation, he will be pressing charges. I'm sure everything will be detailed in the arrest warrant and evidence will be supplied under discovery. Your client should be on his way back here now. I would like to know the reason he opened fire on my deputies." She waved him to a seat. "Coffee?"

"I'm fine, thanks. Why did you send them to speak to him?"

Cross sat down in a chair opposite the table and leaned back, resting one cowboy boot on his knee.

As Sierra was not considered a prime suspect in the murder case, Jenna had no reason to disclose the fact they'd discovered three homicide victims in the forest. She met his gaze. "You'd be aware of the plane crash at Bear Peak?"

"Yes, of course, a tragic accident." Cross' brow furrowed. "Go on."

Jenna nodded. "Dr. Wolfe's daughter Julie was on the flight and she's missing. We can't reach the crash site due to the weather and a significant number of avalanches in the immediate area. I sent my deputies to speak to anyone in the vicinity to ask them if they'd witnessed the crash or had any information about Julie. Both my deputies were wearing sheriff's department vests, with bright yellow lettering back and front. They didn't pull their weapons and identified themselves. The cabin isn't signposted and is the property of the forestry. My deputies did not pose a threat and gave a clear indication of why they were in the forest." She met his gaze. "If Deputy Rowley hadn't been wearing his vest, Mr. Sierra would be facing a murder charge." She raised both eyebrows. "When he turned his weapon on Deputy Kane and Dr. Wolfe, Kane returned fire. He used one shot to disable your client. He received immediate medical attention by Dr. Wolfe. His wound was numbed using local anesthetic to control the pain. We acted by the book."

"I see." Cross' gaze hadn't left her face. "Was my client interviewed after the incident?"

Jenna shook her head. "Not that I'm aware." She picked up her phone and scrolled to the video Kane had sent her. "He was concerned about his dogs. Kane read him his rights and made this video of his permission to enter his premises." She played the video.

"That's very convenient." Cross ran a hand down his face

and rolled up his eyes. "I'll speak to my client. Do you want to speak to him before they ship him off to County?"

The statements had already been lodged electronically. The DA had everything he needed to lay charges. Jenna shook her head. "I don't believe my deputies' stories will differ from the statements. I'll leave the case in the hands of the DA. Maggie will be able to give you copies. Kane is bringing your client back from the hospital now."

"Thank you." Cross stood and pushed on his hat. "I'll wait downstairs."

Jenna stared after him. She wanted to know what Kane wasn't prepared to say over the phone about Luke Sierra and what he'd found or hadn't found in his cabin.

THIRTY-ONE

Jenna took delivery of a box of takeout from Aunt Betty's Café just as Atohi Blackhawk and a man he introduced as Will Cody stepped into the office. Jenna pushed the box onto the counter and turned to wave them to chairs. Will Cody was in his mid-thirties with a boyish open expression and around six-feet tall. Both men appeared cold and weary, melting snow dripped from Blackhawk's hat. "You've both arrived at a fortunate time. There's fresh coffee and a delivery from Aunt Betty's. I'll get the coffee. Please help yourself." She indicated to the carton. Keeping a supply of food in the office in extreme conditions with exhausted men coming and going had become a necessity.

She made the coffee and a decaffeinated brew for herself and sat waiting for them to shed layers of clothes. The men brought with them the scents of a frozen forest and smiled as they collected food from the box. When they sat down, she eyed them hopefully. If only they'd found some trace of Julie. "How bad is it out there?"

"We're used to navigating through blizzards but nature has thrown us a curveball." Cody ate a turnover in three bites. "The earth tremors are increasing and making the entire mountain unstable. Trails we discovered yesterday are blocked today. I imagine we'll be conducting food drops to the people isolated by avalanches before the melt. There's no safe way of clearing them with tons of snow above just waiting to come down." He licked sugar from his fingers. "We didn't find a sign anyone had been by. The snow is covering tracks faster than we can make them."

"It's fortunate we didn't discover any more bodies tied to trees along the way either." Blackhawk cradled a cup between his large hands. "Perhaps the conditions are too harsh even for a killer." He placed his cup on the desk and pulled out three folded pieces of paper. "I know your team is anxious to get out there, so we kept a record of where we've searched. These are maps of hikers' trails throughout the Bear Peak area. I have one for my use, but I've marked up two for you with all the blocked trails we've discovered so far. I've also marked the location of any cabins we have either seen or recall in the area. So where I've used a capital *C* that's a cabin we've seen. *CO* means signs of occupation. The question marks are for the approximate location of other cabins we can recall seeing in the area but couldn't get to. These might range from self-built hunting cabins, forestry, and residences and range in size from one room to many."

Impressed, Jenna stared at the map. "Thank you. I really appreciate you." She frowned. "You'll need to take care out there." She brought them up to speed with the earlier incident. "Rowley is okay, thanks to his vest, and the perpetrator is on his way here now."

"Hmm, if either of these men was involved in the murders, it's unlikely they made it to the crash site." Blackhawk stared at the map. "The access to their cabins is a road maintained by the snowplows. All the accessible fire roads have been cleared. We've been using them as access roads all day." He scanned the map. "Many of the outlying hunters' cabins are on trails leading from fire roads. Hunters leave their vehicles there and use the cabins as a basecamp." He pointed to the map. "Julie would have come from here." He pointed to an area at the base of Bear Peak. "There are many trails leading all over the forest from there and there are many cabins, but all along the edge of the mountain, the avalanches have blocked vast areas. Here and here. So if she's inside that area, she won't be going anywhere for a time. Only a fool would try and make it to the highway through a dense forest in a blizzard." He sighed. "Julie is no fool."

The situation was more complex than Jenna had imagined. "We found bodies along the way to the crash site. Surely the killer must be inside this perimeter?" She circled an area around the crash site with her finger.

"Not necessarily." Cody shrugged. "Atohi's group found a third body closer to the highway, so away from the base of the mountain. If you look at them as a whole, they form part of an arc."

Staring at the map, Jenna could see his point. "Hmm, I guess it makes sense for them to leave the victims close to a place where they could leave their vehicle. So our theory that the killer is using an empty cabin to keep a victim prisoner is wrong. It would be a long hike from the fire roads in the snow to any of these cabins. Even more problematic if he's dragging or carrying someone he plans to murder." She thought for a beat. "This doesn't sound like a Bear Peak resident, does it? They'd have access to their cabins via a fire road and to the highway but there's none we are aware of close to this arc."

"No one is hiking in the snow, Jenna. It's impossible." Atohi met her gaze. "Just like us, he has a snowmobile."

The implications flowed into Jenna. "So those poor women went willingly to their deaths?" She shivered but the room was toasty. "Oh, that goes way past creepy."

THIRTY-TWO

Numb from cold and thirsty, Carolyn didn't believe she could last much longer. Her arms ached and the smell of the rancid mattress seemed to have permeated her lungs, making it difficult to breathe. The idea of mold spores being trapped inside her lungs frightened her, but would she ever get free of this place? She drifted in and out of what must have been unconsciousness over the last few hours. The fire must be almost out by now as the temperature had dropped considerably. Not that it had been tolerable at any time but now she could see the steam rising from her mouth as she took each breath. The sound of the snowmobile coming toward the house filled her with a strange anticipation. A part of her was terrified at what might happen; the other part of her was relieved that it might be over soon. She would never have considered him to be such an uncaring brute. He had been so nice to her when they talked over social media, and unlike others that she'd spoken to in the past, he was exactly the same person as he portrayed in his photograph. She had spoken to other men online prior to meeting him and they'd used an app on their phone to make themselves look better.

When she'd finally made a date to meet them in a public place, of course, she had been horrified to discover they were either ten or more years older than they appeared online, shorter, or fatter. Whatever they had used online to speak to her had changed their appearance completely. Sure, she'd spent a considerable fortune making herself into the woman every man dreamed about, but when they met her, she was the real deal. She had no need to change her appearance in photographs, she had a surgeon to do that for her.

The door to the cabin opened and a rush of freezing-cold air and the smell of the forest wafted through the small cabin. Light flooded the cabin from the lantern he carried. The door shut and she made out the sounds of stamping feet and the creak of the bench beside the front door as the man of her nightmares sat down to remove his boots. His feet echoed across the floorboards and the bucket beside the fire rattled as he tended the fire. Trembling, she closed her eyes as he walked into the room. She couldn't look at him, not after what he'd done to her.

"Oh, there you are, Carolyn." He took a knife from his belt and went about cutting the gaffer tape and freeing her stiff limbs. He dropped her suitcase on the bed between her legs. "Best you get dressed. You'll catch a cold lying around naked." He walked out of the room, his stocking feet silent across the floor. A whistling came from the kitchen, and a clatter of pots and pans.

Carolyn stared after him in disbelief. It was as if nothing had happened between them previously. He'd returned to the cabin a completely different person, and knowing what he was like inside terrified her. Moving slowly like an automaton, every muscle stiff and aching, she fumbled with the opening of her bag. It seemed to take forever to get dressed, but by the time she'd brushed her hair and pulled on a thick woolen hat, heat was returning to her limbs. What was going to happen now?

She had no idea what to say to him after what he had subjected her to. Could he be playing some kind of strange game? What did he want from her? If he planned to kill her, why hadn't he done it already? Maybe this was a power game that some men played?

What should she do? Maybe she'd act completely normal, as if nothing had happened, or should she question him? The latter hadn't gone very well previously, so maybe the best course of action would be to say nothing unless he spoke to her. Right now, her priority was staying alive. Waves of terror gripped her as indecision flooded her dehydrated brain. She stood, but overwhelmed with dizziness, gripped onto the doorframe. A few moments passed before her vision came back into focus and she could see him preparing a meal in the kitchen using the canned goods he had lined up on the counter.

"Sit at the table." He indicated to a rickety old chair. "The coffee will be ready soon. I'm waiting for the kettle to boil and I have a plunger. Without electricity we need to make do with what we have available." He frowned. "It would have been better if you'd added wood to the stove during the day. The fire was almost out when I got home." He chuckled deep in his chest. "I guess you've been a little tied up all day?"

Throat dry and terribly dehydrated, Carolyn indicated to the bottles of water lined up along the bench. "May I have a drink of water please?"

"Yeah, sure." He cracked a bottle and handed it to her with a smirk on his face. "Anything for my girl."

Confused, Carolyn sipped the water and dampened her dry lips. He seemed normal. The same guy she'd been speaking to online. The same happy nice guy who'd picked her up from the airport parking lot. Right now she'd say or do anything to prevent him hurting her. "I'm sorry about the fire. I'll make sure to tend it from now on." She curled her hair around her fingers and smiled at him.

"I know you will." He gave her a long look and turned his head a little to one side. A nerve in his cheek tightened. "There, everything is going along nicely. I know you can't cook but I've gotta go. I'll be back in the morning. I have things to do and people to see tonight."

She stared after him opened-mouthed as he pulled on his boots and coat. "You're leaving me alone again?"

"Yeah, but it's because I need to make plans and it's too dark to share them with you tonight." His hand went to the door. "I'll leave you with the lantern. Be frugal because once the battery is out, you'll be in the dark. Enjoy your supper and maybe save some for tomorrow. I'm not sure when I'll be back." He opened the door. The wind whipped up the flames in the hearth, scattering embers and ash. He partially closed it, holding it with his foot. "There's a blizzard out there. You're fortunate I came by tonight, but leaving you there like that wasn't what I had in mind." He looked at her. "When I come back, I'll take you out to see the view. I've found the perfect place to stop for a picnic lunch."

It wasn't what he had in mind for me. What the heck? Trying to remain calm and appear interested. Carolyn forced her lips into a smile. "That sounds wonderful. Will the blizzard be over by then?"

"I doubt it." He dropped his hand from the doorknob and switched on a flashlight. "For you, it will be like being inside a snowdome." He chuckled as he slipped out the door. "For a time anyway." The key in the lock turned.

Shaking with fear, Carolyn stared at the door. Her heart pounded so hard she wanted to spew. Somehow, she needed to get away. The sound of the snowmobile echoed in the distance. It would warn her when he was returning. She couldn't leave tonight. The temperature outside would kill her before she had gotten far. She needed to eat and make plans. Escaping at first light was her only hope. She went to the door and pulled on it.

Locked. She tried the window and noticed the nails placed evenly along the bottom of the frame. He'd trapped her inside. Panic gripped her and she turned around searching for any weakness in the old log cabin. She must find a way out before he returned or she'd never leave this place alive.

THIRTY-THREE

As Kane peeled off his coat, hat, and gloves, Jenna slid a cup of coffee across her desk. She stared at her cup of decaffeinated coffee. It wasn't so bad but she'd decided to remove caffeine and any other potentially baby-harming substances from her diet. As strange as it may seem, she'd weaned herself from normal coffee a month before she'd become pregnant. It was just one of the things she'd tried as she hadn't been sleeping well and did drink way too much coffee. So if getting more sleep had helped her to conceive, it had worked. She waited for him to drop into the chair opposite her desk. "Okay, what did you find in Sierra's cabin?"

"Nothing." Kane cradled his cup in his hands and sipped. He let out a long sigh and leaned back. "I doubt he's ever had a woman in there. It's bare, with only the necessities, which makes me believe he might move around some. They do. The mountain guys often have cabins for summer and winter. They stick closer to the highway in winter and go deeper to hunt and fish in the warmer months." He sighed. "He hates people. I figure he needs a psych evaluation. I waited outside while Cross was talking to him... by his request I might add. I didn't hear anything but I could see Sierra waving his arms around and yelling. I was expecting Cross to hit the red button for assistance, but he kept his cool. The guards from County were waiting for him when Cross finished. We completed the paperwork and Sierra has left the building. Cross couldn't wait to get out of here."

Jenna eyed him over the rim of her cup. "While you were gone, Blackhawk and Will Cody from search and rescue came by to give me a rundown of what's happening with the search for Julie." She gave him the details. "Of course, Cody doesn't know any details about the murder investigation but Blackhawk made sure he took note of any cabins. Everything he saw or they all recalled they've added to this map." She slid a folded map across the table to him. "It's vast but as the avalanches didn't occur at the same time, we can assume Julie is likely holed up in a cabin that's been recently isolated by an avalanche."

"Hmm." Kane looked at the map. "If I were in the same situation and if I knew the forest like a mountain man, I would find my way around the avalanches. Sure, going through the forest without trails is dangerous but it is possible."

Placing her cup on the table, Jenna shrugged. "It's possible but getting lost out there would be easy without a phone with GPS. We must assume this is the case or someone would have called. Think about it. Everything looks the same. Sure, you could keep the mountain to your right all the way but it weaves around. Trust me, in summer, in daylight, when I was lost in the forest, it was impossible to navigate. Add freezing temperatures and it becomes impossible." She sighed. "Wolfe is convinced she is injured or she'd have left a sign somewhere at the crash site. You've taught her to remain with a wreck unless her life was in danger. It's far easier to find a wreck than a person in the forest, or anywhere."

"Okay, so we assume Julie will recover before trying to find a way out of the forest?" Kane frowned. "I don't figure she'll risk getting lost. She'll wait for the blizzard to pass and then light a fire. She'll keep it going as smoky as possible and hope to see choppers. I've heard Wolfe telling her to do that, so I guess we have no choice but to wait and see what happens." He pushed one hand through his slick black hair. "This doesn't get us closer to the killer. We have two options that I can see. He lives in town and uses the cleared roads into the forest to get to where he leaves his victims. Blackhawk is correct. They're known to him and somehow he manages to trick them into going into the forest. Once there, they are at his mercy." He waved a hand. "The second theory is he does have a cabin or cabins, or he has use of them, so maybe hunting cabins. No one is going to disturb him in this weather."

Jenna looked up as Rio knocked on the office door. "Yes."

"I've finished updating the files." Rio rubbed the back of his neck. He looked exhausted. "I called Kalo and he is having power problems due to the storms. Carter is working on the backup generator. As soon as he can, he'll run those facial recognition files through the software. He figures it won't be until the morning."

Jenna nodded. "Okay, then we'll call it a day. There's nothing more for us to do today. We'll hunt down the whereabouts of the other two potential suspects in the morning."

"Copy that." Rio headed back downstairs.

As Kane collected the cups and rinsed the coffee pots, Jenna gathered her things and pulled on her coat. "We have four potential victims and only three bodies." She pushed her feet into her boots. "We've either missed a body, as they all seemed to be in the same general area, or the killer has her holed up somewhere and like us, he's waiting for the blizzard to pass."

"Maybe he's keeping her for a time." Kane shrugged into his

coat and then bent down to attach Duke's coat as the sleepy dog whined. "The blizzard is his friend; it covers his tracks. At this time, we have no idea how long he keeps them before he ties them to a tree. The waiting and isolation might just be part of his twisted game."

THIRTY-FOUR

The door to the cabin opened slowly and Ben pushed his way inside and stood, waiting for Raven. Julie Wolfe leaned against the kitchen counter, her heart picking up a beat. She hadn't been brave enough to go and look inside the meat locker. Had he stashed a body in there? The idea kept her awake and vigilant. He'd been gone for hours again, and ice covered his eyebrows and beard. "It's dark outside. I figured you'd stopped over somewhere else for the night."

"Nope, but I did try and get around the avalanche." Raven bent to dry Ben before tending to himself. "I smelled smoke about a mile away and tried to track down the source. It was woodsmoke and I climbed up a tree and made out a plume that must be coming from a chimney. I know of a cabin in that direction but it's dilapidated. I figured if I could make it there, whoever lit the fire might have a phone, but I couldn't get through." He sat down on the bench to remove his boots and padded over to the kitchen in his socks. "I've been trying to find a path wide enough to get the sled through so I can get to my storage cabin. The old guy's place I mentioned before. If I can make it there, I can leave the dogs in the barn and come back for you on the snowmobile. The place is closer to a fire road. We could call for help from there and there's a good chance your dad would be able to come and get you. I have a truck there, but I have a very small supply of gas. This is why I don't have the snowmobile here. It's unreliable and I need gas to run it. My dogs I can feed by trapping and they don't break down." He poured coffee into a cup and leaned against the counter. The smell of the forest, pine, and fresh air wafted from him, not the stink of blood like last time. "Did you watch some TV?"

Julie had worked out the way of things in the cabin. Meals consisted of cereal, eggs, and frozen meals of whatever that were oven ready in dishes in the freezer. She'd slid leftover stew into the stove for dinner. She understood about conserving energy and she preferred to have lights. The thought of watching the news raised the hairs on the back of her neck. A killer was in the forest. Should she mention she knew? Maybe ask him outright about what he kept in the meat locker out in the snow. "I watched the news. I was concerned about the power."

"Anything interesting?" Raven checked the stove and smiled. "Thanks for getting dinner. I know it's difficult to get around." He gave her a raised-eyebrow look. "Talking about food, do you eat pork?"

Wondering where this was going, she nodded. "Yes."

"Good." He smiled. "I found a young pig in one of my traps yesterday. It was frozen solid. It's not a wild pig. Some years ago a guy was breeding them and we had a brush fire. He let them all out. They must have run all over and bred like rabbits. We have pink pigs showing up from time to time. I'll cut a chunk off the carcass to roast tomorrow. They make good eating."

A weight suddenly lifted from Julie's shoulders. "A pink pig?" She swallowed hard. "Where are you keeping the meat?"

"In the meat locker out in the snow." Raven smiled. "Now what's been happening on the news?"

Unsure, Julie thought for a beat. So far, he hadn't hurt her.

He'd been kind and considerate. The worry worm in her mind rose up again and whispered a warning. *Ted Bundy was a nice guy too.* "The air crash of course and how they can't get to the site because of the blizzard, and they were asking for the families or friends of women who'd traveled to Black Rock Falls in the past month to check on them and report to the sheriff's office if any were missing."

"So the sheriff's team has discovered a body in the forest when they went to examine the crash site?" Raven refilled his coffee cup and one for her and took them to the table before the fire. He sat down on the sofa and looked at her. "This would tell me that the body was a victim of crime and not carrying identification." He shook his head slowly. "Black Rock Falls is getting a bad reputation for serial killers. You would figure people would avoid it like the plague but they come here in their thousands. It seems that morbid curiosity is a money spinner." He sipped his coffee and bent to rub Ben's ears. The dog was stretched out before the fire. "Do you get involved in the cases?"

Grabbing up her crutches, Julie hobbled to the fire and lowered to the far end of the sofa. "Not usually. Maybe I man the hotline for a time or get everyone food. They work long hours, especially my dad." She leaned back in the chair. "He doesn't talk about the cases at home to me, but he does discuss them with Emily, my older sister. She's studying to be a doctor and will be a medical examiner. She loves working to solve crimes by forensic science."

"And your mom?" Raven raised one eyebrow. "You haven't mentioned her since you arrived."

Julie swallowed the rush of grief that never went away. "She died of cancer about five years ago. When she died, we moved here and Dad was a deputy for a short time. He was waiting for his medical credentials to be accepted. They came through first and then he became a medical examiner for the state of Montana. That's where he met Jenna and Dave. That's Sheriff

Alton and her husband, Deputy Dave Kane. She kept her name to avoid confusion. They're like our family now."

"That's nice and you're studying like your sister?" Raven placed his cup on the table.

He was being so nice, as if he had this special charm that put people at ease. Maybe it was his bedside manner that doctors have. She'd given him her entire life story in seconds. How did he do that? Without thinking, Julie smiled. "Yes." She met his gaze. "Em is three years older than I am and wanted to be an ME from the get-go. Right now, I just want to work with kids."

"That's nice." He stood. "I'll go and see how dinner is coming along."

Without thinking it through, Julie's mouth opened. "Are you married?"

"Nope." He turned from taking the dish from the stove and set it on the counter. "Why?"

Julie's face grew hot. What a stupid thing to ask. It sounded like she regarded him as a potential boyfriend. Admittedly, he was drop-dead gorgeous and in his late twenties, but what if he was a serial killer? She swallowed hard. "Oh, being a doctor and all, I figured some lucky woman would have snapped you up."

"No, I haven't risked bringing a woman into my world." He took silverware from the drawer and turned to get plates. He gave her a long look. "I'm alone in the forest for a good reason."

A shiver went down Julie's spine. Had he just admitted to being a criminal? She thought hard as he scooped stew onto plates and cleared her throat. "Oh, and I figured you were like a knight in shining armor, roaming the forest and rescuing damsels in distress."

"Not a knight, that's never been my style." Raven's brown eyes scanned her face with no hint of amusement. "Well, maybe once I was like Dr. Jekyll, but now I'm more like Mr. Hyde."

THIRTY-FIVE

WEDNESDAY

Seated at his desk in the office, Kane peered over the top of his laptop screen at Jenna. This was the first morning since discovering she was carrying their child that she hadn't spewed. She'd headed to bed early the previous night totally exhausted and risen with rosy cheeks and bright eyes. He'd spent the evening hunting down the other two suspects' whereabouts and found them both on the outskirts of Black Rock Falls. Davis Davidson worked as a ranch hand and Dan D. Williams currently made his money as a barber. From his records, he learned his trade during his stay in County under their rehabilitation program. He rubbed his chin. That would be all they'd need in town, a criminal who was an expert in the use of a cutthroat razor. He wrote their details in his digital notebook and turned as Wolfe walked into the office.

"That darn snow just won't give up this year." Wolfe shook the flakes from his hat and removed his coat. "I dropped by to give y'all an update and see what progress you've made in finding Julie."

"There's no good news on finding Julie." Jenna stood and

poured two cups of coffee and then filled a glass with milk. She set the cups on her desk. "I'll update you with what we know."

"How is Rowley?" Wolfe removed his gloves.

"He's fine but I insisted he stay home today." Jenna frowned. "He must be badly bruised to agree. He hates missing a day."

Kane stood to join them and dropped into a chair beside Wolfe. He listened as Jenna relayed the information from Blackhawk and search and rescue. He turned to look at Wolfe's drawn expression. "You've seen the conditions in the mountains for yourself just yesterday. Blackhawk and the search-and-rescue teams have been working around the clock. Blackhawk has been adding any cabins he came across to the map. Nothing he has checked so far has any sign that Julie or anyone else was there recently. The problem is we can't get close to the crash site. The people out there know the forest well and are doing everything possible to locate Julie and anyone else who might be isolated. It's time-consuming, but once the blizzard slows enough, I know you'll be the first one up searching. Carter and Styles are packed and ready to leave. Julie knows the moment she hears a chopper to light a fire. We'll find her."

"Yeah, she knows, if she's not injured." Wolfe rubbed both hands down his face and his shoulders drooped. "This is my main concern. Where she was sitting in the aircraft was damaged around the leg area. Someone my size would have been crushed, but she could have suffered broken legs, maybe a head injury, if she was bent into the crash position. There was no Mayday call from the pilot. He didn't just go down, he plowed right into the side of the mountain. He must have been flying just above the trees when he went through the pass and dropped to have ended up like that." He gave Kane an anxious look. "I've seen so many crashes. Those who walk away are traumatized. Some have life-changing injuries. I just need to find her, dead or alive. Not knowing is driving me crazy."

"Drink the coffee." Jenna came from around the desk and pushed the cup into his hands. "She is your little girl, but she's also a strong, resourceful, and smart woman. We're all worried, Shane, but all indications point to someone helping her. You need to hold on to that and hope she is somewhere warm and safe."

"Ah, don't y'all forget there's a serial killer out there as well." Wolfe sipped his coffee and held on to it like a life preserver. "Kalo called real early this morning. He asked me to relay the information as they're having problems with power and communications due to the weather." He took out his phone and scrolled through the messages. "He has identified the three victims as Flora Hadley, she was the first body we found; Lorraine Smith, the second; and Abilene Drew was the one found by Blackhawk."

Kane made notes and then looked up at Jenna. "That leaves Carolyn Stubbs as still missing."

"We'll contact the local law enforcement to notify the next of kin. I'll ask them to be in contact with your office." Jenna looked at Wolfe. "You mentioned a report on the victims. What did you find?"

"Nothing." Wolfe leaned back in his chair and met her gaze. "No injuries apart from where they struggled against the tape and nicks from the knife he used to remove their hair. No signs of recent sexual activity. They died of hypothermia and, as far as I can determine, within the last few weeks." He drained his cup and placed it on the desk. "This killer could have Julie. He obviously knows his way around the forest and was in the vicinity of the crash site. That last victim died as recently as seven days ago. The only saving grace for Julie is that she's never had cosmetic surgery. The three victims had multiple procedures: facial, dental, body enhancements, nails... In fact, it would be difficult to know what they were like prior to the many surgeries and other procedures. Unfortunately, this happens. A single enhancement leads to an addiction, if you like, with people wanting more surgeries until they become caricatures of someone they admire. They're seeking perfection but unfortunately often the opposite occurs. It's a sign of the times."

Kane shook his head slowly. "So this guy has a problem with women who have cosmetic surgery?" He took his cup from the desk and drank. "Wow! I wonder what triggers him? The whole look or is it the lips or nails?"

"He removes their hair." Jenna leaned against the desk. "Did they have extensions?"

"Only one, and apart from the hair, no, nothing was touched." Wolfe shrugged. "This is like no other murderer I've seen. He doesn't hurt them prior to tying them to a tree. They were all well fed and had a last meal. Most were the same meals: a meat stew and canned peaches."

"So that sounds like he took them to a cabin first and fed them before taking them out to die." Jenna moved back to her chair and sat down slowly. "So they went voluntarily?"

"It seems so." Wolfe stood and went to refill his cup. "Do you have anything to eat? I missed breakfast."

Kane smiled at Jenna and went to the refrigerator. "I can heat a bowl of chili in the microwave? Unless you want pie. We always have pie."

"Chili." Wolfe nodded. "I've been cold all morning. Thanks."

"We traced them all to the airport and then they vanished." Jenna sipped her glass of milk. "They didn't stay in town. We've checked out every place they might have stayed. So they know this man. They trusted him enough to go off with him in a blizzard, eat a meal in a cabin in the woods, and then go willingly to their deaths."

Kane pushed the bowl into the microwave. "So they've met him before, unless it's one of those dating apps. Would a woman travel here to meet a man she's never met?"

"Yeah, it's normal these days." Jenna leaned back in her chair. "We'd need phone and computer records, but most people have the apps on their phones." She looked from one to the other. "Talk to Rio, he'd know for sure. He'd have friends who use the apps to meet women. It's not like when you guys were looking to meet someone. You'd go to a party or a bar, right?"

Kane exchanged a knowing look with Wolfe. "Nope, for us it would have been at the officers club on base. I personally didn't want a wife at home worrying about me. Being on missions, having someone at home to worry about or who could be used against me wasn't really an option. I dated, but until I met Annie on a mission, I kept my social life low-key."

"My wife, Angela, was the daughter of a general." Wolfe shrugged. "It was how we rolled back in the old days."

"Old days, huh?" Jenna raised both eyebrows. "Kane isn't forty yet and you're, what, forty-five? My goodness, we're having our first baby and what about Norrell? Have you even discussed the possibility of having more kids? She's a young woman."

"More kids?" Wolfe blinked a few times. "The conversation never came up. She loves my kids, and Anna especially is very attached to her. She called her *Mom* the other day. I didn't know what to say as she was so young when Angela died. Both Emily and Julie treat her more like a sister than a stepmother." He looked suddenly perplexed. "Do you figure I'm too old for her?"

"It's bit late to be worrying about that now." Jenna shook her head. "No, you're not too old for her. She's a grown woman and a professional. She knows her own mind and it's not like you rushed into a relationship. Be happy, second chances don't come along very often."

"Okay." Wolfe took the bowl and spoon from Kane and sat down. "So to sum up my report after being sidetracked: This killer isn't the usual violent maniac we've seen in the past. He must be charismatic and have a lot to offer if women are flocking to him."

Leaning against the counter, Kane rubbed his chin. "Add good-looking as well."

"Maybe not." Jenna tapped away on her keyboard. "Rich nerds are popular right now. There, I've sent the details of the victims to their local law enforcement agencies." She looked up. "It doesn't matter what they do now, it's what they say they do on their bio online. They lie all the time, use fake or enhanced images, but I don't believe this guy uses an enhanced or fake image because if he did, the women would be prewarned the moment they met him, so he must look like the real deal." She leaned back in her chair. "I've sent the list to Kalo, but he said with the number of dating sites and if they're using fake names, it will be impossible to hunt them down in a reasonable time, but he'll do his best."

Enjoying Jenna's insights to the case, Kane smiled. "That makes sense. I have the details of the next two suspects. I guess we'd better head out and speak to them. I have addresses and where they work. Both of them work odd hours. So we might be lucky."

"Okay." Jenna looked at Wolfe. "Do you want to ride along?"

"Nope." Wolfe stood and took his bowl to the sink and rinsed it. "I'm running tox screens on the victims, but I haven't discovered anything abnormal. I need to check everything over again just in case I've missed something, but I doubt it." He nodded to Kane. "Thanks for breakfast." He grabbed his hat and coat and headed down the stairs.

Kane handed Jenna her coat and then put on his own. "These two suspects both own hunting cabins. They don't have nine-to-five jobs, so are free to move around. They've had assault charges brought against them in the past. We must be getting close to catching this guy."

"I hope you're right because we still need to find Carolyn Stubbs." Jenna pulled on her hat. "Although I don't like her chances. She fits the general description of the other women. If she is alive, we need to stop this man before he kills her."

THIRTY-SIX

Escape seemed futile. Carolyn searched every inch of the cabin looking for a way out. The windowpanes were too small to crawl through and the front door was solid. There was no way of breaking the lock. After hammering her fists on the wooden panels, she cried out in frustration and then went to sit in front of the fire. The floorboards creaked beneath her feet and she moved back and forth feeling the give in the old wood. She thrust the coffee table to one side and tossed the mat out of the way to inspect the floor. A cold draft seeped through the gap where the boards had shrunk. She scanned the room for something to use to pry up the floorboards and her gaze rested on the poker. She tested the strength in her hand, in truth she'd thought of using it as a weapon, but he was too big. He'd disarm her in seconds.

She fell to her knees and dug the end of the poker down the crack between the floorboards and wiggled it back and forth. The ripping nails whined as she dislodged the floorboard and peered down the hole. She jumped up and ran to the bench to grab the lantern, returned to the hole in the floor, and pushed it into the darkness. Underneath the cabin was dirt, animal scat, and so many cobwebs she couldn't see very far, but the gap between the floorboards and the ground was wide enough for her to crawl through. She attacked the second floorboard and dragged it out to make a gap big enough for her to climb through. The bitter cold rushed through the hole, sending goosebumps running down her arms. If she planned to live through her escape, she would need to protect herself from the weather and take food and water with her, but how much time did she have? She had no idea when her captor would return and he could easily follow her tracks in the snow.

Running into the bedroom for her backpack she dragged out her clothes and dressed in as many clothes as she could fit under her coat. Next, she wrapped bottled water in her PJ's, a few cans of beans, a can opener, and a spoon and pushed them into her backpack. Her boots were waterproof and dry and she had her gloves, a woolen hat, a scarf, and the hood of her coat to keep her warm. She gathered a few other necessities: the lantern, a lighter, and a roll of toilet paper. She didn't have a flashlight but she hoped she would find another cabin along the way before it got dark. The lantern would just have to do. She eased her way down into the hole and shivered as fat spiders ran to get out of her way. Her fear of enclosed spaces gripped her by the throat as she looked around for a way out. The extra clothes had made it difficult for her to move her arms and legs, but by pushing her backpack in front of her to clear her way, she managed to crawl toward the back of the cabin.

Sweat was dripping between her shoulder blades as she edged closer to the back wall. The uneven ground made a gap narrow in places. Gritting her teeth she pushed onward, through the filthy, stinking dirt. She dislodged a bundle of dry grass ahead of her and disturbed a nest of rats that, instead of running away, ran all over her, their tiny claws sticking in her hair. She screamed and they scampered in all directions. Moving as fast as she possibly could, she dragged herself to the edge of the cabin. All around her was a wall of snow and under her the ground had frozen solid. She turned around and, lying on her back, ignored the spiders crawling around in the cobwebs above her and kicked a hole in the snow. She turned around and, using her backpack, punched at the white wall. It was harder than she imagined and took every ounce of her strength to push her way through.

At last she could see daylight and wiggled through the hole. The forest surrounded her, hidden behind a wall of white rain, but to one side of the cabin sat a small rickety shed. Vegetation grew over the roof and the wooden exterior was gray and weathered. Paint flakes still clung to the window frame, but one strong puff of wind would topple it. Shrugging into her backpack, and pulling up her hood, she waded through the thick snow. Flurries buffeted her as the wind whistled through the trees and small pieces of ice battered her hood. Exhausted by the time she'd gone the ten yards to the shed, she pushed open the door and peered inside. It was more difficult walking in the snow than she'd imagined. Every time she had gone out in the snow before it had been on skis or riding in a sleigh. Trying to move through drifts so thick was difficult.

Nervous at what she might find, she peered inside the shed. It was empty and she moved inside, hoping to find a flashlight or something he'd left behind she could use. Her attention settled on two things of interest: the first being a pair of snowshoes, the second an old, dilapidated map stuck on the side of the wall. The map had a date on the bottom, of 1969, so how it had survived for so long amazed her. The rats should have made it part of their nest by now. She grabbed the snowshoes. They were the old type made from leather set in a wooden frame, with leather straps to secure them to her feet. Beside them, covered with cobwebs, two poles leaned against the wall.

After securing the snowshoes, she gently took the fragile map from the wall and laid it on the bench. She peered at a spot marked with an X. Beside it was a hand-drawn house. She looked all over, noticing the marked trails leading in all directions. Some of the trails ended with a little house with people's names attached. This must be a map the owner of the cabin first made when he arrived. His closest neighbors lived in the cabins. Many people lived in cabins or used them for hunting or fishing. She recalled getting here on the back of the snowmobile after he'd parked his truck on a fire road. He'd driven the snowmobile along various tracks to get here. She must avoid running into him at all costs but needed to get to shelter as soon as possible. The highway was clearly marked, as was the river. She stared at the map wishing it could give her advice on which way to go. She measured the distance to the closest cabin. She found two set some distance apart, which ran alongside a track with the name Darcy's Way. That track weaved all the way to the highway.

Determined to get to safety, she folded the map with care and pushed it inside her pocket. She stepped out of the shed, surprised to see her footsteps fading already. With luck, he would never know which way she'd gone. There was a strange silence out in the forest. Visibility was limited to a few yards at best and the sudden blasts of wind sent chunks of ice tumbling down from the trees. Walking was easier with the snowshoes as she headed along the track. Using the sticks to keep her balance, she pushed on for some time, gasping for breath before stopping for a short break. Snow filled her eyebrows and yet a trickle of sweat ran down her spine. Moving through the snow was exhausting and she took the time to pull a bottle of water from inside her jacket and take a few sips. The snow was coming thick and fast, as he'd said earlier. It was like being inside a snow globe. His face drifted into her mind and she pushed away from the tree and kept moving. She'd been walking for what seemed like hours when a slow rumble came in the distance. Snowfall dampened noise. Had she traveled in the wrong direction? Was he coming after her. She looked frantically around. The snow was covering her tracks at a fast rate and they'd be obliterated at the cabin by now. She stood still and listened. Perhaps it was him returning to the cabin and he hadn't discovered her missing yet. Turning back to the path, she kept on pushing forward. A whiff of woodsmoke on the air drifted toward her and she quickened her pace. There must be a cabin just ahead. The sound of a snowmobile roared louder, and it was coming toward her. Help was maybe a few yards away but the snow was like quicksand. She lifted her knees in an attempt to go faster and burst out of the forest. Ahead, she made out a cabin with smoke pouring from the chimney. The area outside had been cleared of snow. She could see a truck in a garage. As she ran toward the door, a snowmobile came out of a curtain of white. Carolyn screamed and ran toward the cabin. She tripped and fell. The snowmobile was heading straight for her. *He's found me.*

THIRTY-SEVEN

After bringing Rio up to date, Jenna followed Kane outside. They'd left Duke inside in the warm. He was more than capable of letting Maggie know if he needed to go outside. She pulled her hood down against the blizzard and, watching her step on the frozen sidewalk, slipped and slid her way to the Beast. "So I guess the first person we'll hunt down is Dan D. Williams. Did you have any luck when you spoke to the barbershop in town?"

"He's due to arrive around ten." Kane backed the truck out of the parking space and headed along Main. "He only comes in for a couple of hours a few times a week to help out if the regular barber is busy. I figured the last thing anyone wants in the middle of a blizzard is a haircut and most men in these parts don't even bother to shave when it's this cold."

Jenna couldn't remember when she'd ever seen Kane disheveled or unshaven. "Maybe you're not the only man in town who likes to look slick all the time." She grinned at him. "You have no idea how many times I had the urge to ruffle your hair, especially when you were angry with me."

"I don't recall ever being angry with you, Jenna." Kane

glanced at her before returning his gaze to the road. "Exasperated when you put yourself in danger and refuse my protection maybe, but it takes a whole lot more than that to make me angry." He sighed. "I figure the last time I got angry was when Tauri's life was threatened. It rose up on me white-hot, and I needed to drop into the zone to calm down before I did something stupid, but I handled it." He pulled to the curb. "This is the place. Now I'm going to annoy you again because I want you to wait for me to help you climb over that mound of ice. If you slip and sit down heavy on your butt, I wouldn't be able to forgive myself, so bend a little, huh?"

Although she'd never told him, Jenna quite enjoyed being protected by the man she loved. At first, he'd taken a lot of getting used to, and when chasing down serial killers with him, she'd constantly needed to remind him that she wasn't going to break. After discovering many years later that he'd spent most of his time alone on missions, and his family had raised him to respect and protect women, she'd needed to show him how capable she could be in the field. He'd countered by improving her skills across the board with morning workout sessions and time at the firing range. The one thing she did value was his respect for women. He might be old-school, but being a gentleman suited her just fine.

She took Kane's hand and slipped and slid over the hard-packed ice alongside the sidewalk, finally making it to the heavy coating of sand and salt. They crunched into the barbershop and she ran her gaze along the row of men waiting to be served. She bit back a smile when she read a notice on the wall: *Half-price haircuts Wednesdays and soup of the day.*

She hung back as Kane smiled at the proprietor. He had his hair cut here regularly and had since arriving in Black Rock Falls.

"I'm pretty busy today, Deputy." The barber waved a hand to the waiting men. "Tomorrow is good, but I cut your hair only two weeks ago. You sure you need a haircut already?"

"No, I'm good." Kane smiled. "I just want a quick word with Dan Williams when he's through with that customer. It will only take a few minutes."

"I'm done here." Dan Williams, ruggedly handsome, well built with dark brown eyes, flicked a glance at Jenna. "Is there a problem? Someone die?"

Jenna moved forward. "Is there a place we can talk?"

"Sure, out back, but I can't be long. I have people waiting." Williams led the way to a back room. He turned and shut the door when they walked inside. "What's this all about? You trying to make me look bad in front of my boss? Do you know how hard it is for an ex-crim to get work?"

"No, you can tell him whatever you need to explain why we're here, but we need to know the location of your cabin in the forest and when you were last there." Kane leaned against the door and stared him down.

"I'm not sure." Williams rubbed his chin. "Why, and do I need a lawyer?"

Jenna exchanged a meaningful look with Kane and slowly took out her notebook and pen. "Is there something you need to tell us about, Mr. Williams? You seem a little jumpy. We only want to know if you've been out to your cabin lately. You've heard about the air crash at Bear Peak? Well, we have people missing. If they made it out alive, they're likely to take shelter in one of the cabins. Right now, we're speaking to people who own cabins in that area and collecting information, such as is there a CB radio in the cabin or a landline? With the blizzard, hunting down survivors is proving impossible."

"Okay, okay." Williams let out a long breath. "I was out there earlier. Well, I've been out there a few times this week. I have a meat locker and been dropping by to collect meat, mostly to feed my dogs. I didn't see anyone. I only made it there and back because the fire road has been cleared. I can't drive my truck all the way to my place but I can use the snowmobile."

"So what time did you start work this morning?" Kane's grim expression bored into him.

"A little after ten." Williams indicated to the door. "That was my first client."

Jenna stared at her notes. "Just out of interest. Do you use dating apps?"

"That's a leading question. Say if I do?" Williams chewed on a thumbnail, tearing it and spitting out the broken nail. "It's not a felony to use them. Everyone does."

"Okay, so let's say you do use one, do you know or have been in contact with Flora Hadley, Lorraine Smith, or Abilene Drew over the last few weeks?" Kane straightened. "They are listed as missing."

"No, can't say I've spoken to them." Williams shrugged. "But you do know most of them have phony names. No one uses their names, do they? I mean, if a girl checked me out, I wouldn't stand a chance of meeting her, would I?"

Jenna folded her notebook. "I guess not. Do you have a problem with us dropping by your cabin and making sure it's empty?"

"Yeah, it seems that I do." Williams shook his head. "I'm sorry about the people from the air crash, but if you want to search my cabin, you'll need a warrant and you don't have probable cause. I don't trust cops. They plant evidence and people like me go away for things they didn't do." He headed toward Kane one hand extended. "Now, let me out of here before I lose my job."

"Sure." Kane stood to one side and waited for him to go. He turned to Jenna. "He's just moved to the top of our list."

THIRTY-EIGHT

In sheer terror, Carolyn plunged into the deep snowdrifts and lay still as the sound of the engine got closer. She realized after a few minutes that the sound was coming from more than one snowmobile. They rumbled to a stop and she chanced a look at the cabin. Frozen with fear, she covered her mouth with her scarf to hide the steam from her panting breath. The man could easily be her captor. Maybe he'd brought back a few friends with him. He'd proved untrustworthy, with a weird side she couldn't explain. The idea it might be him frightened her and she hid behind a tree. One of the men climbed off his ride and went to the door. He spoke for a few minutes to the occupier, before returning to the snowmobile and then they turned around and headed back the way they'd come. Heart pounding and too afraid to move, she watched them disappear into the wall of swirling white, If that wasn't him, had she missed the chance of escaping the forest?

She made her way across the clearing to the cabin. On the mailbox was the name Brindley. She pounded on the door. The door opened and two whippets stuck their heads out, tails wagging. A blonde-haired lady gave her an astonished look. Carolyn smiled at her. "Mrs. Brindley?"

"Yes, I'm Martha Brindley." She stared at her and then blinked. "Are you the missing girl?"

Sagging with relief, Carolyn pressed one hand against the wall of the cabin. "Yes, that's me. Can I come inside to get warm for a time?"

"Yes, yes, of course." Martha waved her into a mudroom. "You can hang your wet clothes there, but bring your boots inside and set them beside the fire in the kitchen."

Unable to control her emotions, Carolyn burst into tears. "I've been walking for hours. I figured I'd die out there. Do you have a phone? I need to call my folks."

"There, there. You're safe now." Martha put one arm around her shoulder. "People are out searching for you. I wish I could let them know you're okay, but in this weather I can't get any bars, I'm afraid." She walked into the kitchen. "I have fresh coffee and muffins. I bet you're starving."

Glad to be inside the neat, warm home, she peeled off her coat and followed. The dogs sniffed her and wagged their tails. "I love your dogs."

"They are great company but they don't like the blizzard either." Martha took down two cups and poured coffee. "When you've rested up and had a meal, you'll feel better. Later, we can try and make it down to Nancy Marin's cabin. She isn't far and has a CB radio, but I'm not venturing out in a blizzard on foot. I don't have one of those snowmobiles. When it's snowing, I stay home or wait until we get a turn of the snowplow so I can drive my truck."

Exhaustion dragging at her, Carolyn nodded. "I don't believe I can walk another step right now. Thank you so much for taking me in. I really appreciate it." She inhaled the aroma of fresh-baked muffins and dropped into a chair at the table.

"I'm glad of the company." Martha placed the coffee fixings

on the table and two plates. She added a plate piled with blueberry muffins. "Help yourself."

Trembling, Carolyn added fixings to her coffee and took a sip. Everything seemed surreal, as if she'd fallen down the rabbit hole. Was she really in a kitchen with a lovely woman, sipping coffee and eating muffins or had she fallen asleep and was slowly freezing to death? She took a bite of the delicious muffin and allowed the taste to explode across her taste buds. It was the best muffin she'd ever tasted and the coffee was like nectar of the gods. She ate slowly, savoring every bite, her eyelids grew heavy. Drained of energy and now in a warm cozy environment, all she wanted to do was sleep.

"Oh, dear, don't fall asleep at the table." Martha stood and walked around the table to grab her arm. "My spare room is made up. You'd better rest before you venture outside again." She smiled at her. "Get out of those wet clothes and I'll dry them for you."

Totally exhausted, Carolyn dragged leaden feet along a passageway to a beautifully furnished room. She pulled off another layer of sweaters and her damp pants and lay them over the back of a chair. "Thank you so much."

"It's a pleasure to have you." Martha pulled back the thick comforter and plumped up the pillow. "Lay your head down. You're safe now."

The bed looked so inviting. Carolyn sat on the edge of the bed, and by the time her head hit the pillow, sleep surrounded her in a warm hug.

* * *

Disorientated, Carolyn opened her eyes. It was still daylight and she glanced at the clock beside the bed. She'd been asleep for two hours. Shaking her head, she climbed out of bed. She needed to get a message to her folks and the sheriff to tell her about what had happened to her. She made her way out and back to the kitchen. Her clothes were hanging on a rail in front of the fire and Martha was knitting in a rocking chair. "Thank you so much for letting me rest but I must get a message to my folks."

"Oh, I understand, my dear." Martha pushed to her feet. "Have a cup of coffee and some cookies before you brave the cold again. It won't be an easy walk to Nancy's but you'll make it."

Nodding, Carolyn pushed her long blonde hair from her face and gathered it into a ponytail, securing it with a band from around her wrist. "Thank you, I'd appreciate it."

She drank the coffee and ate the cookies and they chatted about the dogs. A short time later, she stood and gathered her still damp but warm clothes and pulled them on. Bundled up against the cold with a pair of thick woolen gloves Martha had offered her, Carolyn pulled on her snowshoes and stumbled out into the blinding-white vista. She bent her head against the onslaught of snow driven by wind that swirled the flakes in all directions, making it difficult to see the trail ahead. Even with the snowshoes her feet sank into the powder coating and each step became harder than the next. When she noticed the outline of a cabin in the distance, she punched the air with excitement. She'd made it and soon she'd be safe. She stumbled to the front door and knocked hard. When a woman opened the door and stared at her wide-eyed, Carolyn pulled down her scarf and smiled at her. "Nancy? Martha sent me to ask if you could send a message to get help."

"Oh, my. You're the missing girl." Nancy waved her inside. "Wait right there in the mudroom, I'll get you a towel and then make the call." She hurried away and disappeared into a back room. Carolyn looked around the neat cabin. It was very cozy, and heat radiated from the wood fire burning in the hearth in the family room. It made her want to own a cabin but maybe one not so isolated. Within minutes Nancy came back carrying a towel and handed it to her. She dabbed at her face and hair. "Thanks."

"The snow tracks are everywhere." Nancy smiled. "You get off those wet clothes and I'll contact search and rescue and they'll be right along. You'll be back in town before you know it. The snowplows have been clearing the fire roads to give people access to their cabins. There are quite a few of us who live here permanently." She turned away and hurried along the passageway.

Carolyn stiffened at the sound of a snowmobile. She peered out the side of the drapes and gaped in disbelief at the sight of the man nightmares were made of heading toward the cabin. His blue snowmobile had a bright yellow stripe down one side and his helmet resembled a skull. It was clearly visible even through the curtain of snow. Panic gripped her and she fled through the cabin, her snowshoes clattering on the polished wood floor. She reached the back door and Nancy came into the passageway.

"What's wrong?" Nancy stared toward the front door.

Heart racing, Carolyn turned and looked at her. "A man is chasing me. I have to hide. He'll see my tracks and come here."

"He won't get inside my cabin." Nancy stared at her. "I have a shotgun and I know how to use it."

Carolyn shook her head. "He's dangerous. I can't risk your life. Get help and I'll run."

"If you must. I've cleared the path to the woodshed." Nancy pulled open the back door. "It has two doors, hide inside or run into the forest from the other door. He won't see your tracks. Click the lock on the door before you leave. It will need a key to open it. If he goes inside, he won't think you went out the other door. Head north toward the mountains, and I'll tell the rescue crew when they arrive."

Carolyn stared out into the blizzard. "He'll know someone has been here."

"I'll hold him off." Nancy patted her arm. "Trust me. I can do this. If you get the chance to double back when he's gone, come here and wait here for search and rescue. I'll go and call in an update and get the sheriff out here."

Nodding, Carolyn ducked out the door. She didn't want to involve Nancy in her troubles and she could avoid the man chasing her for a little longer. Help was on the way, she just needed to survive until the sheriff arrived. Heart hammering, she dashed across the yard and into the woodshed. The snowshoes, like flippers, hampered each step, but she edged around the piles of split firewood and dragged open the door. She opened the lock and fell out the door and rolled into a massive snowdrift. Struggling to her feet as the sound of the snowmobile grew louder, she lifted her knees and pushed through the freezing white until the trees broke up the drift. A blind man could find her from her tracks, but she turned away from the fire road and zigzagged through the trees until she came to a trail. The freezing air cut into her throat and lungs with each step. The brightness made her dizzy but she kept going. She had to get away. It was her only hope. The longer she could run the more time she gave the sheriff to save her. How long would it take them to get here? She let out a sob and pressed one hand against a tree, gasping the freezing air. A gunshot blasted the silence. Heart racing, she turned to look behind her. Had Nancy shot him? Trembling, she waited, listening. A few minutes later the roar of the snowmobile started again and it was getting louder by the second.

Ahead, the trail spread out white and pristine, there was no way he wouldn't be able to follow her. At the speed he was traveling, he'd mow her down before she got far. Frantic, she searched ahead and, seeing overhanging branches, ran at them and leaped into the air. Her hands locked on the bough of a large pine. In desperation, she swung her legs back and forth. On the upswing she let go. The momentum swung her away from the trail and into the forest. Miraculously she didn't hit one of the trees but fell between a space and landed flat on her face. Winded, she staggered to her feet and ran wildly away from the oncoming noise of the snowmobile. The snowfall wasn't so deep here, but she kept zigzagging between the trees and trying to head in the same general direction.

As she ran, she searched around for deep undergrowth. Lungs bursting from overexertion, she kept moving. She must find a place to hide. It would be impossible to outrun him on a snowmobile and hiding in the undergrowth was her only chance. Maybe when he went past, she could risk trying to get back to the cabin. Trembling with terror, she grabbed a fallen branch and dragged it across her footprints and then rolled beneath a dead bush. With luck, the heavily falling snow would cover all trace of her. Heart threatening to burst from her chest, she curled into a ball on the frozen ground. The noise of the snowmobile was getting louder by the second. He was coming.

THIRTY-NINE

Visibility was down to zero as Kane turned the Beast onto the road to the Big D Ranch. The wipers could barely shift the torrential snowfall building up on the windshield. He glanced at Jenna. "This is getting impossible. Even the Beast is having trouble shifting all these drifts. I can't see Davidson moving back and forth to the forest in this weather."

"At least we have a great heater." Jenna zipped up her jacket as the truck came to a halt at the barn. The sign pointing to the manager's office hung just inside the entrance. "We'll go and speak to the manager. He might give us the lowdown on Davidson."

Kane pulled his double woolen cap over his ears and pressed his Stetson over the top. He turned to Jenna and saw his reflection in her sunglasses. He pushed his up his nose. In this weather, snow blindness was a sad reality. "You can wait here if you want. I'm leaving the engine running and the heat on, anyway. I don't want to risk being stranded out here for heaven knows how long."

"Oh, I'm coming with you." Jenna unclipped her seatbelt and then pulled on thick gloves. "We have no idea what we're walking into or how many people are involved in the murders. We always assume it's one man. What if it's two or more?"

Raising both eyebrows Kane shrugged. "It's always a possibility, I guess." He indicated with his chin to a middle-aged man standing in the entrance of the barn eyeing them with interest. "We have an audience already." He pushed open his door and waited for Jenna to climb down before walking toward the barn.

Not wanting to be overprotective, he suppressed the desire to take her hand in case she slipped in the snow. Although everyone had told him to treat her normally, he couldn't imagine falling over in the snow could be good for her or the baby. It hadn't been that long for her to get pregnant, but for Jenna it had been an eternity. He hoped it would be the first of the three she yearned for, but now after adopting Tauri, perhaps she could be content with one or maybe two. He smiled to himself, however many she wanted, he'd be overjoyed. Having Tauri showed him how much he enjoyed being a father. Removing his sunglasses, he stepped inside the barn with Jenna close behind and nodded to the man. "Deputy Kane and this is Sheriff Alton. We'd like to speak to the manager." He slid the sunglasses into his pocket.

"That's me." The man held out his hand. "Joe Plant. Come into my office." He led the way past bales of hay and a tractor to a door marked with MANAGER written in paint by hand. "Okay, has one of my hands run afoul of the law?"

"That remains to be seen." Jenna moved forward to stand beside Kane. "You recall the air crash at Bear Peak? We have people missing and we're hunting down the owners of cabins in Stanton Forest around the Bear Peak area. It makes sense that the victims would go to the cabins for assistance. Mr. Davidson owns a cabin in that area. We discovered he works and bunks here on occasion and would like a word with him."

"He's not here." Plant dropped into a chair behind a large cluttered desk and, resting his elbows on the wooden arms, towered his fingers and looked at them suspiciously. "Hmm, I figure there's something you're not telling me." He looked from one to the other. "I'm aware of his assault charges against women and that he did time. So you believe he's involved in a crime?"

Kane wrinkled his nose. The small room smelled of cow turds and male sweat. Plant's clothes didn't appear to have been changed in a long time, unless he'd been mucking out a pigpen. "We don't have any evidence to suggest that Davidson is involved in a crime at this time."

"Not everyone living in the forest welcomes strangers, but they might have seen or heard something." Jenna folded her arms across her chest. "We need to know if Mr. Davidson noticed any strangers passing by or if he knows the location of other cabins in the immediate area." She waved a hand. "The weather is making searching for them impossible and some of the trails are blocked by avalanches."

"There's not much I can say." Plant poured three fingers of bourbon into a glass and sipped it. "He came in for a few hours yesterday and said he'd be making repairs to his cabin. I told him I'd need him on Friday and he said he should be through by then."

Kane wondered if the owner was on site and allowed his manager to drink on the job. He pushed the thought to one side. "Does Davidson have a wife or someone sharing his cabin with him?"

"He takes girls there." Plant leaned back and scrutinized Kane's face. "There's a river in walking distance and it's secluded. He comes back with stories about his conquests. Seems the girls he attracts like to go skinny-dipping in summer." He chuckled. "Nothing wrong with being a ladies' man."

"What's he like?" Jenna glanced at the DMV image on her phone. "This is him, right?"

"Yeah, that's him. He's just what the city women like, a big strong cowboy." Plant squinted at the screen. "He has a beard right now. Most of the hands grow one in winter. Me, I can't stand the itching."

Kane narrowed his gaze. "Where does he meet all these city women? This time of the year they're all out at the ski resort and chasing after the ski instructors. I don't figure a ranch hand would fit into that crowd."

"Maybe you're right." Plant poured another drink and smiled at him. "He showed me how he meets his women. He uses the dating apps on his phone." He belly-laughed. "Have you looked at one of those apps? It's like a smorgasbord of women. You can just scroll through and pick a few, link them to your file, and wait for them to call or message you. Not like the old days of picking up women in the bars, right?" He smirked at Kane.

Kane ignored him and pushed on with the questions. "Does he have many friends? Does he take guys to his cabin as well?"

"No, he's a loner unless he's found himself a woman." Plant turned the glass around with the tips of his fingers as if contemplating another drink. "He probably has one at his cabin now. I haven't seen him for a few days."

"I hope he hasn't been trapped by an avalanche. It's dangerous in the mountains right now." Jenna frowned. "Do you know the location of Davidson's cabin? All we have is a road we can't find on a map and the location of Bear Peak. We should drop by and do a welfare check."

"It just so happens that I do." Plant grinned, displaying yellowed teeth. "One time, a girl he'd met on a dating app refused to go anywhere without her friend. So Davis used me as his wingman and took me out to his cabin for the weekend. He collected the women from town. They seemed well pleased with him but not so much with me." He stared into space grinning like a monkey. "Things worked out just fine." He searched in his drawer for a notepad and a pen. "This is the highway. You go past the warden's station, take the fire road. The trail to his cabin is on the left, not the first or second trail, but the third trail. It winds around some. You won't get through in your truck with the snow and all. You'll need a snowmobile. Davis usually parks his truck on the fire road and drives his snowmobile from there."

Kane nodded. "I know the area. We were close by a couple of days ago. Thanks for your help." He handed him a card. "If he shows, give me a call. We'd like to know he made it out of the mountains okay."

"Yeah, sure." Plant looked puzzled. "I'd call him but since the blizzard started, I can't get through to anyone outside of town."

"Yeah, we're aware of the problems." Jenna nodded and followed Kane outside. As they walked back to the Beast, she tugged on his arm. "Call Aunt Betty's and order takeout. We'll grab it on the way back to the office to eat on the way. I'll grab the snowmobile trailer and then head out there. Davidson sounds like our man."

Kane nodded. "I want to know if he's home or out in the forest murdering women." He looked up. "The snow is getting worse. If it's our killer, we'll need to hunt him down without delay."

FORTY

Unable to wait for news, Wolfe and Emily headed for the forest warden's station. It was the closest one to Bear Peak and they wanted to make sure they'd been informed about Julie's disappearance. With the phones out, he'd go and tell them personally. The wardens could ask any hunters who came by if they'd seen any signs of her. It was a shot in the dark as he figured no one would be stupid enough to be out in this weather. They'd gotten almost to the parking lot when his phone buzzed and his truck's screen lit up with an incoming call. It was Maggie from the sheriff's office. "Wolfe."

"This is Maggie, I had a call from search and rescue to say Julie had walked into a cabin up near Bear Peak but there's a problem. The woman that called it in said a man on a blue snowmobile with a yellow stripe was chasing her down. The poor girl had to run out the back door while the woman distracted him. He knocked her down and searched her house. She grabbed her shotgun and ran after him and fired a warning shot. I've notified the sheriff and they're on their way. I'll text you the coordinates of the cabin."

Wolfe tossed his phone to Emily and accelerated toward

Bear Peak. "We're close by, contact Jenna and tell her we're going after her." He waited for his phone to signal a message and then disconnected.

"Okay, I've punched in the coordinates." Emily waited for the GPS to recalibrate and glanced at her dad. "The off-ramp to the fire road is just ahead. It should be clear. Jenna told me earlier the snowplows are working around the clock to keep them open."

Wolfe punched a fist on the steering wheel. "We should have thought to bring the snowmobiles."

"The snowplow attachment you have will help. We'll go as far as we can and walk." Emily gripped the door as the truck slid sideways down the off-ramp. "If Julie can run through the drifts, then so can I."

Pushing his truck as fast as possible, Wolfe drove along the fire road. "I can see snowmobile tracks. Whoever is chasing her came this way."

Ahead, a cabin appeared out of the flurry and Wolfe pulled to a halt. He slid from the truck, strode to the door, and banged on it with his fist. When the door opened a crack and a woman peered out, he nodded to her. "I'm Dr. Shane Wolfe. You called search and rescue about a missing girl and a man chasing her? Which way did she go? I'm her father."

"Oh, thank goodness. She didn't get time to mention her name but she was blonde like you." The woman opened the door, one hand clutching a shotgun. "She went north toward the mountain." She pointed in the direction. "There's a trail behind my woodshed. You can drive along it with the snowplow on your truck. She went that way but that man was on her tail."

Wolfe nodded. "Thanks. The sheriff is on her way. Point her in the right direction." He hurried back to the truck. "I know where she's heading but she's smart enough not to stick to the trail. She'll hole up somewhere until the guy goes past."

Spinning the wheels, he took his foot off the gas a little and eased the truck forward. The trail was just where the woman had indicated, and from the marks in the snow, the guy chasing her down had found the trail as well. He pushed the truck as hard as possible, the deep snow giving way to the snowplow attached to the front of his truck. When the trail ended in a clearing, he turned the truck around facing the way back. In front of them were two smaller trails, one to the right and one to the left. The snowmobile had gone right. He looked at Emily's determined face. "Grab a backpack and the snowshoes from the back of the truck. I'm following the snowmobile."

"I'll go left." Emily jumped out and was dragging on snowshoes. She grabbed a backpack and tossed it to him. "I know her. She'll go through the forest if he's on her tail. She might be down here and hiding somewhere."

Reluctant to let his daughter go alone, he shook his head and suited up. "It's not safe."

"It's safer than you think." Emily patted a bulge under one arm. "I'm carrying. Just like you. I'm not planning on taking any risks." She pressed a kiss to his cheek and took off bounding through the deep snow.

Emotion welled up inside Wolfe as he watched her go. "Please, God, don't let me lose two daughters out here today."

FORTY-ONE

Jenna thrust supplies into their backpacks on the fly as Kane pushed the Beast harder along the slippery roads. The traffic was slight on the highway with only a few people venturing out in the blizzard. They made good time and soon bumped along the fire road at high speed. Kane kept the Beast sitting in the middle of the road and it never faltered as its powerful engine roared. They cut through the powder snow with ease and headed for a cabin in the distance. All around it, footlong icicles like daggers hung down from the gutters and snow spread over it like frosting and piled up along the windowsills. Before they reached it, a woman ran out carrying a shotgun waved them down. Kane slowed the truck and Jenna buzzed down her window. "I'm Sheriff Alton."

She listened as the woman explained the situation and indicated where Wolfe had gone. She turned to Kane and pointed. "That way."

"Wolfe won't get far and hasn't brought his snowmobiles. They were still at the office when I collected ours." Kane gunned the engine and they slid around the trees and followed a wide track.

They traveled for five minutes or so along the trail when Wolfe's white truck loomed up out of the blanketing snowfall. Jenna shook her head. She'd never known Wolfe to be irresponsible. "He must be on foot. Does he keep snowshoes in his truck?"

"I think so. Grab the backpacks. I'll unload the snowmobiles." Kane leaped from the Beast and had the snowmobiles on the ground in minutes. He gave Jenna a long look. "Maybe you should ride with me?"

Jenna pointed to the two sets of tracks slowly disappearing under the snow. "It looks like Wolfe followed the snowmobile and Emily went this way just in case. I'll follow Em. If the killer is down that track, Wolfe will need backup." She squeezed his arm. "I'll be fine. The girls need my help right now. We must split up." She removed her hat and tossed it inside the Beast and pulled out a helmet. "Go now."

"Yes, ma'am." Kane pulled her close and kissed her hard. "Use your com if you need me. He pushed an earbud into his ear, climbed onto the snowmobile, and took off along the winding track.

Jenna attached her earpiece and then pushed on her helmet. She raised the visor, preferring her sunglasses, and sighed with relief when the snowmobile started. She'd find Emily and they'd both be safer riding the snowmobile. Moving off, she ducked under low branches but kept her eyes on the fading footprints. How far ahead had Emily gone? They'd only been ten minutes or so behind them. Concern gripped her as the footsteps were crossed by the marks of a snowmobile. She tapped her com. "Dave, I have snowmobile tracks. There must be a crossover track somewhere close by."

"Copy, I can see Wolfe. I'll pick him up and try and find the cut-through. Hang back if you see the snowmobile. Don't tackle him alone."

Unable to see far ahead or hear much over the noise of her

snowmobile, unease slid down Jenna's spine. The killer could be just ahead and she'd never know. "Copy."

The images of the frozen women flashed through her mind. There was no way Emily was going to be his next victim. Throwing caution to the wind, she followed the tracks. After what seemed like forever, in the distance she made out flashes of color. She recognized Emily's bright yellow hat bobbing along and her orange puffy jacket following the tree line. The wind was blowing the snow in flurries, making visibility difficult. Surely, Emily could hear her coming. The next second, there was a flash of red in the trees. The killer was heading their way. Fear for Emily's safety gripped her, and she accelerated. The snowmobile spluttered and stalled. Jenna leaped from the vehicle and waded through the thick snow. "Oh, please, let me get to her in time."

FORTY-TWO

Terror gripped Carolyn as she ran through the trees, the dense forest had shielded the ground to some extent and made the going easier, but a monster was out there searching for her tracks and trying to find a way through with his snowmobile to get to her. She'd ran one way and then the other, ducking down to hide from view, but her tracks in the snow would be easy for him to follow. Her only chance was to confuse him by crossing over her tracks so he couldn't know which way she'd gone. The roar of the engine came close and she ducked under a low branch piled high with snow and pressed her back to the trunk. Daring to peek around the tree she made him out in the pelting snow, standing up on the snowmobile and peering all around. As long as the snow kept falling, she had a chance to double back. Horrified, the next moment she heard him laugh with glee and take off along a parallel track, when suddenly he parked and started to wade through the thick snow. Not able to see clearly from her position, she moved from her hiding place to stare in amazement as a woman came moving swiftly down the trail, her blonde hair flowing out from under a knitted cap.

Fear had her by the throat. Was he going to grab this poor

woman and hurt her too? Seconds later he bounded out of the forest. He lunged at the other woman and grabbed her by the hair. The woman let out a piercing scream and fought back like a wildcat. Watching in terror, Carolyn moved forward with her fists clenched ready to fight, but would she get there in time? The next second, a man came out of the trees bellowing like a charging bull. Amazed, Carolyn gasped as the other man dragged the woman from her captor's grasp and then punched him in the chest. The stranger was huge, and the monster staggered back and then held up both hands in front of him as if in surrender, and then without a backward glance, he turned and ran back into the forest. The engine of his snowmobile roared as he took off in a cloud of white. As the noise of his engine got louder, terrified Carolyn searched for a place to hide. The snowmobile was coming straight for her. She must get away. Surely, the man and woman would help her if she could get back to them, but how could she get past him?

Panic gripped her as she scanned the white landscape. Everything in the forest looked the same and she had no idea how to get back to the cabins. She must try something or she'd die anyway. Maybe if she tried to run in a circle, she might get back to them. It was her only chance to survive. Exhausted, Carolyn ran zigzagging through the trees, pumping her arms and lifting her knees. She must get away. Lungs burning, she stopped and bent over, hands on knees, and glanced behind her. The snow was falling so thick and fast, she couldn't see a thing. *Think. I could be walking around in circles. What can I do?* White smoke surrounded her as she moved off again and then she slowed and broke some branches on the tree beside her. Moving more slowly, she did the same every few trees. In the distance she could hear a snowmobile. It sounded as if it was coming from two different directions. Terrified, Carolyn ran blindly and burst out of the forest onto a wider track. The snow was thicker here and snowmobile tracks cut deep into the clean white crust. She heard a noise and opened her mouth to scream. Her captor was right behind her.

"Oh, there you are." As if he had all the time in the world, he climbed off the vehicle and grinned at her. "This is a perfect place. Why wait any longer?"

FORTY-THREE

Moving into the forest to avoid the thick drifts, Jenna's heart had missed a beat at Emily's screams. Her legs ached from negotiating snowdrifts like quicksand, but she'd seen the huge man go to Emily's rescue. He was standing with one arm around her waist now, helping her to a fallen log. Not trusting anyone, as Jenna moved closer she pulled her weapon and slid a bullet into the chamber. She held out her gun at arm's length and approached with caution. "Sheriff's department. Put your hands where I can see them." She looked at Emily. "Stand away from him, Em."

"I'm okay, Jenna." Emily's face was sheet white.

"Good to see you." The man stood and held up both hands. "I've been trying to find a way to contact you, but we've been isolated by the avalanches. I just found a way through the forest before. My name is John Raven."

"He saved me from a lunatic that called me Carolyn." Emily lifted a trembling hand to her head. "He ripped out my hair and this man saved me."

That name was familiar. Jenna took in the man, the same size as Kane and strikingly handsome. She shook her head in disbelief and lowered her gun. "Johnny Raven? Ex-military medical corp. You know Ty Carter?"

"Guilty as charged." He indicated toward Emily. "You must be a relative of Julie Wolfe. You could be sisters."

"Yes, I'm Emily. Julie is my younger sister." Emily removed her sunglasses and stared up at him unblinking.

Concerned, Jenna didn't holster her weapon. She stood her ground. "How do you know Julie Wolfe, Mr. Raven?"

"Raven is fine, ma'am. I found her in the plane wreck out at Bear Peak and took her back to my cabin." Raven narrowed his gaze. "She's okay, but her leg is likely broken. I'd have stabilized her and then called for assistance, but I couldn't get through to my other cabin. It has a CB radio but is on the other side of the avalanche. I've been going out daily since and trying to find a track wide enough for the dogsled. It's been an impossible task. The moment I figure I can get Julie through, there's another tremor and the snow slides again."

"I can't thank you enough." Emily smiled at him. "You saved my life and Julie's. Is she far from here? Can we go get her? My dad isn't far away and we have snowmobiles."

"Yeah, sure. It's some ways away but I've marked the trail. It's easy to get turned around in the forest." Raven bent and picked up her hat, brushed off the snow, and fitted it to her head with a tenderness that surprised Jenna. "Are you okay?"

"Yeah, I'm fine." Emily was staring at him like a lovesick puppy.

Clearing her throat, Jenna holstered her weapon. "Can I remind you, the man who attacked you is likely the suspect we're hunting down for a triple homicide? He mentioned the name Carolyn? She's one of the missing persons. He likely kidnapped her and is planning on killing her. Keep your weapon close at hand. I'll bring Dave up to date. He's close by with your dad."

FORTY-FOUR

Kane stopped to collect Wolfe and they hurtled along the pathway following the snowmobile tracks. "This must be the man hunting down Julie. Are you armed?"

"Yeah, and so is Em. She went down the other track. If Jenna went after her, she would have found her by now."

"Dave, do you copy?" Jenna's voice came through his com.

Kane tapped his com. "Copy. I've found Wolfe. We're following the tracks."

"A man wearing a skull helmet attacked Em, but then a guy jumped out of the forest and saved her. His name is Johnny Raven, the guy Carter mentioned. The helmet guy took off. I heard a snowmobile starting, and I figure he's heading back your way. Julie is fine. Raven says he has her in his cabin. She's safe but has a broken leg. The man called Emily by the name, Carolyn. He must have mistaken her for Carolyn Stubbs, the other missing woman. She is blonde too and about the same size. I bet Carolyn is the woman who showed up at the cabin looking for help. Everyone assumed she was Julie."

Dammit. That's all I need. Kane frowned and pushed the snowmobile along as fast as possible. "Copy. Stay where you are with Em. I don't want either of you in the crossfire. Stay with the snowmobile so we can see you."

"Copy. I love you." Jenna closed her com.

If this was the killer, they didn't have much time. Kane stared ahead at the tracks where they crisscrossed, so which way should he go? He stopped and removed his helmet, listening. The forest was eerily quiet and then came a piercing scream. He turned to Wolfe. "Julie is safe. This guy attacked Em, but she's okay. Some guy saved her. That scream is from the next victim."

"Well, let's take him down." Wolfe's face was grim as he pulled back the slide on his Glock.

Nodding, Kane hung his helmet from the handlebars and turned to Wolfe. "We'll run in the snowmobile tracks. I don't want to give him notice we're coming for him. He might kill the girl. We know he likes to cut off their hair and strip them, so we'll have time to sneak up on him." He pointed through the forest. "That way." He pulled his M18 pistol and took off through the trees.

As he ran, adrenaline flooded his muscles. No longer cold or tired, Kane increased his speed and Wolfe kept up beside him as they moved through the forest. He tapped his com. "Jenna, we're on foot heading toward the screams. Take cover. We don't know if he's armed."

"Copy. I so want to be there when you take him down."

That was so like Jenna, wanting to be slap bang in the middle of danger. Anything to take down a killer. Kane smiled to himself. He admired that about her. "Emily needs you, and you have no idea why the guy who saved Julie is holed up in the forest. You could be in more danger than us. Stay sharp."

"You too."

"I see them on the edge of the river." Wolfe pointed ahead. "What the heck is he doing?"

Taking in the situation, Kane kept his voice low. "We'll

circle around and come in from both sides." He indicated with his hand for Wolfe to go right.

The snow crunched under his boots, and branches cracked as he moved between frozen limbs, but the man in the skull helmet was so engrossed in what he was doing he didn't notice them approaching. The man had gaffer-taped a woman's mouth and wrapped both arms around the tree. Tears ran down her face but she was taking in air through her nose and still screaming behind the tape, but the sound was little more than a muffled squeak. With her back to the tree, she could see Kane coming, and he pressed a finger to his lips. As the killer secured her waist and then went down to her legs, she went quiet and stood still. Her eyes fixed on Kane pleading for help.

"That's better. You know you can't do a thing to stop me. I'm going to strip back your mask and show the world what's really underneath." The man looked up at her and lifted his visor. "Now this is done, those awful clothes must go." He pulled a knife from his belt and went to slide it under the arm of her jacket.

Close by, Wolfe emerged from the trees weapon drawn. A twig snapped under his boots and the killer's head spun in his direction. Kane froze midstride. Now the girl was in mortal danger. He'd try and use her life as a bargaining chip. It was a classic move.

"Stop right there or I'll slice her throat." The killer's voice was conversational. "Can you imagine hot blood spurting over the snow? The steam rising, the smell as she dies? Do you want to know how that makes you feel? The sight will stay with you for a lifetime and haunt your dreams. I'll do it. Drop your weapon. This one is mine."

"You'll be dead before you hit the ground." Wolfe took aim. "You don't know me. I might enjoy blowing a guy's brains out. You wanna risk it?"

"You don't have the guts." The killer waved the knife, indicating toward the woman. "We can share her. What do you say?"

"I like my idea better." Wolfe smiled. "I'll have you and the girl. It's a win-win."

Shifting his weapon to his left hand, Kane walked silently up behind the man with the knife. He grabbed the wrist holding the blade and pushed the barrel of his gun hard into the man's spine. "Sheriff's department. He's with me. You lose. Drop the knife."

"Not now. I'm not finished." The man threw back his head to headbutt Kane.

Moving away just in time, Kane bent back the man's hand until it snapped. The man wailed in agony as the knife tumbled from his trembling fingers. The next instant, Wolfe was beside him and aimed his gun at the man's face.

"Just give me an excuse." Wolfe's aim was steady. "No one lays hands on my girls. No one."

After holstering his weapon, Kane dragged off the man's helmet. "Try headbutting me again and I'll break your neck." He pulled zip ties out of his pocket and cuffed him.

"You've broken my wrist. You can't cuff me." The man's knees buckled. "Oh, that hurts. You can't do that. Stop."

Shrugging, Kane pulled him upright. "Seems that I can."

When he spun him around, the identity of the man surprised him. This man was on the bottom of his list. "Well, if it's not Steven Oberg. What a twisted individual you are." He looked at Wolfe. "Maybe we should tie him to a tree and leave him out here. Poetic justice, don't you think?"

"Yeah, it is, but if you keep on talking that way, people are gonna start believing you're the Tarot Killer." Wolfe was referring to a mysterious criminal who killed serial killers that escaped justice. He holstered his weapon and went about cutting the woman free. "One vigilante is more than we need right now."

FORTY-FIVE

Cold seeped through Jenna's boots as she pressed her com. "Dave, what's happening?"

"It's okay. We have the suspect. It's Steven Oberg. The girl is Carolyn Stubbs and she's okay." Kane cleared his throat. *"We'll come to you."*

Jenna nodded. "Copy. I've called Rio and the paramedics to meet us at the cabin. They'll be there by the time we get back. My snowmobile stalled and won't start."

"Don't worry about it. Get close to Emily and keep one eye on Raven. We don't know him. Keep your weapon within reach."

A shiver ran down Jenna's spine. "Copy." She walked closer to Raven and Emily. "Dave and Shane are heading this way with the prisoner and Carolyn Stubbs. I don't mean to pry but why is a primary-care physician holed up in a cabin at Bear Peak without any form of communication?" She leaned her back against a tree. "We have one doctor in town, and he's getting on in years. Sure, people can go to the ER, but Wolfe often needs to take up the slack and being ME is a full-time job.

You could really do some good if you opened a practice in town."

"How much did Carter tell you about me?" Raven's gaze narrowed. "And how did my name come up in the conversation?"

Surprised by the stiffening of his posture, Jenna rested a hand on the butt of her weapon. "Not much, only that you left the service and train dogs for protection and prefer to work off the grid." She shrugged. "Your name came up as a person of interest as you own cabins in the area. What you don't know, as you've been isolated, is that three women were murdered recently. Tied to trees and left to freeze to death, so we were checking out people living in the area, is all."

"Oh, now everything makes sense." He shook his head slowly and a smile creased his face, making him look charming. "Julie knows about the murders, right? That would be why she's been acting like a cat on a hot tin roof around me."

"No, she doesn't know." Emily looked up at him from her perch on the log. "We found the first body when we went to the crash site. You must have walked right past it."

Jenna thought for a beat. "She's just finished reading Jo Wells' series of books about serial killers. Jo Wells is the leading behavioral analyst with the FBI."

"Yeah, I've read her work." Raven raised both eyebrows. "So Julie was afraid I was a serial killer and keeping her against her will? Oh, the poor girl. No wonder she headed out in the snow on her crutches a couple of times. She refused decent pain relief and I know she was hurting bad." He tugged at his beard. "I've been out daily, searching for a way around the avalanches wide enough for my dogsled. I recalled there are cabins close to the fire road on this side of Bear Peak, so today I followed the river hoping that I'd find one occupied and could call for assistance. My cabin is close to the mountain, not far from the crash site, but that first tremor brought down a wall of snow on each side of me." He looked from Jenna to Emily. "I live here because I needed time to escape a traumatic episode in my life. Seeing all my team die in a chopper crash caused PTSD and being like that isn't conducive to being a doctor in a small town. People need to rely on me and I wasn't reliable. Now, it's not so bad, but training dogs keeps me active and brings in a decent income. I have a contact in town and when I have a dog ready I can call her on a CB radio. It's far enough away in a second cabin where it won't cause a problem. My snowmobile is there at the moment, and my truck. It has a nice big shed to keep everything safe over winter. The woman at the animal shelter knows where I live. If a suitable dog comes into the shelter, she drives out here to see me."

Having stood in the presence of many psychopaths, he didn't need to convince Jenna. This guy was the real deal and he'd saved and protected Julie. She nodded slowly. "Did you train K-9s?"

"Yeah, it was part of my rehabilitation." Raven rubbed his hands together and stamped his feet to keep warm. "I have Ben. A fully trained K-9 but he's not for sale. He's my buddy. He's waiting just over yonder with the dogsled team. When I heard the snowmobile, I walked ahead on foot rather than risk driving the dogs out in front of a vehicle traveling at high speed."

A doctor, with a K-9 and military training—how interesting. Jenna's mind was working overtime. Johnny Raven could be just the man she needed to join her team. As a consultant, she could call him when they needed help. She'd discuss the idea with Kane and Wolfe and then get a full background check before she made any decision. She smiled at Raven. "Oh, I can't wait to meet him. You'd know about Carter's dog, Zorro?"

"Yeah, I do." Raven smiled ruefully. "They brought Zorro to me for treatment as we had no vet in the field when Carter was MIA. The dog refused to eat. He'd drink water, that's all, and howled most times. If anyone tried to touch him, he'd bite them, so the guys in the kennels kept him muzzled. When I discovered Carter had been wounded, I flew Zorro to see him. Right there at Carter's bedside, I filled a bowl with kibble, and the moment Carter gave the command, Zorro ate. I've never seen anything like it. That dog refused to leave his side. Carter figures Zorro was knocked unconscious in the explosion, came around, and walked for days until he made it back to base, but Carter had been flown to a medical unit."

"Are you a chopper pilot as well?" Emily looked at him wide-eyed.

"Yeah, but it's been a while." Raven stared into the distance. "I hear a snowmobile."

Jenna smiled as Kane loomed out of the heavy curtain of snow with the prisoner tied to the snowmobile facing backward. Behind him, Wolfe had Carolyn hanging around his waist. She eyed Oberg with distaste. "Do you want me to call an attorney to meet us at the sheriff's office?"

"What's the point?" Oberg indicated with his chin toward Carolyn. "I should have killed her the day I picked her up from the airport. Tell the DA I want to make a deal."

Surprised, Jenna raised an eyebrow. "Sure." She turned to Kane. "Great job. My snowmobile decided to quit on me right when I needed it. I'm not sure how we're going to collect Julie and get back to the Beast. There's too many of us."

"Did it stall?" Kane lifted one leg over the handlebars to dismount and walked away from Oberg to speak to her.

Jenna nodded. "Yeah, I turned the throttle to full and it just died." She frowned. "You said not to do that and I forgot. Then it wouldn't start, so I ran here."

"It was probably flooded with gas." Kane shrugged. "It will start now it's been sitting for a time. Just remember next time not to panic. Wait, don't touch the throttle, and then start it."

"Where is Julie?" Wolfe was off the snowmobile and eyeing Raven with distrust.

"She's safe in my cabin." Raven looked from him to Kane. "My dogsled is back there and my dogs have been waiting in the cold for too long. Now I know there's a way through here, I can drive back and get her."

"Not without me you're not. I'll follow you on Jenna's ride." Wolfe headed off in the snow.

"That's not gonna work." Kane looked after him and sighed. "What about Emily? Wolfe can't go off alone."

Jenna shrugged. "Then I'll go with him." She looked at Kane's annoyed expression. "I have a satellite phone to send you the cabin's coordinates when we arrive. I'm armed and I'm wearing my vest. Nothing is going to happen to me. I'll be safe with Wolfe. You go and meet Rio and the paramedics. Carolyn will need to go to the hospital. Emily will go with her so they'll know she's a crime victim."

"I'd like to see Julie, but sure, I'll take her." Emily climbed onto Wolfe's snowmobile. "Lead the way, Dave."

Jenna turned to Kane. "Rio can get Oberg into a cell. Rowley was heading into the office and will be there by now as backup. You can follow us to the cabin when Rio leaves and we can all ride back together, if Julie can travel."

"That sounds like a plan." Kane indicated toward Oberg. "I broke his wrist. He'll need medical attention."

Blowing out a breath, Jenna peered at his eyes shielded behind mirrored sunglasses and only saw her own face and red-tipped nose. "Get the paramedics to look at him. We'll follow up when we get back to the office."

"Okay. I'll be interested to hear Julie's side of the story and I want to know more about Raven." Kane climbed back onto the vehicle and pulled down his visor. "Catch you later." He sped off toward the cabin with Emily close behind.

A snowmobile roared and moments later Wolfe came through the snow. Jenna waved him down. "I'm coming with you. Dave will follow later."

FORTY-SIX

Apprehension and concern gripped Wolfe as he rode toward Raven's cabin. Although Raven had mentioned that he was a medical doctor, his worry for Julie consumed him. If her leg had been broken as Raven had mentioned, going this long without treatment could be fatal or she may suffer permanent disability. What kind of physical or mental torture had she gone through over the last few days? He only had Raven's word that she was safe and well and he didn't trust anyone with his girls. The dogsled moved along the trail faster than he would have expected and soon they arrived at what could only be called a complex rather than a cabin in the woods. The cabin was spacious and had many outbuildings. He noticed solar panels on every available space. The roofs angled in such a way it was difficult for them to be covered completely in snow, but the snow was everywhere and icicles hung from all around the cabin. Before Jenna had dismounted behind him, the cabin door flew open and Julie stood in the opening on crutches. Her face was thin and drawn with bright red patches on each cheek.

"Daddy! Jenna!" Julie staggered forward. "I knew you'd find me."

Grinning, Wolfe grabbed his medical kit and ran toward the cabin. Julie hadn't called him Daddy since she was ten years old. Handing his kit to Jenna, who was on his heels, he scooped up Julie and carried her inside. "Thank the Lord. We thought you were dead or taken by a serial killer." He deposited her on the sofa and then pulled off his coat and gloves. "Let me take a look at you."

"I figured Raven was a serial killer for sure." Julie stared at him, her eyes brimming with tears. "He was so kind and nice, I figured it was a psychopath's charm. You see, he kept disappearing for hours at a time, sometimes all day."

Seeing his daughter so distressed tore at Wolfe's heart but he needed to calm her. "He was out searching for a trail around the avalanches wide enough to get the dogsled through so he could get you some help. We found him making his way to a couple of cabins not far from the highway. He was very happy to see us and saved Emily from a serial killer."

"He did what?! Is she okay?" Julie rose up from the sofa.

"She's fine." Jenna eased her back down. "It's complicated. We found three bodies in the forest, and Dave and your dad stopped the killer from murdering another victim. Emily is with the victim and Dave, and they're heading back to meet the paramedics and Rio. The suspect is strapped to Dave's snowmobile. He'll call me when they have everyone settled. Emily is heading to the ER with the victim, and Rio will take the prisoner into custody. Dave will be back here soon. The main thing is you're safe."

"Where's Raven?" Julie winced as Wolfe removed her bandages.

"Tending his dogs." Jenna indicated with her chin toward the door. "He'll be along soon."

Impressed by the makeshift splint, Wolfe examined Julie's leg. "I don't figure it's broken, more likely a crack, which is painful. X-rays will tell the tale." He pulled out an air splint from his kit and eased it over her leg before inflating it. "There, that will be more comfortable. I won't give you strong pain meds as you'll need to hang on behind me on the snowmobile, but I'll give you a local anesthetic to numb the injury before we leave. It's going to be a bumpy road back to my truck." He handed her two pills. "These will help." He passed her the bottle of water on the coffee table. "Do you remember the crash?"

"Before but not during." Julie rubbed her temples. "The pilot said a storm was coming and it was going to be rough. I put my head down and then everything went black. I woke up here."

"She had an egg on the back of her head." Raven stamped the snow off his boots and dropped them into a plastic tray by the door. "No concussion, she was lucid and as angry as a wildcat. I've figured all along she must believe I'm some type of crazy man. Now, after seeing what happened in the forest before, I'm not surprised she's wary."

"Bad things happen in Black Rock Falls." Jenna frowned. "Have you come across any human remains in your travels?"

"Nope or I'd have contacted you. Well, I would have anytime but the present." Raven sighed. "I did try and get a message out but all my pathways were blocked. I know about the crime rate in town. I have orders for ten protection dogs but they take time to train." His hand went to a large dog at his side. "This is Ben. He's a K-9. I trained him myself when I was in the service. I've had him since he was a pup. He failed his final test, that's why I have him. Since then he's aced every trial I've put him through. He was a little immature before but now he's good."

Wolfe stood and held out his hand. "You did a fine job with Julie's leg. I can't thank you enough for saving her life and Emily's as well. I am in your debt. Anything you need, you only have to ask."

"I did what anyone would do." Raven shrugged. "Agreed,

my medical skills are a little rusty but the basics are still there. It's like flying a chopper: you never forget."

A snowmobile roared toward the house, setting the dogs barking. Wolfe turned toward the door. "That will be Dave Kane. He has a military background as well. I flew choppers in my time as well. Have you ever thought about a career in law enforcement?"

"I've heard of Dave Kane and Sheriff Alton—the dynamic duo of Black Rock Falls, as my neighbors refer to them. I'm not too sure about changing my lifestyle. I'm pretty busy with my dogs and I'm a doctor not a cop." Raven grinned. "Although, taking down bad guys might be an interesting distraction. Are you looking for a new deputy, Sheriff?"

"More like a consultant but they'll be deputized and on the payroll. I need someone we can call in when required." Jenna frowned. "I'll need to discuss it further with my team. Training would be required and that includes fitness."

"That's more my style. Maybe we'll talk later then when you make a decision." Raven took a towel from a hook on the wall and rubbed Ben all over before straightening. "I'm sure you'd all like a hot beverage before you leave."

Wolfe rubbed his hands together. His feet had been numb all day and the tingling sensation as they slowly came back to life crept through his toes. "I would love a cup of coffee, thank you."

A knock came at the door. Wolfe looked at Raven. "That will be Dave."

"Ah, you must be Deputy Dave Kane." Raven stepped to one side as Kane stamped his feet before stepping inside. They stood eye to eye. "Your reputation precedes you."

"Johnny Raven, I presume?" Kane stared him down. "Carter gave me the rundown about you." His gaze narrowed and his mouth turned down. "Why have you kept Julie holed up here for so long?"

"It's a long story." Raven shrugged but a growl rumbled in Ben's chest. The dog recognized Kane as a threat. "Dr. Wolfe is satisfied with the explanation."

The two men were like bulls ready to lock horns. Wolfe could imagine having these two working alongside him in the team. He'd really need to speak to Jenna. This man was an asset they could use in an emergency. He moved toward them and looked at Kane. "I'll tell you later. Did you bring the spare satellite phone and charger from my truck?"

"Yeah." Kane fished it out of his pocket, but his gaze was still locked on Raven. "Julie and Emily are like my sisters."

"Hey, he saved both their lives. If he wasn't there, Oberg would have grabbed Emily." Jenna squeezed Kane's arm. "He's one of the good guys."

"Maybe." Kane let out a snort. From his expression, he'd need more convincing.

Wolfe took the phone from him and handed it to Raven. "Take this. One day you might break your leg and need help. My number is on speed dial."

"Thanks." Calm as a lake on a summer's day, Raven took the phone and walked into the kitchen with Ben close to his side. "Now who wants coffee and who'd prefer hot chocolate?"

FORTY-SEVEN

As the Beast roared back to the office, Jenna stared at Kane. "Okay what's stuck in your craw?" She sighed. "I've never seen you take an instant dislike to anyone in all the time we've been together... well, apart from a few serial killers."

"I *know* Johnny Raven. This is why I didn't want him as a suspect." Kane's fingers gripped the steering wheel and he stared straight ahead.

Astounded, Jenna turned in her seat. "Why didn't you tell me?"

"You know why." Kane shook his head slowly. "He flew an evac chopper during one of my missions. He wasn't supposed to be behind enemy lines but he risked his life to save me." He flicked her a glance but his expression was hidden behind his mirrored sunglasses. "The chopper was hit and somehow he managed to put it down. We spent ten days avoiding the enemy. He's very good at his job. Yeah, he's a doctor but he's a damn fine soldier as well. Special ops would have taken him in a second. He's smart and has a brilliant memory for details. He's younger than me but not by much and he made it through from medic to doctor and was still flying missions." A nerve in Kane's cheek twitched. "He'll see through the surgery I've had. My eyes are the same. Sure the scars and tattoos are gone, but although my accent is slightly different, he's no fool. I can't disguise my size or my skills, and if he runs my prints, I'll be relocated."

Horrified, Jenna gaped at him. "You had tattoos?" She caught his mouth twitch into a smile and then fade. "Why didn't Wolfe mention him?"

"Because Shane doesn't know." Kane drummed his fingers on the steering wheel. "It was around the time his wife first got sick. I had another handler during that mission. That's probably why I came close to being captured. Trust me, I'm alive because of Shane. He thinks one step ahead all the time. If he'd known Raven, the moment his name came up he'd have shut him down."

Astonished, Jenna stared at him. "You mean kill him?"

"If he's a threat to national security, yeah. It happens all the time." His shoulders hunched. "That was one of my jobs, in case it slipped your mind."

Trying to grasp the enormity of the situation, Jenna stared at him. "What can we do?"

"He can't use a retina scanner on me if he suspects something. I mean, he might consider me a security risk, as in, I faked my death to spy for a hostile country, for instance. If he reports me and they run my prints, all hell will break loose. My DNA isn't on file anywhere. Wolfe was able to pull that, but my prints will be under my real name because if they suddenly vanished, it would send up reg flags in the military." Kane sucked in a breath and shook his head. "This guy isn't going away now, is he? I'll ask Wolfe about altering my fingerprints."

Swallowing hard, Jenna stared at him. "That's practically impossible. Burning them off with heat or chemicals doesn't work for long. Eventually they grow back."

"It's okay. Shane will have a way. There are all types of new technology now. He'll come up with something." Kane slowed as they reached Main. "I'll be sore for a week, maybe less. I'll wear gloves and tell people I got frostbite. It's the only way, unless you figure killing a man who saved Julie, Emily, and me is the only way out of this mess." He sighed. "Personally, I believe that's a little harsh, but we need to do something before the shit hits the fan." He drove into the parking lot behind the office. "I'll unhitch the trailer and you go inside in the warm."

Fear clenched Jenna's belly and she closed her hand around his arm, feeling the tension in his muscles. "They'd take you from me and our kids? Would they really do that?"

"To keep you safe, yeah, they would." Kane slipped from the truck and came around the hood to wait as she climbed out. He held out his hand. "I'll take whatever steps to make sure that doesn't happen." He pulled her close. "You are my world, nothing else matters. I'll do whatever it takes to protect my family."

Holding back tears threatening to spill, Jenna walked carefully to the back door and scanned her eye. The door clicked open and she hurried inside, glad of the warmth and familiar smell of the office. Rowley met her as she walked into the ground floor. Although panic for Kane ripped into her, she must act normal and she smiled at him. "I'm glad to see you up and around. How do you feel?"

"A little sore but I'm okay." Rowley scrutinized her face. "You look exhausted. Oberg is safely locked away in interview room one. He wants to talk to the DA. Rio called him and he is waiting for you. He said, to speak to Oberg, make sure you give him his Miranda rights on video and then he'll do his thing. He'll watch the interview from the conference room." He frowned. "First, you need to get out of those wet clothes. Sit down and I'll get you something to eat and drink. Is Kane on his way? I just had a delivery from Aunt Betty's and the peach pie is still hot."

Jenna smiled at him. "Oh, that will be wonderful. I'll go and change." She headed for the stairs.

* * *

Twenty minutes or so later Jenna and Kane walked into the interview room. Rio had searched Oberg and relieved him of a few personal items, but what was interesting was the Glock, a roll of gaffer tape, a hunting knife, a lipstick, and his phone. The most interesting was his phone, complete with images of the women he'd murdered. All items had been entered into evidence.

"Jenna." Kane pulled her to one side. "This guy is a jerk. He has no respect for women. I figure we do the good cop, bad cop ploy with him."

She stared at him. "What do you mean?"

"Look, I need to get inside his head and find out why he's doing this, so I might need to sink to his level and say some pretty derogative things about women. It will be as offensive to me as it is for you, but it's for a good reason. These guys often trash-talk if they believe they're getting sympathy. So if I say anything disrespectful against women, you know darn well that's not what I really believe. Will you be comfortable with this line of interrogation? It's used all over with success."

Nodding, Jenna understood cops used every means of legal persuasion, even lies to get a prisoner to talk, and if this worked, she'd swallow her distaste. Her husband was a good and respectful man, and if he needed to sink to the level of a monster to get him to confess, well, so be it. "Okay, I'll grit my teeth because I know you're only doing your job. Let's get at it."

Jenna switched on the video, which fed to the conference room, and gave the date, time, and who was present. She read Oberg his rights and sat down beside Kane. "Are you waiving your rights to have a lawyer present?"

"Yeah, I don't need one just for an interview." Oberg chuckled.

Jenna took a legal pad from the drawer and a pen from inside her pocket. "Okay, Mr. Oberg, tell me all about the women in the forest." She gave him a direct stare. "How did you meet them?"

"I don't want to say." Oberg looked away and his mouth turned down.

Flicking a glance at Kane, Jenna stood. "Then I'm wasting my time. You agreed to talk to me so I could speak to the DA about a possible deal. I'll need something to give him, Mr. Oberg. Details are important and will make or break a deal."

"Okay, sit down." Oberg rolled his eyes. "But I don't like your attitude toward me. Bossy women are a pain in the butt."

"Either answer the questions or we walk." Kane scraped back his chair. "I'd rather be eating peach pie than talking to you."

"I met them through dating apps, okay?" Oberg rolled his shoulders. "Everyone does it these days."

Jenna sat down and made a few unnecessary notes. "How did you get them to Black Rock Falls?"

"I offered them a vacation at a ski resort." Oberg grinned. "They couldn't get here fast enough, but when they arrived, I put them on the back of my snowmobile and took them into the forest to admire the view. They all came willingly."

"Describe what happened next." Kane rested his clenched hands on the table.

"I told them to lean against a tree and look at the view. I pulled out my phone to take a pic and then walked behind them, grabbed their wrists and wrapped them around the tree." Oberg grinned. "They got nasty but when I pressed my Glock into their faces they went real still." He looked at Kane and shrugged. "I didn't rape them or hurt them, just maybe scared them a little. I tied them to the tree, covered their mouths if they wouldn't stop screaming, and cut off their clothes. Next, I took their hair, drew a smiley face on their foreheads, and took a pic and showed them." He chuckled. "You should have seen their faces. Their hair was like a puppy they couldn't stop stroking. It drove me crazy watching them preening like damn birds all the time."

Jenna looked up from writing. She'd written a confession for him and all he needed to do was to sign it. "Then what? You drove away and left them to freeze to death?"

"Yeah, I guess I did, but wildlife might have gotten there first. It's happened before. Not here but in Colorado." Oberg shrugged. "Is that classified as murder? I guess by hacking off their hair and clothes it might be classified as assault, but I didn't murder them. The weather did that all by itself."

"Did you intend for them to die?" Kane's voice was low and almost cordial. "I mean some women nag, nag, nag, and I guess tying them naked to a tree in twenty below would be a way of shutting them up for a time."

"Yeah, I didn't want them showing up again and causing me strife." Oberg thought for a beat. "I guess deep down I couldn't stand the sight of them."

Hating hearing Kane speak like this but impressed he was getting the prisoner on his side, Jenna leaned forward, resting her hands on the desk. "Do you recall their names?"

"Nah, as soon as I walk away, they are erased from my mind." Oberg frowned. "I take photographs so I can look at them and sometimes I go back later to see if the critters have eaten them and take more pics. They look so funny staring out into the snow."

"Women can be annoying." Kane leaned back in his chair and waved a hand. "They have all these weird habits. What did they do to make you want to take them into the forest?"

"It was the hair. They were always touching their hair." Oberg rolled his eyes. "Normal people don't play with their hair all the time. The fake women, you know the types, with big puffed-up lips, eyebrows hitched up so high they looked startled or like clowns all the time, the puffy cheeks, implants all over, long fake nails. They are the ones who do it all the time. It's like they are sending out alien signals. Like it's, 'Look at me hiding behind the mask. Really I'm an ugly old crone.' I strip them off and show the world what's underneath."

Horrified, Jenna tried to compose herself. "Were the women you left to die horrible to you? I've known many women who look beautiful because of a little cosmetic surgery. It increases their self-esteem. It's not meant to be a mask."

"No not horrible but demanding." Oberg sighed. "As if breaking a nail was criminal, or if they couldn't get their hair or nails done, it was the end of the world. They were obsessed with how they looked all the time. It was look at me, look at me. Every five minutes they were taking selfies and they couldn't walk past a mirror without stopping to admire themselves. It's not normal. They're all freaks. Crazy self-absorbed freaks." He swung his gaze to Kane. "He understands. I bet he likes his women natural, just like I do."

"Maybe not." Kane rubbed his chin. "Are we done here or do you want to go into more detail before we call in the DA? He's watching the interview and knows you've cooperated. I guess you'll need to speak to him, but first we'll need a signed confession given freely without duress."

"Sure." Oberg shrugged. "Whatever, to get it over with. My wrist hurts and it will be difficult to sign it."

"That will be fine. We'll witness the document and we have it on tape." Kane straightened. "It's all good. You did the right thing."

"Okay." Jenna finished the written confession by adding a list of the women they'd discovered dead in the forest. She mentioned the attempted murder of Carolyn and the attack on

Emily Wolfe. She slid it across the table. "Read this aloud, and if you agree, sign it and I'll call in the DA."

"I confess to taking Flora Hadley, Lorraine Smith, Abilene Drew into the forest, tying them to trees, stripping them, cutting off their hair, and leaving them to die. I also confess to keeping Carolyn Stubbs prisoner and taking her into the forest to do the same thing. I attacked Emily Wolfe on the trail." He looked at Jenna. "I had no idea who she was. I figured she was Carolyn." He signed the bottom and smiled. "There, now can we do a deal?"

Jenna took the legal pad and pen and stood. "The DA will be right in."

Following Kane outside, Jenna leaned against the wall. "I guess we'd better inform all the law enforcement offices in Colorado and tell them about Oberg."

Footsteps announced the DA with a colleague and Rio. Jenna nodded. "He's all yours."

"I can't believe he gave up all that evidence so easily." The DA rubbed his chin. "The slip about Colorado is interesting. I figure this guy's crime spree goes wider than we imagined." He looked at Jenna. "I've already called County to collect the prisoner. I'll formally charge him and sort everything from hereon. Make sure you have all Carolyn Stubbs' details, parents, friends, everything in case we need her. I believe Oberg will plead guilty, but if he changes his mind, she'll be a crucial witness. Rio can handle everything from here. Why don't you head on home, you look exhausted." He walked inside the interview room.

Jenna turned to Rio. "That's a good idea. You can handle all the details and for once, we'll head home early. Christmas is just around the corner and after running through snowdrifts all day, I need time to recuperate."

"Don't worry, the office is in safe hands." Rio grinned and headed into the interview room.

Bone weary, Jenna climbed the stairs. As they walked into her office, Duke came out of his basket, tail windmilling and giving them a doggy smile. She bent to rub his ears. "Guess what, Duke? We get to head home early." She straightened and smiled at Kane. "Why don't you get his coat on? I'll call Nanny Raya and tell her we're on our way to collect Tauri. He wanted to see the Christmas decorations along Main, so we'll drive slowly so he can see them."

"That sounds like a plan." Kane bent to kiss her. "This has been one long day."

EPILOGUE

TWO WEEKS LATER

Everything had changed once the blizzard stopped, although there was no guarantee it wouldn't start up again. Snowfall had been almost daily, which made the skiers happy and the townsfolk impatient. With choppers flying into the crash site and checking on residents trapped by the avalanches, life was getting back to normal. The investigation of a light plane crash had been conducted by the Federal Aviation Administration and their findings would be sent to the National Transportation Safety Board. A report would be sent to Jenna at a later date, but although to her it was obvious that the blizzard caused the crash, every small detail would be examined. Answers would be given to the families of the people who'd perished in the wreck.

Jenna had visited Carolyn Stubbs in the hospital. Her ordeal had left her distraught and her family was coming to collect her. Although she'd only suffered a few scrapes and bruises, the time with Oberg would mean she'd need a long time in therapy. The law enforcement offices in Colorado were following up on Oberg's confession and searching for similar crimes in the state. Wolfe had released the bodies of the victims to their next of kin and confirmed the women had all died of exposure within two weeks of each other. Jenna had noticed how exhausted he'd been after finding Julie, and the holidays would give them all time to recover. She just hoped nothing bad would happen over the holidays this year. They all needed time away from crime for a week or two. The office would run on a skeleton staff, with each person responsible for taking the 911 calls in turn and calling for backup if the need arose, but so far peace and goodwill had come to Black Rock Falls.

She placed a hand on her belly, wishing she could feel the baby's movements, but it was too early yet. The ultrasound had shown a healthy baby and a strong heartbeat. Even at this early stage it was big for its age, and secretly Jenna wished it was a boy. She'd always wanted a big family, lots of boys and maybe one girl they could all spoil like crazy, but if two children was the hand she'd been dealt, she'd still be happy. Kane was an amazing father. He excelled at everything he did and fatherhood was no different. She giggled, maybe his kryptonite was changing dirty diapers?

The house smelled of the aromas of delicious food. Kane had been baking for hours with the help of Special Agent Jo Wells, who was staying in the cottage with Ty Carter and her daughter Jaime. Jenna stood and took a box of glass baubles to the tree and attached them. It was an artificial tree, but it looked just the same as a natural pine. Why kill an oxygen-giving tree when a plastic one would last a generation? They'd had fun decorating it and she had taken a picture of Kane lifting Tauri to place the star on the top. Their laughter and love shone from their eyes. She'd loved the picture so much that she'd printed a copy and mounted it in a frame on the mantel. It would be something she'd keep forever. She peered out of the window to watch Kane and Tauri, bundled up so much they resembled a bear and a cub, making a snowman. She'd taken two pieces of charcoal from the grate earlier in the morning for the eyes and had a large carrot for the nose. It was time to go outside and add the trimmings. After pushing her feet into boots and dragging on a thick waterproof coat and hat, she stepped outside.

Immediately her men attacked her with snowballs, both laughing and ducking away from her attempts to throw some back. She pulled her decorations from her pocket and attached them. Suddenly the snowman looked real. "He needs a mouth."

"We've got one, Mommy." Tauri handed her a piece of bent twig. "Now he has a smile."

"And this." Kane pulled a green beanie with a red pom-pom from his pocket and stretched it over the head. He added a straw broom from the barn and nodded. "Now that's a snowman."

A horn sounded and the gates to the ranch opened. A stream of vehicles came along the driveway and parked outside the house. Wolfe, Norrell, and his family piled out first. Julie, wearing a Moon Boot, had a cracked leg but she was doing just fine. Rio and his family were followed by Rowley, Sandy, and the twins. An older pickup rolled into the yard and Johnny Raven climbed out, carrying a box of wine. Jenna turned to Kane and raised one eyebrow. "Really? After all your concerns, you invite him to our home."

"For now, he gets the benefit of the doubt." Kane moved closer. "He saved lives and he's all alone right now. It's the least we can do and I'm covered." He wiggled his fingers. "The changes to my fingerprints are healed thanks to Wolfe's tissue soldering. Yeah, it was painful and permanent, but we'll never need to worry about my prints showing up again." He sighed. "Hopefully Raven might figure I remind him of a guy he knew years ago who died in a bombing. We all have our ghosts, Jenna, and hopefully that's all I'll ever be to him. There is another thing: by keeping him close, we can keep an eye on him, and so can Wolfe."

Jenna nodded. "Well, if he does prove to be trustworthy, he might well be a very useful asset to our team."

"I guess time will tell." Kane smiled and waved at the visitors. "We need a picture." He pulled a camera from his pocket. "Don't laugh, this is a darn good camera and it has a delay."

Giggling, Jenna stared at it. "So does your phone." She took in his amused expression. "I'm sure it will be just fine."

When Carter, Jo, and Jaime came running from the cottage, everyone milled around the snowman. Although Jenna would miss Atohi Blackhawk, Nanny Raya, and Maggie, they all had families to spend the holidays with, and Blackhawk would no doubt drop by later. He was part of her family now and they enjoyed many Sunday lunches together. She smiled at everyone. "Gather around. Dave, set up your camera to take a photograph of us all together."

"I'll set it for sixty seconds." Kane placed the camera on the porch railing and ran back to the group.

They all squashed together giggling like a gaggle of geese, gifts in hands, with the snowman in the middle. Laughter filled the air. Jenna slid an arm around Kane with Tauri cuddled between them. Light snow dusted the scene. It was picture-postcard perfect. "Altogether now for a photo to remember. One, two, three." Jenna stared at the camera. "Merry Christmas!"

A LETTER FROM D.K. HOOD

Dear Reader,

Thank you so much for choosing my novel and coming with me on another of Kane and Alton's thrilling cases in *Their Frozen Bones*.

If you'd like to keep up-to-date with all my latest releases, just sign up at the website link below. I will never share your email address or spam you, and you can unsubscribe at any time.

www.bookouture.com/dk-hood

I love writing about winter and snow. Living in Queensland, Australia, now, I actually miss the snow. I can recall as a child being excited when I woke to see the first snow and many happy times skiing, which was a passion of mine. Now our winters pass in a blink of an eye and are very mild. As I write this and another book is finished, the next story is ready to be written. There are so many exiting adventures for Jenna and Dave yet to come. I hope you'll come along with me to enjoy the ride.

If you enjoyed *Their Frozen Bones,* I would be very grateful if you could leave a review and recommend my book to your friends and family. I really enjoy hearing from readers, so feel free to ask me questions at any time. You can get in touch on my social media or through my website.

Thank you so much for your support.

D.K. Hood

www.dkhood.com

ACKNOWLEDGMENTS

Many thanks to all the readers who took the time to post great reviews of my books and to those amazing people who hosted me on their blogs.

The D.K. Hood Readers' Group has been a wonderful way for me to communicate with my readers on a different level and show my appreciation. I am truly blessed to find so many friends from across the sea and in Australia. To each and every one of you, thank you for your support. It means such a lot to me.

Many thanks to Helen, my wonderful editor, and every member of #TeamBookouture, who are listed below. They take my books and make them special.

D.K. Hood

PUBLISHING TEAM

Turning a manuscript into a book requires the efforts of many people. The publishing team at Bookouture would like to acknowledge everyone who contributed to this publication.

Audio

Alba Proko

Sinead O'Connor

Melissa Tran

Commercial

Lauren Morrissette

Hannah Richmond

Imogen Allport

Cover design

Blacksheep

Data and analysis

Mark Alder

Mohamed Bussuri

Editorial

Helen Jenner

Ria Clare

Copyeditor
Ian Hodder

Proofreader
Claire Rushbrook

Marketing
Alex Crow
Melanie Price
Occy Carr
Cíara Rosney
Martyna Młynarska

Operations and distribution
Marina Valles
Stephanie Straub

Production
Hannah Snetsinger
Mandy Kullar
Jen Shannon
Ria Clare

Publicity
Kim Nash
Noelle Holten
Jess Readett
Sarah Hardy

Rights and contracts
Peta Nightingale
Richard King
Saidah Graham